Fyfa's Sacrifice

GUARDIANS OF ALBA
BOOK TWO

JAYNE CASTEL

All characters and situations in this publication are fictitious, and any resemblance to living persons is purely coincidental.

Fyfa's Sacrifice, by Jayne Castel

Published by Winter Mist Press

ISBN: 978-0-473-58422-1 (Paperback)

Edited by Tim Burton
Cover design by Winter Mist Press
Cover photography courtesy of www.shutterstock.com
Dagger vector image courtesy of www.pixabay.com

Visit Jayne's website: www.jaynecastel.com

***

To my darling Tim.

***

Historical Romances
by Jayne Castel

DARK AGES BRITAIN

The Kingdom of the East Angles series
Night Shadows (prequel novella)
Dark Under the Cover of Night (Book One)
Nightfall till Daybreak (Book Two)
The Deepening Night (Book Three)
The Kingdom of the East Angles: The Complete Series

The Kingdom of Mercia series
The Breaking Dawn (Book One)
Darkest before Dawn (Book Two)
Dawn of Wolves (Book Three)
The Kingdom of Mercia: The Complete Series

The Kingdom of Northumbria series
The Whispering Wind (Book One)
Wind Song (Book Two)
Lord of the North Wind (Book Three)
The Kingdom of Northumbria: The Complete Series

DARK AGES SCOTLAND

The Warrior Brothers of Skye series
Blood Feud (Book One)
Barbarian Slave (Book Two)
Battle Eagle (Book Three)
The Warrior Brothers of Skye: The Complete Series

The Pict Wars series
Warrior's Heart (Book One)
Warrior's Secret (Book Two)
Warrior's Wrath (Book Three)
The Pict Wars: The Complete Series

Novellas
Winter's Promise

MEDIEVAL SCOTLAND

The Brides of Skye series
The Beast's Bride (Book One)
The Outlaw's Bride (Book Two)
The Rogue's Bride (Book Three)
The Brides of Skye: The Complete Series

The Sisters of Kilbride series
Unforgotten (Book One)
Awoken (Book Two)
Fallen (Book Three)
Claimed (Epilogue novella)

The Immortal Highland Centurions series
Maximus (Book One)
Cassian (Book Two)
Draco (Book Three)
The Laird's Return (Epilogue festive novella)

Stolen Highland Hearts series
Highlander Deceived (Book One)
Highlander Entangled (Book Two)
Highlander Forbidden (Book Three)

Guardians of Alba series
Nessa's Seduction (Book One)
Fyfa's Sacrifice (Book Two)

Epic Fantasy Romances
by Jayne Castel

Light and Darkness series
Ruled by Shadows (Book One)
The Lost Swallow (Book Two)
Path of the Dark (Book Three)
Light and Darkness: The Complete Series

*"If it is not right do not do it;
if it is not true do not say it."*
—Marcus Aurelius

1

STRANGERS

Stirling Castle, Scotland

Early July, 1304

SHE LOOKED ACROSS the table at her husband—and into the face of a stranger.

As usual of late, Hume avoided her gaze. Instead, he stared down at his noon meal of turnip and onion pottage, a grim expression upon his face.

Stifling a sigh, Fyfa tore her attention from the man she'd wed five years earlier, a man she'd never truly been honest with, and looked down at her own unappetizing meal. Supplies were running dangerously low, and that meant it was pottage most days.

A familiar rumble split the air then. An instant later, the entire fortress shuddered.

"That damn monstrosity must have gotten close to the walls again," Hume muttered, to himself rather than his wife.

He spoke of the great wooden siege tower the English had assembled in the early days of their attack, four months prior. The defenders had set fire to that cursed contraption, had peppered it with crossbow bolts and missiles, and yet their attackers merely patched it up. The siege tower came equipped with a heavy wooden battering ram—and it sounded as if that had just started to pound the walls once more.

Boom. Boom. Boom.

Fyfa set her jaw. Why did everything come in threes?

Hume cursed under his breath. A 'clunk' followed as he set down the spoon he'd been stirring his pottage with.

Fyfa looked up once more to see that her husband's brow was furrowed. "I'd better go up and see what they're doing," he announced after a pause.

Fyfa swallowed a mouthful of pottage. "Ye know what they're doing, husband," she chided him. "Attempting to knock a great hole through the curtain wall." His frown deepened at her words, yet she pressed on. "Why don't ye finish yer meal before going up onto the walls so the English can take shots at ye? Ye can't be everywhere, or ye will exhaust yerself."

Hume's broad shoulders tensed. His moss-green gaze met hers then and held for a long moment. A nerve flickered in his cheek.

Fyfa had always considered her husband handsome. He was tall and strongly built, for despite that his role as steward didn't require much physical strength, he trained regularly with the garrison to keep fighting fit.

However, of late, Hume just looked severe. He kept his dark-auburn hair shorn short—unlike most Scotsmen, who wore theirs long—and a scowl scarred his face most days. He wasn't old—having just passed his thirtieth winter—yet deep grooves bracketed his mouth and nose. And now, as often, his lips were pressed together in a hard, thin disapproving line.

Disapproval. She saw it in his eyes every time he looked her way.

She was a disappointment to him.

"The English take shots at *all* of the men on the wall," he growled. "The least I can do is help them defend this castle."

Fyfa held his gaze, her own ire rising. At least he was reacting to her today though. Over the past months, he'd taken to pretending she hadn't spoken when she asked him things—a behavior that made her palm itch to slap him. His mutinous silence these days chafed at her like a sore that wouldn't heal.

"Then ye might as well do it on a full belly," Fyfa replied, biting out the words.

"I'm not hungry." He shoved back the bowl of pottage and rose to his feet. Suddenly, the solar in which they shared their meals seemed overly small as he loomed over the table. Tension rippled through the air between them for an instant, yet Fyfa boldly held her husband's eye.

Frustration burned in the depths of his mossy eyes. He was vexed with her—and she knew it had nothing to do with the noon meal or the battering ram that was now hammering the walls.

It had to do with her presence in his life and the ruin that was their marriage.

Tearing his gaze from hers, Hume stepped away from the table, turned on his heel, and stalked from the chamber, leaving Fyfa alone. The door thudded shut behind him while she sat, listening to the heavy tread of his footfalls moving away.

Muttering a curse of her own, Fyfa leaned back in her chair and dragged a hand down her face.

Crone's tears, she was tired of all of this.

She was bone-weary of the siege. Sir William Oliphant had defended the castle admirably, yet those English bastards were relentless.

Months earlier, Sir William had tried to put Longshanks off attacking by saying that he couldn't surrender the castle without the permission of Sir John Soules, the Guardian of Scotland—who just happened to be currently residing in France. Longshanks had thrown the excuse back in Oliphant's face and launched his attack.

She was tired of the assault itself—day after day, the whoosh of the trebuchets, the thunder of missiles hammering the castle walls, the choking smoke of Greek fire—and the constant fear that today would be when their defenses failed.

She was tired of eating coarse bread and tasteless pottage. Nearly all their food reserves were exhausted; it had been two weeks since they'd finished the last of their salted beef, and their final wheel of cheese had been consumed a few days earlier.

But most of all, she was tired of trying to be Hume Comyn's dutiful wife.

Trying and failing.

Fyfa choked down the last of her pottage—for, unlike her husband, she wasn't about to waste their precious food reserves—and rose to her feet. She cleared up the dishes, placing them upon a tray for the servants to collect, and left the apartments she shared with her husband.

She didn't follow Hume up to the walls. He'd forbidden her from going there anyway during daylight hours while the attack raged. Instead, she went downstairs. She didn't take the main stairwell, but a smaller one used by servants to bring food up from the kitchens in the basement.

Descending to the lowest level, Fyfa emerged into the busy kitchens. Although the noon meal had just completed, there was always bread and bannocks to be baked and vegetables to be prepared. Supper was a much lighter meal, yet a wedge of bannock with a boiled egg—fortunately, the keep had a clutch of fowl—was more appetizing than the pottage.

Greeting the cooks with a wave and a tight smile, Fyfa strode through the kitchens before taking the main stairwell that led up to the entrance hall. It took her past a number of storage alcoves. Glancing nervously over her shoulder to make sure she wasn't being followed, she ducked into one of them. She then moved to the back and lifted a pile of old jute sacks, revealing a trapdoor.

Fyfa cast another look behind her. Even after years at Stirling, she was careful. The last thing she wanted was the folk here to learn who she really was. She murmured a charm, releasing the lock upon the door. Lifting the trapdoor, she climbed down the ladder into her sanctuary.

A small space, carved out of the stone beneath Stirling Castle, greeted her.

Breathing in the cool, damp air, and allowing the tension of the morning and her husband's dour company to unravel, Fyfa let her gaze travel around the space. She'd located the disused storeroom soon after her arrival at Stirling and wasted no time in making it her own.

She was tidy by nature and liked to keep the quarters she shared with Hume organized. Likewise, everything in her 'sanctuary' had its place. Narrow shelves—on which sat baskets of dried herbs and candles of different shapes, sizes, and colors—lined the chamber, which had once been used as a cheese store. However, she'd kept the center of the space empty and had drawn a neat pentagram—a five-pointed star inside a circle—upon the stone floor with charcoal. Each point of the star represented one of the elements: spirit, water, fire, earth, and air.

Gazing upon her sanctuary, Fyfa's chest tightened. She was a skilled druidess, one of her order's best—and yet she was trapped within Stirling's walls, helpless to do anything but watch as the English slowly eroded their defenses.

Her expression pinched at the thought. She hated feeling so useless.

Picking up a small red candle from one of the shelves, Fyfa examined it. She'd used this one, five years earlier, when she'd pursued Hume.

The young steward of Stirling, although big and formidable looking, was shy with women. He'd literally run off the first time she'd flirted with him, his face blushing bright pink.

To aid herself in capturing his heart, Fyfa had burned a crimson candle on a new moon, with Hume's name written from the top down. Fyfa had been working within Stirling Castle as a scullery maid, and as such her difference in rank hadn't made her a natural choice of wife for Hume Comyn. But the working she'd used broke down the man's shyness and defenses.

And when they'd lain together two days later, she'd discovered that she was his first. Guilt had swept over her that night, for she hadn't realized just how timid the steward was around women.

She felt as if she'd manipulated him—which she had. To her, he'd been little more than a target—a way into Stirling's secrets. If she were wed to the steward of Stirling, she'd be privy to the decisions made within these walls and the rumors that circulated the castle.

Fyfa stared at the candle, her throat thickening.

Aye, she'd used her natural wiles and comeliness to their full advantage in gaining Hume's affections—but she'd also had some help from witching.

When Hume had fallen for her, he'd fallen hard.

She inwardly cringed at the way she'd viewed him then, the faint disdain she'd felt for the puppy-like way he'd once idolized her. How she wished he still felt that way. His withdrawn attitude now stood in stark contrast.

Fyfa swallowed, setting down the candle on its shelf with a thud. It was tempting to use candle magic again, to woo her husband as she once had, and to end this war between them. She couldn't do the task she'd been sent to Stirling for if he refused to confide in her. He'd once spoken to her of his meetings with Oliphant and other men of power, yet these days, he remained stubbornly silent.

It frustrated Fyfa, but using the craft to manipulate someone into loving her had already backfired once. She cringed to think what damage it might wreak if she used it again.

Drawing in a deep, steadying breath, Fyfa listened to the rumble of the continuing siege high above. It sounded as if a great storm were breaking over Stirling.

She sighed. No, she was stuck in this mess—one of her own making—and she would need to find another way out of it. One that didn't use witching.

The truth was that, despite everything, she cared for Hume. Her feelings for him were complicated. She'd long decided that there wasn't space in her heart for both Scotland and a husband—and as such, she'd held a piece of herself in reserve from the beginning. Hume didn't know who she really was, in all senses.

But surely they could still be happy together? Aye, reconciliation would make her task here easier, yet it would also ease the knots in her belly and the ache that rose under her ribs whenever her gaze alighted upon her husband's shuttered face.

Resolve straightened Fyfa's shoulders and made her jaw firm, chasing away the weariness that pressed down upon her. She couldn't do anything about the enemy at present, but perhaps she could take steps to mend her marriage. She wanted to see Hume Comyn smile again, to make things right between them.

I shall begin today.

2

DOUBT

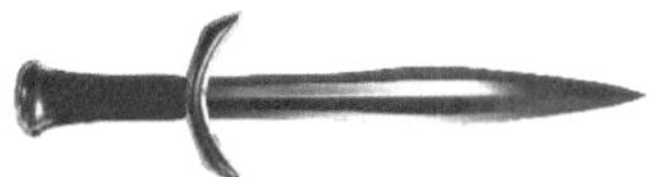

HUME COMYN HADN'T known what true misery was—until he got married.

Taking the stairs to the ramparts, he reflected on just how much unhappiness Fyfa had brought into his life. Of course, it hadn't always been that way. There had been a time when just a look from the fire-haired lass who'd joined the kitchen servants as a scullery maid years earlier had brought all his senses to life, excitement sweeping through him, desire tightening his belly.

But these days, the only urge he had when he looked upon his wife was the desire to rail at her, to demand to know why she had married him at all.

He was sure Fyfa didn't love him. He doubted she ever had.

Jaw clenched, Hume stepped out onto Stirling Castle's walls. The latest attack had died away, leaving an eerie silence in its wake—an indrawn breath before the next assault began. Dark smoke drifted across the ramparts, stinging Hume's throat as he approached the merlons—the high battlements edging the wall—and peered through a crenel, the narrow gap between two of them.

Sunlight sparkled off the rippling surface of the River Forth below, and the banners and flags of the English fluttered in the breeze. The hillside below the eastern walls crawled with mail-clad men.

Hume's brow furrowed. For months now, the English had camped beneath the castle. They'd arrived upon the first day of April, and once Sir William Oliphant, Governor of Stirling, had refused to surrender the fortress, Edward Longshanks had begun his attack.

Now, with summer inching by, Hume wondered just how long it would continue.

"I wouldn't stand there for too long, Comyn, if I were ye," a voice intruded then. "A crossbow bolt is likely to hit ye between the eyes if ye do."

Hume glanced up to see that Cameron Stewart, Captain of the Stirling Guard, now stood at his shoulder. The captain moved quietly; it unnerved Hume that he hadn't even heard him approach. Leather-clad and wild-haired, his strong jaw covered in a thick layer of dark stubble, Stewart was lean rather than brawny.

The sight of the captain made Hume's mouth flatten. However, he took his warning and stepped back so the merlon obscured him once more. In truth, Stewart was the type of man Hume had always aspired, and failed, to be—and he'd secretly envied him for it. Confident, to the point of arrogance, and a warrior of renown, Stewart had spent years working his way up through the ranks before becoming captain of Stirling's garrison. The men respected him deeply—and by his reputation, he'd also bedded half the women in this keep.

Hume's jaw clenched at this last thought. He wasn't entirely sure that this man hadn't had a dalliance with Fyfa. He had no proof, but he'd noted how the rakish captain's eye tracked Hume's lovely red-headed wife on the occasions they'd banqueted in the great hall together. And since the siege had begun and they'd all been locked inside the walls of this castle, his suspicions had grown. But, Hume's misgivings aside, it was the captain's arrogance that needled him the most.

Hume never failed to feel lacking in his presence.

"Yer concern for my well-being is touching, Captain," Hume replied, his tone dry, "but surely, ye have more important matters to concern yerself with this morning?"

Stewart cocked an eyebrow. "I do, *Steward*," he replied, "but we don't want to leave that pretty wife of yers a widow just yet, do we?"

Hume snorted, even though tension rippled through him at the jibe.

God's teeth, it vexed him how easily the captain got under his skin.

They'd occasionally sparred together in the practice yard, for although Hume's role in the castle didn't require him to defend it physically, he'd decided a long time ago that he needed to keep his body fighting fit should the need ever arise. The role of steward was an important one—one he was proud of—but it was as if the captain sensed that he secretly felt less of a man for conducting what was, in essence, an administrative role.

The bastard can't make ye feel worthless … not without yer permission, Hume reminded himself, irritation spiking through him. He'd worked hard over the years to overcome his old insecurities. To most folk, he appeared the confident, if a bit stern, steward of Stirling. But underneath it all lurked self-doubt, and Cameron Stewart knew it.

"How much longer will our store of missiles hold out?" Hume asked then, deliberately bringing matters back to the siege itself.

"It's hard to tell," the captain admitted. His stubbled jaw tensed then. "We use whatever they lob at us, but we're starting to run low … and their Greek fire has done significant damage to our trebuchets."

Hume scowled. Stewart wasn't exaggerating. And yet, their catapults weren't the only losses. Men fell daily, and the stables had burned down three days earlier when a cluster of Greek fire landed upon its roof. They'd managed to save some of the horses but not all. The screams of the dying beasts still haunted Hume.

"The day is coming when Oliphant is going to have to talk to Longshanks again," Stewart said then. "None of us want to surrender … but perhaps he needs to start considering it." The captain paused, a groove forming between his dark brows. "Has he said anything to ye of his plans?"

Hume shook his head, his belly tightening. Throughout the siege, Stewart's confidence had been unshakable. Things were indeed dire if the brash captain was talking negotiation—and surrender.

"The governor keeps his own counsel at present," he replied gruffly.

In truth, William Oliphant was worried. They'd held out admirably, but the English weren't giving up. Many Scots had come to the defenders' aid over the past months—far more than they'd anticipated. Warbands of Highland warriors had descended upon Stirling, conducting raids of the enemy camp both in daylight hours and at night. Some of their raids against the English had been a great success.

Nonetheless, Edward of England was relentless. Over the past month, their Scot allies had dwindled, and they'd witnessed more English troops arriving from the south.

"Oliphant can't hide away forever," Stewart continued. "He needs to face this."

Once again, Hume tensed at the captain's bluntness.

Unfortunately, Stewart was right—William Oliphant had taken to locking himself away in his solar, deliberately avoiding the castle walls. In the early weeks of the siege, he'd ventured out every morning, rallying the men, keeping morale high.

But now Oliphant left that task to Hume—and the steward wasn't sure he was the right choice for the job. The men didn't look at him with hope in their eyes, the way they did when Oliphant stepped out onto the walls. And they didn't stand alert and listen, the way they did when Cameron Stewart walked by.

"Oliphant knows what he's doing," Hume replied with a frown. He couldn't let the undercurrent of despair in Stewart's voice get to him. "We have trusted him so far, and he has not led us astray."

Cameron Stewart scowled. "Aye," he muttered. "But barring a miracle, Stirling *will* fall, Comyn."

A nearby shout warned them that the siege was resuming. Both men ducked as missiles—chunks of lead and stone—hit the ramparts. An instant later, a boulder sailed over the merlons and collided with one of the wooden trebuchets on the wall, shattering it.

Hume left the wall a short while later, brushing dust and chunks of mortar off his clothing. He descended the narrow steps leading down from the battlements, his jaw clenched as he listened to the 'swoosh' of catapults releasing below the castle and the whistle of cross-bow bolts.

Danger crackled through the air—although since the siege had been going on a while now, he'd gotten used to living with it.

Hume had nearly reached the bottom of the steps when he encountered a small, lanky figure, clad in oversized plate armor, rattling toward him. Somehow the lad had gotten hold of a sword; however, it was so heavy, he had to grasp it with two hands.

Blocking the boy's path up onto the walls, Hume scowled. "Craig ... where do ye think ye are going?"

Craig Duncan straightened, squaring his thin shoulders, and pushed back the visor that had fallen over his eyes.

"I'm going to join the men," he announced, "and do my part."

Their gazes fused for a long moment. Hume fought the urge to smile, for Craig's expression was painfully earnest. However, the seriousness in the lad's blue eyes checked him. The lad was at that awkward age of around twelve winters—the time when he was walking the path from boy to young man. He could easily take offense at well-meaning advice.

Many years had passed since Hume had been that age, yet he remembered well what it had felt like to be neither a child nor a man. And he'd hated being patronized. Like Craig, he too had been fatherless.

Graham Duncan, one of the Stirling Garrison, had fallen during the first month of the siege. Craig's mother, a castle cook, hadn't coped well with her husband's death, and her son had been set adrift. Hume had done his best to make sure Craig was kept busy—but of late, the relentless siege had taken up most of the steward's attention.

It didn't surprise him that Craig wanted to fight on the walls. However, he wasn't going to let him.

"Give me that sword," he said softly, holding out a hand. When Craig hesitated, his lean face turning mutinous, Hume gave him a quelling look. "It won't do ye any good up there anyway ... a blade won't stop Greek fire, cross-bow bolts, and balls of lead."

Craig glared back, their gazes dueling, before the defiance drained from his features. "I just want to help," he said roughly. "I feel so useless hiding in the keep with the *women*."

Hume sighed at this comment, taking the sword from the lad and stepping close to him. He then looped an arm around Craig's shoulders and steered him in the direction of the keep. "Come away from the walls."

He could feel the tension in the boy's thin shoulders. He was vibrating with it.

They walked toward the keep, while the fortress shuddered under the onslaught of missiles and acrid smoke drifted across the inner-bailey. Reaching the back entrance to the kitchens, Hume released the lad and turned to him.

"Don't be so keen to rush toward death, Craig," he said then, meeting his eye once more. "Fear not, the time will come, when ye will be able to fight the English ... but until then" —he reached out and placed a firm hand on the lad's shoulder— "Ye can help in other ways."

Craig's mouth thinned. "Aye, by emptying slop-buckets," he muttered bitterly.

Hume's mouth quirked. "I've emptied plenty of those in my time too," he chided. "However, that wasn't the task I had in mind. I'm going to the stables to collect stones for our trebuchets." The stables were nothing more than a heap of charred rubble—and Captain Stewart had mentioned they were low on missiles. "Ye can assist me."

Hume stepped inside the steward's apartments to see his wife seated at a table in the center of the space. She was studying a book by candlelight.

It was late. After spending most of the day toiling with Craig to collect missiles for the trebuchets, Hume had just been up on the walls to survey the damage the day's siege had wrought. He'd stepped over chunks of stone and around pools of congealing blood before examining a hole in the ramparts where a large ball of lead had hit earlier in the day. Stewart and his men were out there now, doing their best to repair the damage.

"Isn't that my ledger?" he asked, his brow furrowing. He noted then that she had a scrap of parchment by the book and appeared to be scribbling notes down upon it.

Fyfa glanced up, favoring him with a smile. However, her gaze was wary. "I thought I'd make myself useful and tally up the remainder of our grain supplies for ye." An awkward pause followed before Fyfa cleared her throat and motioned to a cup on the table, covered by a square of cloth. "I managed to purloin some goat's milk this evening too ... I know that ye have missed it of late."

Hume had. Nonetheless, he wouldn't let himself be distracted.

"Aye ... thank ye," he murmured. Drawing close, he looked down at the open ledger before her. He saw that she had been viewing the list of grains they had remaining in the castle. Just two more sacks of oats, and the same of barley. A hollow feeling settled within him at the sight.

"I had no idea supplies were this low, Hume," she said, her tone turning grave. "We'll get through this grain within the fortnight."

"I'm aware of that." Reaching out, he closed the ledger firmly before pulling it away from her.

Fyfa angled her chin up, meeting his gaze. Her eyes were dark blue, the hue of the sea on a summer's day. As always, the impact of their gazes meeting, something that happened rarely of late, made Hume's breathing catch. Even now, her proximity affected him. It was two years since they'd last lain together, two years since they'd shared a tender touch or a kiss. And yet meeting his wife's eye still heightened Hume's senses.

The only difference these days was that he resisted the pull. It was torture, going so long without a woman, and he hadn't sought solace in another's arms, but the gulf between husband and wife was too wide for him to cross.

Aye, his body still craved her, yet the trust that had once lain between them had gone.

He tried to stay away from the apartments he shared with Fyfa and focus on other matters as much as possible during the day. The rare moments in which he saw her were a punch to the gut. Every time his gaze settled upon his comely wife, every time he saw her favor someone else with a smile, caught her laughing over something with one of the other women, something deep within his chest twisted.

Had he ever made his wife laugh?

"Why have ye said nothing of this to me?" Fyfa asked softly.

Hume drew back, gripping the ledger. "Such things don't concern ye, wife."

"Do they not?" Fyfa slid back her chair and rose to her feet. She had to angle her chin high to continue to meet his eye. Hume towered over most folk.

The moments drew out, and despite that he did his best to keep his wife far from his thoughts, Hume's gaze drank her in. She had a body like a siren, and although it had been two years since he'd seen her naked, the memory was etched on his mind forever. She had long legs, a generous swell of breast and hip, and a nipped-in waist. His wife also possessed soft, milky skin; a lovely, heart-shaped face; and fiery hair that drew gazes wherever she went. Quite simply, Fyfa was unforgettable.

She could have had any man, so why had she chosen him?

Hume had his theories. The one that he'd fixed upon, the one that plagued and tormented him daily, was that his lovely wife was ambitious and scheming. She'd been a scullery maid when he'd met her, and now she was a castle steward's wife. Fyfa had risen through the ranks in a way few women did.

These days, Hume was convinced she'd wed him to elevate her position.

Hume moved past Fyfa then, inhaling the scent of lilac. It was her favorite perfume, although he imagined the reserves of it, and the scented soap she liked so much to bathe with, would be nearly exhausted by now. Curse him, but he found himself dragging the sweet scent into his lungs. He couldn't help himself.

"Aye, wife." Hume shifted to the bookcase behind them and replaced the leather-bound book. "The ledgers are my business, not yers."

He then went to the bench seat on the opposite side of the room and, without another word, opened the basket next to it—pulling out a cushion and a blanket. It was a signal that he was retiring for the night and that so should she. They'd once shared the large comfortable bed-chamber, but these days, it was her domain. Instead, Hume bedded down on the long padded bench seat in the solar. It wasn't the most comfortable of beds, yet Hume put up with it.

Long moments passed while Hume arranged the covers, back turned to his wife. He'd expected her to move away, but she didn't. Eventually, he stiffened and straightened up, casting her a look over his shoulder. Fyfa was watching him, her lovely face taut, her gaze veiled.

When Fyfa broke the weighty silence, her voice was husky. "Things used to be good between us, Hume ... can we not go back to those days?"

The knots in Hume's gut tightened. Lord, how he longed to cast aside all the mistrust, suspicion, and hurt of the past years and act as if none of it mattered. But that wasn't Hume's way. He was a man who bruised deeply, and he bore countless scars on account of this woman.

Aye, he wanted to reach for her, to bury his face in his wife's lilac-scented hair and forget everything that had passed between them. But he couldn't. "No," he said softly, his voice catching once more. "I don't think we can."

3

THE WARNING

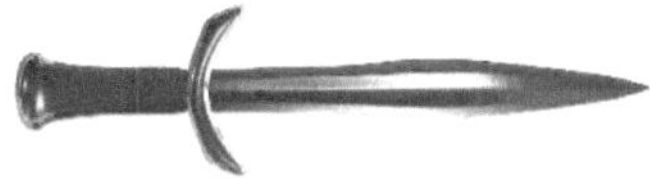

THE CROW WAS waiting for Fyfa when she entered the solar, a basket of laundry clutched to her breast. Halting just inside the doorway, her eyes widening with surprise, she kicked the door shut behind her and set down the basket.

"Eclipse, is that ye?"

Perched upon the stone window ledge, the large black crow inclined its head, obsidian eyes fixed upon her. Indeed, this was the High Bandruì's familiar.

"I wish I had better news for ye," Fyfa murmured moving toward the open window. Outdoors it was a bright, sunny day—bonny summer weather. Yet, the sunshine was marred by the pall of dirty smoke that drifted over the walls and the constant boom and rumble of the siege that shook the castle to its foundations. It seemed an odd thing, to go about one's daily chores while fire, stone, and lead besieged the castle walls. But life went on, and there was still soiled clothing to be washed and dried, meals to be prepared, and the dwindling livestock within the walls to be tended to.

"We're running dangerously low on food supplies," Fyfa continued. "And I've just heard that more troops have arrived at the enemy camp." She scowled then. "The Hammer isn't giving up."

The Hammer—it was the name her order used for Edward of England, the 'Hammer of the Scots' and their thrice-cursed besieger.

Eclipse gave a soft caw and shuffled toward her on the stone ledge. Fyfa frowned. How she wished she was powerful enough to draw a familiar to her—only the strongest druidesses did so—and how she wished she could decipher the noises the crow made, as Colina could.

Fyfa's gaze took in the bird's blue-black feathers and streamlined shape. And it was then that she noticed something she'd missed on entering the chamber. The crow carried a scroll attached to one of its legs.

Shuffling closer to Fyfa on the window ledge, Eclipse raised his left claw, offering it to her.

Fyfa's pulse accelerated. She'd thought Colina had sent Eclipse south to gain news on how the siege was progressing, although she probably didn't need details from Fyfa to know that the castle was close to falling. Their allies, who had done their best to slow and even stop the siege, would have sent word north. But instead, the High Bandruì had now sent *her* a message.

Reaching down, Fyfa untied the leather band that secured the small scroll. Gently, for she didn't want to rip the parchment, she unfurled it. She then held it up, so she could read it in the sunlight streaming in through the window. There were a few lines written in tiny script. Fyfa had to squint to decipher it. Colina had taken great care to teach them all their letters as bairns—for Guardians of Alba needed to be able to read and write in order to send and receive messages from each other.

A moment later, she read the missive aloud. "Beware of Lamia Delamare, the witch at the Hammer's side. She knows who we are. Nessa has left the camp. Gain what news ye can."

Fyfa's pulse quickened further, her skin prickling. "A *witch* ... with the English?" she whispered. "Nessa must have discovered it."

She thought then of her sister. The druidess had been sent to intercept the English army and regain the trust of the man she'd once seduced. In the spring, Nessa had arrived at Stirling, bringing news of the impending English attack. She'd also carried word that their leader had learned that Robert Bruce, the Seventh Lord of Annandale and Earl of Carrick, would one day be the savior of Scotland. The discovery had come to Colina in a vision—however, when she'd cast the bones later that day, she'd found out that forces were moving against Bruce and that he had to be protected.

Armed with this news, Nessa had bravely gone back into the wolf's lair.

Fyfa glanced out the window, her brow furrowing. She often wondered of late what had become of her sister—the three of them, Fyfa, Nessa, and Breanna were especially close. She hoped Nessa hadn't put herself at too much risk in making such a discovery. Nevertheless, she was relieved to learn that her sister no longer resided in the English camp; it was a dangerous place for a Scotswoman.

Whispering an oath under her breath, Fyfa glanced down at the missive once more, re-reading the words, committing them to memory.

The whisper of the opening door made her turn then.

Hume strode inside, one of his precious ledgers stuffed under his arm. He'd been to see Oliphant—to discuss how to utilize their dwindling resources. She imagined that was why he'd taken the ledger with him, although Hume made a point of not telling her anything these days.

Their exchange of the night before still stung. It had hurt when he refused her attempt to reach out the hand of truce between them. She'd gone to bed afterward and lain awake for hours, staring up at the darkness. Her husband was so wary of her these days—and she realized it would take more than just words to mend their relationship. She was going to have to *show* him she wanted a reconciliation.

However, now wasn't the right moment. His entrance into the solar had been ill-timed indeed.

Seeing her standing there by the window, Hume halted, his gaze shifting to the crow perched on the ledge. Puzzlement filtered over his face before he spied the parchment in her hands. "What's that?" he asked.

Fyfa glanced down, cursing herself for not tucking the scroll away the instant she heard the door open.

"Nothing," she said lightly, her fingers closing over the missive.

His gaze narrowed. "It doesn't look like *nothing*, wife." A moment passed, and then Hume slammed the ledger down on the table between them. "Is it a message?"

"No," she replied, marveling at how steady her voice was. How adept she had gotten at lying since she'd taken residence at Stirling Castle. The line between truth and fiction had become blurred over the years. "It's just a list I was making."

His dark-auburn brows crashed together. "A list of what?"

Fyfa's heart started to beat a tattoo against her ribs. "Just of chores that need doing. Nothing of importance."

Hume moved around the table toward her. "If it's not important, then ye shall let me see it." He held out a hand. "Give it to me."

Panic flared like a beacon within Fyfa. She could see the suspicion in his eyes. He believed she was keeping secrets from him—and she was. She'd promised herself she'd try to mend things between them, yet she couldn't let him read this missive from Colina.

She had to do something.

Acting on instinct, Fyfa dove forward, covering the distance between the window and the hearth in just three strides. She then threw the parchment upon the glowing coals, watching as it shriveled to black.

An instant later, Hume stood over her, his gaze burning. "What the devil are ye doing?" he demanded roughly.

"I've just realized I've done everything on the list," Fyfa replied, her tone brittle now. It was getting difficult to maintain the façade. "So ... I thought I'd burn it."

Her husband glared down at her. "Ye burned it because ye didn't wish me to see what was written upon it."

Fyfa snorted, even if her belly was now tying itself up in knots. "Don't be a dolt, Hume. I hate it when ye act like some jealous knave."

And she did. Over the years, she'd noted the way her husband glared at any man who glanced in her direction—even in the years since they no longer shared a bed. If anything, the problems between them had caused his mistrust to grow.

Hume reached out then, his fingers wrapping around her arm.

Fyfa stifled a gasp. It was the first time in months he'd touched her—and the last time, a brush of hands during supper, had been an accident. The heat of his hand burned against the bare skin of her arm. It was a hot day, and so she wore a sleeveless kirtle. "What didn't ye want me to read?" he growled, his grip tightening.

Fyfa's chin kicked up, her lips parting in wordless surprise. This behavior was completely unlike Hume. He was a big, brawny man—built more like a warrior than a steward—yet she'd always thought him as gentle as a lamb. But right now, he was at the point of crossing a line.

As if sensing this, Hume released her arm then and stepped back, his gaze guttering. A nerve flickered under one eye, betraying the emotions he was trying to tamp down.

Long moments drew out. The castle shuddered, and shouting followed, drifting across the keep from the eastern walls. Yet husband and wife continued to stare at each other.

"It was nothing important, Hume," Fyfa replied eventually. "Trust me."

Guilt twisted inside her then. *Trust me.* He had once.

His jaw tightened. "Was it a note from a lover?"

Lover. Fyfa's mouth pursed. Here it was—the accusation that simmered in the silences between them, the suspicion that had ruined their marriage.

Fyfa had indeed hidden something from him, yet she couldn't believe he thought she was carrying on with other men. She knew she could be a flirt, and her confident manner could be misconstrued—but since the day she'd first lain with Hume Comyn, she had taken no other man to her bed.

Still, she could see from the look on his face that he didn't believe her.

Despite Hume's withdrawn manner toward her the evening before, she continued to hope they could mend things. However, she had to admit that her behavior just now certainly made her look guilty.

Fyfa drew in a deep, steadying breath. "I know our rapport has been strained of late, Hume," she murmured. "But let me assure ye, even though we no longer share a bed, I have not betrayed ye."

That, at least, was the truth.

He stared down at her, his gaze shadowing. And in those eyes, she saw a flicker of vulnerability, of doubt.

Fyfa's throat constricted. Hume didn't deserve this treatment. He was a good man but wasn't as thick-skinned as most folk thought. If his mistrust of her had built a wall between them, it was the man's self-doubt that had put their relationship on shaky ground to begin with. Once, during an unguarded moment, he'd revealed to her that he couldn't understand why she'd chosen him.

His words had twisted like a boning knife to the chest.

The wrong woman could break a man like Hume Comyn. And with a sinking sensation, Fyfa realized she was well on the way to doing so. He'd loved her once, and she sensed that he still had feelings for her.

Why else would he be so jealous?

"I don't know what ye expect me to think," he murmured then. "When ye act in such a secretive fashion."

"Ye know I am a woman who likes my freedom," Fyfa replied. "Yer overbearing manner made me panic … and throw the parchment into the fire." She paused, realizing just how weak the argument was.

Long moments passed, and then he took another step back, widening the gulf between them.

With a sinking sensation in her belly, Fyfa realized he didn't believe her. She didn't blame him—she wouldn't either in his position.

Hume's lips parted as if he was going to reply, and yet he stopped himself, choking back whatever words he was going to utter. Bestowing her with a lingering, hurt look, he spun on his heel and stalked from the chamber.

Heart beating fast, Fyfa turned back to the window. She wasn't surprised to see that the High Bandruì's familiar had already departed.

4

NO SURRENDER

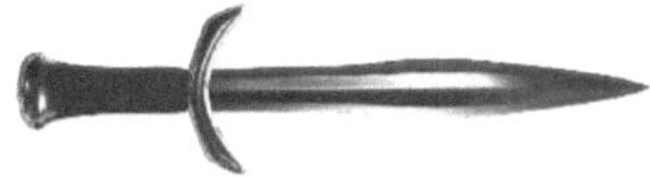

"I WON'T YIELD the castle, not yet."

Sir William Oliphant's gravelly voice carried through the solar before fading away into silence.

Seated at the table in the center of the richly furnished space, Hume regarded Stirling's governor over the rim of his pewter goblet. "I don't think Captain Stewart was suggesting that," he replied. "He just wishes to know what yer plans going forward are."

Hume too was impatient to hear how the governor wished to proceed.

Across the table, Oliphant frowned. He then reached for the jug of wine and topped up his goblet. Watching him, Hume wondered if the governor realized just how low their wine reserves were. They were down to their last barrel now. And while the rest of the keep drank boiled water drawn from the well, for the small herd of goats within the keep were too stressed to give much milk, the governor and his wife were the only folk here who had the luxury of wine with their meals.

Hume raised his goblet to his lips and took a sip. And of course, he and Fyfa could indulge this evening as well. They'd joined William and Estelle Oliphant in their large solar for a light supper. It had been a while since the last occasion the couples had dined together.

Looking upon Oliphant's face, Hume reflected how tired the man appeared these days. It was a huge burden he shouldered. Oliphant was less than a decade older than his steward, and yet his haggard features, illuminated by cressets on the wall behind him, made the governor look much older. To his right, his wife Estelle picked at her supper of turnip and kale pottage, served with boiled eggs and coarse bread. They were indeed fortunate that the castle grounds included the Nether Bailey, a large grassy area they'd had the foresight to plant out with vegetables in early spring.

Without it, the inhabitants of the castle would have surely starved.

Silence drew out before Hume cleared his throat. "Stewart has concerns," he began, "perhaps it's time the pair of ye met to discuss them."

Oliphant scowled. "And what says he?"

Hume fought the urge to return the scowl. He was getting tired of being the go-between. The governor and the captain had locked horns more than once over the past months. These days, they preferred to relay messages via Hume.

Oliphant's absence from the walls also hadn't gone unnoticed. He was starting to lose the respect of the Stirling guard—something he couldn't afford to do.

"Stewart's been paying close attention to the English camp," Hume replied, careful not to let his irritation show. "And he has noted that their numbers have swollen in the past few days. More pavilions have gone up. He thinks they are preparing for something. As such, he believes ye should at least consider negotiating with Longshanks again ... sooner rather than later." Hume paused there, before adding. "The English king isn't known for his clemency ... although if we approach him before things go any further, he may decide to spare us."

Oliphant took another gulp of wine before muttering a curse under his breath. "When did ye and Stewart turn into such old women?" he growled. "No matter what the enemy is plotting, we shall continue to defend this fortress." The governor's attention then shifted to where Fyfa sat at Hume's side. She was usually vivacious company at these suppers, yet this eve, she'd spoken little. "What say ye, Lady Comyn? Ye have always been steadfast in yer conviction that we shouldn't yield to those English dogs."

Hume's gaze roamed over Fyfa's face. She looked unusually tense this eve, her dark-blue eyes veiled. She then glanced over at Hume before focusing on the governor once more. "My husband's counsel is wise, Sir William," she replied with a demureness that was quite unlike her. "Perhaps, ye should heed Captain Stewart?"

Surprise feathered through Hume, lightening the weight that usually settled upon his chest whenever he looked at his wife. Fyfa's support meant a lot to him—especially after their argument earlier in the day when he'd found her with that missive. The woman had been lying through her teeth—he was sure of it. Nonetheless, he hadn't meant to grab her arm like that. Truthfully, the violence of his reaction had scared him. He didn't want to lose control or frighten her.

Fyfa's talk of remaining true to him contrasted with the guilt on her face as she had thrown that scroll onto the fire. She'd indeed taken a lover, and he was determined to find out just who the bastard was. There were many virile warriors within these walls, many of whom went out of their way to flirt with the steward's comely wife. The thought made Hume's belly cramp.

Across the table, Oliphant's brow had furrowed. "Not ye too, Fyfa." He snorted then. "Months of besieging us, and they're still no closer to breaching the walls. Stirling is strong, and it will hold out. There will be no parley. Stewart has clearly turned craven."

And so have ye, Comyn. The words were unspoken, yet they vibrated through the solar nonetheless.

Hume drew in a deep breath as he sought to remain patient. The governor's blinkered view on matters wasn't going to aid them in the coming days.

"Stewart is the defender of this castle," Hume replied after a pause, injecting a warning note into his voice. Aye, the captain rubbed him up the wrong way at times, yet Stewart was on the front line; he knew how badly things were going. "I think we would all be foolish to dismiss his words."

Silence fell, tension settling over the table. Eventually, Estelle Oliphant spoke up, her voice soft and imploring. "I agree with Hume and Fyfa, my darling. Perhaps ye should hear Captain Stewart out?"

Moments passed while the governor locked gazes with his wife. Estelle Oliphant was a small woman with a sweet face and soft blue eyes. Yet for all her softness, Hume knew that Sir William heeded her. He'd often felt a trifle envious over the years, at just how close the two of them were.

Estelle reached out then, placing a hand over her husband's forearm. "Ye can still refuse to negotiate, William," she reminded him gently. "Why don't ye call him to ye on the morrow … and hear his counsel?"

Next to Hume, Fyfa shifted in her seat. Glancing at his wife once more, he noted her face had tensed. Her lips parted, as if she wished to speak, before she pressed them shut.

Meanwhile, the governor and his wife continued to gaze at each other. It was as if the surroundings had faded and only the pair of them remained. Hume suddenly felt as if he and Fyfa were intruding. What he would give to have his wife look at him with such open adoration, such conviction.

William Oliphant's shoulders slumped then, before he nodded, a weary sigh escaping him. "Very well, my love."

Fyfa walked from the solar, bristling. The evening had been a disappointment. Hume appeared bent on getting Oliphant to re-open negotiations and contemplate surrender, and Estelle, a woman she usually agreed with, had taken Hume's side.

How she'd itched to support Oliphant. It had taken every inch of her self-control not to contradict her husband, yet for the sake of their marriage, she'd held her tongue.

It hadn't been the best of days. The altercation with Hume after she'd thrown Colina's missive into the fire had put her out of sorts—and the High Bandruì's message was worrying indeed. The news that Longshanks had a witch aiding him gnawed constantly at Fyfa, as did their worsening situation here. Surely, more Highlanders would come to stand with them at Stirling? They'd already aided them to keep the English at bay. But the defenders needed more of their allies to harry the enemy. Just a while longer, and the English might abandon the siege.

Fyfa had been relieved earlier when the governor had invited her and Hume to join him and his wife that evening. It had been too long since they'd had an invite from the Oliphants. However, her relief had soon turned into frustration.

When Estelle had convinced William to speak with Captain Stewart, and hear his concerns out, Fyfa had actually opened her mouth to urge him to remain steadfast. However, such a comment would contradict her earlier words. She'd also seen Hume's swift glance in her direction—a reminder to hold her tongue.

Even so, once they were out in the corridor, and heading toward the landing that would take them down to the next level and back to their apartments, Fyfa found herself simmering. Part of the reason she'd chosen Hume as her husband, alongside the fact that he was steward of Stirling, was the man's steadfast belief in the Scottish cause. In the early days of their relationship, he'd confided in her that he'd rather die than see his homeland ruled by the English.

But now both Hume and the formerly unwavering Captain Stewart seemed to be losing heart. She couldn't believe it.

They had nearly reached the stairs when Hume glanced her way. "Ye were quiet during supper," he observed.

"Was I?" she replied, deliberately keeping her tone light.

"Aye." He paused then, his attention still upon her face. "Thank ye for supporting me back there ... I didn't think ye would."

Heat flowered in Fyfa's chest. "A husband and wife should stand united," she replied stiffly.

Mother's milk, keeping her mouth shut was proving harder than she'd thought. She dearly wanted to support Hume, and yet she hated the thought of Oliphant contemplating a surrender to the enemy. Her role here was to help fight for Scottish freedom, but her desire to reconcile with her husband had put her in a difficult position indeed.

"Surely, ye too realize that Stirling will fall eventually?" Hume went on.

Fyfa clenched her jaw. She wished he'd stop talking. She wasn't sure how much longer she could keep her opinions to herself.

"And what of Longshanks?" she finally managed, surprised that her voice didn't show the ire that now boiled in her breast. "Do ye really believe he'll show us mercy when it does?"

Of course, the pair of them had first-hand experience of The Hammer. He'd taken Stirling a few years earlier and had forced her husband and the other Scots residing inside the castle to serve him. Anyone who'd opposed him had been dealt with ruthlessly.

Hume's green eyes shadowed. "He may not," he admitted. "But one thing is certain ... if we don't negotiate a surrender, every soul in the keep is likely to die."

Frustration coiled tighter still within Fyfa, and she looked away so that he wouldn't see the chagrin in her eyes.

Hume lapsed into silence. His wife was, indeed, in a strange mood this eve. Tension vibrated off her, and she kept avoiding his eye. Having his wife as an ally for once had eased his resentment toward her a little, yet as they walked down the hallway toward the steward's solar, Hume wondered if her demureness was merely a ruse to placate him.

A chill settled in the pit of his belly.

Perhaps she didn't agree with him at all, but had merely kept her opinions to herself? He'd seen the spark in her eye just now, and he'd lived with this woman long enough to sense when she was holding back.

Hume reached the door to their apartments, disappointment souring his mouth as he took hold of the handle. Didn't she realize he was trying to protect her? Didn't she understand what danger she, and everyone else in this fortress, was in?

Despite the rift between them, he couldn't bear the thought of his wife coming to harm. Of late, nightmares had plagued him—of what would happen when Stirling finally fell. On one night, in particular, he'd dreamed that he'd been held down by English soldiers and forced to watch as they raped and murdered Fyfa. The dream had been startlingly vivid and so real that Hume had awoken, heart pounding, in a cold sweat.

Aye, Longshanks would be truly vexed by now. The siege was drawing out far longer than he'd initially intended. He'd lost many soldiers during the fighting, and humiliation must have cut him to the quick.

The only way the bastard would show any mercy would be if Oliphant negotiated surrender.

Pushing his way inside the solar, Hume went to the basket beside the bench seat and pulled out his bedding.

"Are ye going to bed so soon?" Fyfa asked behind him. "I thought we could have a game or two of knucklebones before retiring." She paused then. "I could let ye win for once, if ye like?" There was a playful edge to her voice now, one that he hadn't heard in a while.

Hume straightened up, his gaze shifting to the window. Indeed, it wasn't late. Outdoors, the last blush of the long twilight still graced the sky. The attack had ceased for the day, and as always, an eerie quiet settled over the fortress while Stirling drew its breath and readied itself for the following day.

It had been a while since they'd played at knucklebones together, and the mention made him recall long winter evenings huddled together in front of the hearth.

Fyfa played knucklebones better than anyone he'd met.

Aye, he was tempted. Suddenly, he wanted nothing more than to sit with his wife and enjoy her company.

But then he recalled the tension in her face as they'd walked back from supper, the stilted way she'd responded to him, and how she'd avoided his eye.

The chill returned, slithering down his spine like an icy finger.

He wasn't a complete fool. Fyfa was trying to appease him—she was trying to *play* him like a lyre. And all the while, she was still keeping secrets from him.

His throat constricted, and he coughed to ease it. "I'm tired, Fyfa," he replied. Indeed, the weariness in his voice wasn't feigned. "I'd like to retire now."

A pause followed, and when Fyfa replied, her voice was subdued, the playfulness extinguished like a tender flame in a draft. "Very well … goodnight, husband."

"Goodnight." Hume resumed making up his bed, deliberately not glancing her way. Moments later, he heard the whisper of her foot-falls as she went through into the bed-chamber and closed the door behind her.

Alone, Hume abandoned making his bed and sank down on the edge of the bench seat instead, raking both hands through his hair. He then whispered a curse. What was happening to him these days? His life, his marriage, was falling to pieces—and he felt powerless to stop it.

5

A JEALOUS HUSBAND

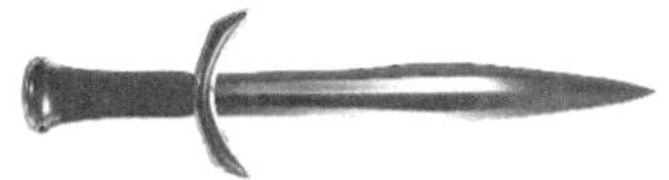

"WOULD YE LIKE some honey, Hume?" Fyfa asked, breaking the heavy hush in the solar.

Her husband glanced up from where he'd been contemplating the rough wedge of oaten griddle cake before him. However, when Fyfa held out the earthen pot of heather honey, he frowned. "There's barely any left … ye have it."

Fyfa made an impatient noise in the back of her throat. "I've already had my fill," she lied. She'd spread the barest film of honey onto her bannock so that her husband could have the rest. "Go on."

Tentatively, he took the pot from her. The wary look on his face, as if he were accepting a gift from a leper, made Fyfa's breathing constrict.

She'd tried her best the evening before to back her husband, even to her own detriment, yet he'd withdrawn from her shortly afterward. She'd seen the suspicion in his eyes and the stiff set of his shoulders.

She clearly hadn't hidden her feelings as well as she'd imagined.

Hume now thought she was trying to manipulate him.

She wasn't—she was attempting to reconcile with him.

"So, this is the last of the honey then?" Hume asked, as he scraped out the pot and spread the amber-hued paste upon his bannock.

"It seems so ... but I will see if the cooks are hiding any in the kitchens." Memories intruded then, and Fyfa smiled. "Do ye remember those delicious honey shortbreads we helped ourselves to when we conducted that midnight raid on the kitchens?"

Hume's gaze met hers, and to her surprise, his mouth quirked. "Aye, it was at Yule, if I remember ... just two months after we were wed." He paused then, his gaze glinting. "The shortbread was worth it ... although I didn't appreciate being chased out of the kitchen by an enraged cook wielding a rolling pin."

Fyfa laughed, warmth spreading through her. It pleased her to be able to make her husband smile. Alpin, the head cook, had indeed been furious with them. She recalled how close she'd felt to Hume that night, clutching his hand as they'd raced up the stairs to escape Alpin's wrath.

Watching her husband's face as he took a bite of bannock, Fyfa favored him with another smile. She wouldn't let his reticence put her off. Once she put her mind to something, she could be single-minded in her focus.

Hopefully, we can feel close like that again.

The castle shuddered. Fyfa stumbled, bracing herself against the stone wall as whatever had collided with the keep shook it to its foundations.

"Crone's tears," she muttered. "What was that?"

A moment later, she heard anguished voices echoing down from above. Fyfa's pulse quickened, and she hurried to the stairwell before taking the steps to the top level of the keep. On the way, she passed two panicked female servants, who fled in the opposite direction.

Ignoring their pleas to follow them, Fyfa pressed on. Above, she found chaos. A huge lump of stone had hit the eastern side of the keep, tearing a great hole in the wall. Daylight now streamed through the billowing smoke. Rubble covered the floor.

Through the settling dust, Fyfa spied two figures staggering toward her. The governor and his wife had emerged from their apartments farther along the corridor.

"Come," Fyfa called out to them. "It's not safe here … we must get to the lower levels."

Husband and wife heeded her and started clambering over the rubble, careful to keep close to the interior wall. It was wise, for Fyfa wasn't sure how stable this corridor actually was. She reached for the wall as well, bracing herself as the floor flexed under her feet.

The enemy was still hammering the walls.

Boom.

Another missile hit the castle, and the floor bucked, nearly throwing Fyfa to the ground.

Clutching at her husband, Estelle scrambled over the pile of rubble. Grim-faced, William Oliphant dragged his wife after him, joining Fyfa on the other side. Together the trio hurried toward the stairwell. They'd almost reached it when Hume erupted from the stairs.

"Thank the Lord," he gasped when he saw the governor and his wife were safe. "I was outside in the bailey when that boulder hit … I was sure I was going to find ye both flattened."

Oliphant huffed a wry laugh. "A few more yards to the right, and ye would have."

"Ye were fortunate indeed," Fyfa agreed. "Although let's not test yer luck by lingering up here."

"Aye." Hume cast his wife a pointed look. "Let us *all* get to safety."

They descended into the lower levels of the keep, to where hysterical servants gathered on the landing. Some of them were weeping, while others were ashen-faced. Like Hume, they'd dreaded the worst.

"All is well," William Oliphant boomed, taking charge for the first time in weeks. "As ye can see, my wife and I are unharmed. Please return to yer duties." In an instant, the shroud of exhaustion that had diminished the man of late disappeared, and the old Sir Oliphant, the man who had taken a stand against the English, returned.

Noting the glint in his eye, Fyfa allowed herself a relieved smile. Perhaps all was not lost, after all.

Leaving her husband, the governor, and his wife to calm the servants, Fyfa made her way down to the kitchens—which had been her initial destination before the missile hit. Around her, the rumble of the siege continued to vibrate the walls. The day was waning, but the attack continued.

The enemy was relentless.

Down in the kitchens, she let the cooks and servants know what had transpired upstairs. After that, she went through the meals planned for the coming days: depressing, meager fare indeed. Fyfa kept up a friendly banter with the cooks and scullery maids, although it was hard to concentrate, for worries plagued her. She'd seen Hume's ledgers—they weren't far away from starving. Yet nothing could be done, for there was no way to get supplies into the castle. The English had them surrounded.

Defeat. The very word was ashes in her mouth. She still couldn't bear to think of the possibility. *How has it come to this?*

Eventually, she left the kitchens. Climbing the stairs to the landing that would take her up to the higher levels of the keep, Fyfa was so intent on her thoughts that she didn't notice the figure that stepped out into her path.

Colliding with a lean, leather-clad man, Fyfa skidded to a halt.

"Hades," she gasped, looking up into Cameron Stewart's handsome face. "Where did ye come from, Captain?"

"Apologies, Lady Comyn." The captain inclined his head yet didn't step out of her way. "I was on my way down to the kitchens. I haven't eaten since dawn."

Studying him, Fyfa's brow furrowed. The captain's face was more strained than she'd ever seen it. There were dark circles under his eyes, and his unshaven jaw gave him a roguish look. She hadn't seen Stewart often of late—in truth, she'd taken to avoiding him, as the man had gotten a little too attentive to her in the past months. It seemed that defending a castle under siege wasn't nearly enough of a distraction for him.

Of course, the captain's prowess abed was the talk of the servants, although Fyfa hadn't been one of his conquests—and she didn't intend to be.

"I'm sure the cooks will prepare ye something," she replied with a smile. She then went to slide past him.

However, he forestalled her with a question. "Are there any eggs left?"

Fyfa halted. "I'm afraid not … the fowls have stopped laying."

His mouth thinned at this. "So, it's pottage and hard bannock, is it?"

"Aye."

His gaze lingered on her face then, and Fyfa tensed. The man was exhausted and hungry, yet she spied the naked interest in his eyes. "It's been a while since we have spoken, Fyfa," he murmured. "I've missed yer bonny face."

Fyfa favored him with another smile, although this one was a trifle strained. The thrice-cursed man had shifted so that she would need to push him aside to move past. "Aye … well … we've all been occupied of late."

"Aye … but life should be about more than just war, lass." His voice had lowered to an intimate rumble. He stepped closer then, and she moved back to find her back up against the wall. There was nowhere else to go; the man effectively had her cornered.

Their gazes held, and Fyfa considered her next move.

She wasn't one easily intimidated or flustered by men. She had a naturally playful manner, and there had been a time when she'd enjoyed the attention. But with everything that had happened of late, she found it hard to flirt or to respond to the smiles and comments of the men within this castle.

She had no patience for the likes of Cameron Stewart.

"Aye," she replied, her tone cooling. "It's about survival."

The captain favored her with an arch look. "We'll survive."

Irritation spiked through Fyfa. *No wonder he's keen to surrender to the English,* she thought bitterly. *I bet the fazart's keen to save his own hide.*

She didn't voice her thoughts aloud though—few men enjoyed being named a coward.

Oblivious to her ire, or perhaps drawn to it, the captain grinned and reached out, stroking her cheek with the back of his hand. "Don't worry, Fyfa, when the castle falls, I shall protect ye."

Fyfa clenched her jaw. *Men.* Crone's tears, she was tired of them. She wasn't useless and feeble, and she didn't want the captain's protection. She had a husband to defend her, and her own skills to call upon.

"Stewart!" A male voice intruded then, rough with anger. "Get away from my wife."

The captain dropped his hand and stepped back, swiveling toward where Hume strode toward them.

Pulse fluttering in the base of her throat, Fyfa watched her husband approach. Hume's broad shoulders were rounded, his hands clenched by his sides. His face was set in fierce lines, and his moss-green eyes blazed.

Cold washed over Fyfa. She didn't want him to think she'd been flirting with Stewart. His jealousy was really getting too much.

"We were just sharing some words, Comyn," Stewart said lightly, a rakish grin splitting his face. He didn't appear remotely concerned by the fact that Hume was bearing down upon them. "No need to get yer braies in a knot."

"Ye don't need to stand over her to do that," Hume snarled. "Or touch her."

"Hume," Fyfa interjected, stepping between them. "It's not—"

"Stand aside, Fyfa." His voice reverberated against stone. "Let me deal with this."

"I will not, ye great clodhead," she countered, her own ire rising. "The captain was indeed crowding me, yet nothing happened ... and nothing was going to. Please calm yerself."

Hume halted, looming over her. His eyes narrowed, and a nerve bunched in his jaw. Her breathing quickened. She didn't like upsetting him—but it seemed that was all she did these days. Everything she said and did roused suspicion. And now Cameron Stewart, with his flirtatious behavior, had just made matters worse. If things continued in this vein, there would soon be an unbridgeable gulf between them.

"If ye wish to take a swing at me, be my guest, Comyn," Stewart drawled from behind her, his voice amused. "However, I warn ye that I shall strike back."

"Cur!" Hume's face contorted, and he lunged forward, moving to push Fyfa aside.

"No!" Digging her heels in, she slammed her palms hard upon the stone wall of his chest. "Stop it ... both of ye!" Her pulse now thundered in her ears. "God's teeth, Hume ... enough of this," she said between gritted teeth. "I swear, ye have nothing to worry about."

The keep shook then, the thick stone walls trembling under the impact of another missile.

A heartbeat followed, and then cries erupted upon the floor above them, the shouting drifting down the stairwell that lay just a few yards away. Moments later, someone started screaming, the shrill noise echoing through the keep.

Captain Stewart muttered a curse under his breath and pushed past Fyfa and Hume. "This will have to wait, Comyn," he muttered. All trace of goading and amusement had disappeared from his face.

The captain strode off, taking the stairs two at a time.

Spitting an expletive of his own, Hume stepped back from Fyfa. "Stay down here," he ordered. Then, before she could answer him, Hume swiveled on his heel and took off after the captain of the guard.

Alone in the hallway, Fyfa watched her husband disappear. A heartbeat passed, and then she picked up her skirts and hurried across the wide hall and toward the doors that would take her out of the keep.

She needed to warn their healer to ready the infirmary.

6

WHY DID YE MARRY ME?

FYFA WENT UP to the walls as dusk settled. Smoke wreathed across the ramparts, making her cough as she picked her way through the debris.

She took in the damage—the missing chunks out of the merlons, the blackened frames of trebuchets upon the walls that had been incinerated by Greek fire—and her skin prickled. The last few months had left a deep scar upon Stirling Castle. Every night, after the assault ended for the day, men climbed up here and did their best to repair the walls. But she could see that it was like trying to patch up a storm-tossed birlinn full of holes.

Sooner or later, their ship would sink.

Don't ye lose despair too, she inwardly berated herself. *Scotland needs ye!*

And it did.

Moving to a sturdier section of the wall, she peered east through the crenel between two merlons, at the patchwork of tents and fluttering flags that carpeted the hillside. Her gaze narrowed. Aye, the English camp did seem to have grown in size since she'd last ventured up here.

Fyfa swallowed, her throat constricting. *How I wish my sisters were here to advise me.*

She missed Nessa and Breanna constantly these days. The three of them were the same age. Colina, the High Bandruì of the Guardians of Alba, had found them all in the same year—all foundlings, all unwanted bairns that she had taken in and raised as her own daughters.

However, as much as she wished to be calmed by Nessa's steadying influence, and to be bolstered by Breanna's defiance, Fyfa was relieved that her sisters weren't in Stirling. This was the most dangerous place in Scotland right now.

She remained there at the wall for a while longer, surveying the English camp, and as she did so, for the first time ever, Fyfa felt doubt creep through her.

She and her sisters had been tireless over the past years, but had things gone too far? Would Scotland fall, despite all the work they'd put in, all the sacrifices they'd made?

"No," she whispered aloud. "I won't let that happen."

Fyfa lived to protect her homeland. Ever since she'd been old enough to know who her mother and sisters were, and the shared mission that bonded them, she'd dedicated herself to their goal entirely. Fyfa had no idea who her blood kin, her clan, were. Colina had found her abandoned, on the banks of a burn on a chilly spring morning. The druidess had told her it was most likely the large leaf-shaped birthmark she bore upon her left thigh that had scared her parents into abandoning her. Some superstitious folk believed such bairns, who carried 'the mark', were changelings.

Fyfa rarely dwelled upon her origins. It didn't matter who her blood relatives were; the Guardians were the only family she'd ever known. The only family she needed.

And what about Hume … is he not family too?

Fyfa drew in a deep breath before reaching up a fist to rub at the ache that had risen beneath her breast bone. Aye, he was. Despite that she couldn't share the truth with him, she and her husband still had a bond, one she would fight to preserve.

Pushing thoughts of Hume aside for the moment, and trying to ignore the lingering ache in her breast, Fyfa peered into the gloaming. Something was going on down there. Beyond the English palisade, they appeared to be erecting something. There was a scaffold of sorts.

Had Hume noticed it?

Fyfa turned from the wall. She needed to find her husband and tell him what she'd just spied.

Fyfa stepped into the solar and abruptly halted. She'd sought Hume out here, although she'd expected to find him seated at the table eating his supper or resting on the bench seat.

But instead, he stood before a washbowl by the window, naked to the waist as he bathed.

Fyfa's gaze ranged over the broad muscles of his back and shoulders, and her breathing stilled. It had been a long while since she'd seen his naked torso, and he was even stronger and more muscular than she remembered. She knew he'd taken to training with the men every dawn, yet he'd bulked up even more than she'd realized.

His pale, lightly freckled skin glistened with water, and Fyfa found her belly tightening with awareness. A dizzying wave of desire followed. Two years was a long time to live without any intimacy with her husband.

When Hume turned to her, her traitorous gaze slid across his sculpted chest, watching the water that trickled down his flat belly to the waist band below. His braies sat low on his hips, so low that her gaze settled upon the vee of muscles that angled down to his groin and the curls of dark-auburn hair that peeked over the waistband.

Fyfa's heart lurched into her throat.

Maiden's Blood, what am I doing? She yanked her gaze upward, and the heat of desire that had pooled in the cradle of her hips dissolved.

Hume Comyn's face was stone-hewn this evening. Of course, after the incident with Cameron Stewart, she'd expected as such.

Fyfa licked her lips, nervousness stealing upon her. "Have ye eaten yet?" she asked. It wasn't an empty question, for she did sometimes worry that her husband didn't take proper care of himself. Of late, he'd become so focused on helping defend the castle, he seemed to have little time for anything else.

"No," he replied, his tone guarded. "I'm about to."

He reached for a drying cloth, deftly removed the distracting rivulets of water from his chest and abdomen, and hauled on a loose lèine.

"I've just been up on the walls," she said after a pause.

Hume's gaze narrowed. "Ye shouldn't—"

"Don't worry," she interrupted him before he could reprimand her. "I waited till the siege had ceased for the day." She drew in a breath. "Ye do realize the English are building something down there?"

Hume stilled. "They are?"

"Aye … there's a large scaffold behind the eastern perimeter."

"Another siege tower?"

"Perhaps … but it might be worth alerting Captain Stewart and Sir William about."

Silence fell between them before he nodded. However, his expression didn't soften.

Fyfa cleared her throat. Moving to the table, she pulled out a chair and lowered herself down into it. "We need to talk, Hume," she said softly.

"Aye, we do," Hume helped himself to some pottage and a wedge of bannock and took a seat opposite her. He then glanced up, his brow furrowing. "Aren't ye eating?"

Fyfa shook her head. "I had my supper earlier," she lied. In truth, she had little appetite this evening. "Ye go on."

She watched as he dipped the bannock into the vegetable stew to soften it before taking a bite. He then chewed without any sign of enjoyment.

"The pottage is a bit watery, I'm afraid," she said in an attempt to ease things between them. "The cooks are running low on turnips and onions."

He gave a nod, yet she could tell he wasn't paying any attention to his supper.

"Look, Hume," she began, deciding that it was best to start talking. The weighty pauses were getting to her. "Ye got the wrong end of the stick today … nothing happened between me and Captain Stewart … and nothing ever will."

Hume swallowed before reaching for a cup of boiled, cooled water. His gaze was shuttered when it met hers. "That bastard has had an eye on ye for a while now."

"Aye, that hasn't escaped my notice either," she replied, careful to keep her tone low and even. "But that doesn't mean I've encouraged him. The man believes he's the Lord's gift to women ... and he cornered me today."

Silence stretched out between them, and the urge to apologize fluttered up within Fyfa. Irritation followed swiftly behind it. She had nothing to say sorry for—whatever Hume thought, she had never taken a lover.

"What was I supposed to think, Fyfa?" Hume asked eventually. His voice was low yet held a rasp. "Seeing the two of ye standing so close."

Fyfa dragged in a deep breath. "I know how it must have looked, but—"

"And what if he'd tried to kiss ye?" he cut her off. "Would ye have stopped him?" Her husband's face was pale and strained. He still hadn't raised his voice. Nonetheless, she could feel his tension; it shimmered between them.

Heat flooded through Fyfa as her irritation slid into anger. "Of course, I would have," she replied, her voice clipped now.

"Would ye?"

Fyfa's heart started to pound against her ribs. Curse him, he wasn't listening to her. "I can see that nothing I say will make any difference to ye, husband," she bit out between clenched teeth. "But I repeat ... I have spread my legs for none other than ye." The words were crude, yet they spilled out of her. She'd hidden many things from her husband—including her real identity—and guilt often pulled at her chest when she thought of just what a sham their marriage was. But she'd never cuckolded him.

Hume stared back at her, his gaze widening.

An instant later, Fyfa was on her feet and heading toward the door to her bed-chamber. "I'll bid ye good eve now."

However, she was just a foot from the door when Hume spoke once more. "Why did ye marry me?"

Pulse thundering, Fyfa spun around and met his eye. His expression was hard, yet the raw pain in his eyes made her anger momentarily dim. In that instant, she hated herself for what she'd done to him. She'd never given Hume's feelings much thought, years earlier, when she'd sought to win his heart and his hand in marriage. He'd merely been the key she needed to secure herself a place at Stirling Castle and unlock the secrets her order needed.

And her position had yielded many secrets over the years. She'd been able to provide the Guardians with a lot of information that had aided their fight against the English.

But it had come at a cost—and tonight, she wondered if the price had been too high for both of them.

"Why would ye ask me that?" she choked out. "Ye *know* why I wed ye."

Hume rose to his feet and approached her. Fyfa moved back, only to find herself flush against the closed door.

"Do I?" he said roughly. "I was entranced by ye at the time, Fyfa ... it was only later that I questioned what my beautiful, fire-haired wife ever saw in me."

Fyfa's breathing caught. Hume's words brought her back to the first time they'd lain together just over five years earlier. They'd danced around each other for a while, and then, frustrated that he wasn't aggressively pursuing her, Fyfa had come to his bed-chamber one night.

Hume had been both delighted and unnerved by her boldness, and when he undressed her, she'd noted how his hands had shaken. And when they'd lain together, naked, upon the bed, he'd admitted that she was his first.

He was five and twenty and had never lain with a woman.

The knowledge had surprised her. Hume was a tall, strong man with rugged good looks and a gentle, if slightly dour, temperament. She couldn't imagine why he hadn't tumbled a number of lasses by that age. But afterward—when she'd shown him how to please her, before they'd both found their release—he'd admitted that he'd always been cripplingly shy around women.

He'd grown up the only son of a bitter widow who'd taken out her hatred of men upon him.

It had shocked her to learn he'd believed no woman would want him.

"I saw many things in ye, Hume," she whispered. And it was the truth. "Ye are honest, stout-hearted, and loyal."

His throat worked. "Aye … like a hound."

Fyfa's breathing hitched. This wasn't going well. He wasn't touching her, yet his proximity was unnerving and distracting her. The scent of lye soap and clean male enveloped her. Crone's tears, it had been so long since she'd been this close to him—and she felt a fluttering sensation low in her belly at his nearness.

"I'm not to blame for yer lack of trust in women," she murmured. "Ever since we wed, ye have watched me like a hawk … it's almost as if ye *want* me to cuckold ye."

He shook his head, his gaze guttering. "What I want is a wife whom I can trust." He stepped nearer still, his closeness overwhelming now. Fyfa's chin kicked up as she struggled to hold his gaze. His breath feathered across her ear when he leaned in. "Do I repulse ye, Fyfa?"

"No," she whispered honestly. The Three strike her down, it was quite the opposite. Her core tightened at the roughness in his voice. Maybe that was what they both needed—to rid this tension between them with a good tumble? Initially, it had been good between them. In those first months, they'd spent long, sweaty nights enjoying each other's bodies—and then the rot had set in. She reached up then, her palm splaying against his chest. "I meant what I said the other evening, Hume. I want us to start again."

And she truly did. An ache now rose deep within her, as she realized how lonely she was. Beneath her brave front, sadness dogged her steps. She wanted Hume to be her safe haven, especially now when things were looking so dire for them all.

Her husband's face shuttered. An instant later, Hume stepped back from her. "How can we?" He moved back farther, his broad chest rising and falling sharply. "When ye keep secrets from me."

7

NOTHING TO HIDE

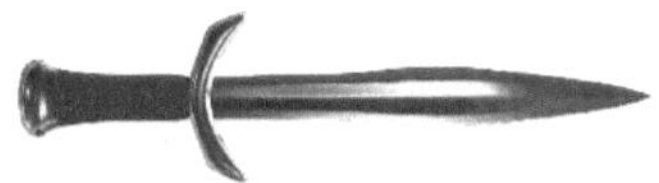

FYFA AWOKE BEFORE dawn, listening to the muffled shouts of men at combat practice in the bailey below. It was a daily routine for them—for it limbered the muscles and eased tension—before the defenders of Stirling Castle went up onto the walls.

Hume would be down there with them.

Lying there, staring up at the rafters, Fyfa wondered if she'd ever be reconciled with her husband. Events seemed to conspire against her: first the missive she'd thrown into the fire, and then the awkward scene with Captain Stewart. For every tentative step she and Hume took forward, they seemed to be taking three strides back.

Fyfa's throat tightened as she pushed herself up in bed and kicked off the covers. Of course, underneath it all, she knew she was largely to blame for this mess.

Ye shouldn't have married him. Indeed, Hume was a decent man, and he deserved better.

Her single-minded pursuit of Scottish freedom meant that there wasn't space for much else in her life. Her secrets and lies had slowly eroded Hume's trust, but she couldn't tell him who she really was—she'd sworn an oath to her order to keep her identity secret.

Muttering a curse, she swung her legs over the side of her bed and rose to her feet, reaching for her clothes.

"Focus, Fyfa," she murmured aloud. "Ye have more than just Hume to worry about at present."

It was true. She was letting herself get distracted. She'd spent a restless night, her thoughts entirely upon her husband: the sight of him standing there by the window the night before, half-naked, his skin glistening with water; and the way he'd stood close to her, not touching her, yet with his breath feathering against her cheek.

Maiden's blood, how she'd wanted him in that moment. She'd ached with need at the gruff timbre of his voice and the musky scent of his skin.

But, instead, she should be thinking about the warning Eclipse had brought her, and about that odd-looking scaffold she'd spied in the English camp. And what of Robert Bruce? If she survived this siege, he would need to be her priority.

Fyfa's jaw firmed as she laced up the bodice of her kirtle.

She'd prepare some bannock now, for Hume upon his return from combat practice—and then she would go to her sanctuary and cast the bones to see what the Goddesses had in store for them in the coming days.

Hume silently forced down a lump of dry bannock—there was no butter or honey to spread upon it now, and they were forced to use stale, coarse grain. It was barely palatable.

Yet Hume choked it down with the same doggedness he used in daily life.

Across the table, Fyfa was strangely subdued. Although things had been strained between them for a while now, his wife usually had a light, easy presence. Yet not so this morning. Her face was pale, the hollows under her eyes hinting that she hadn't slept well the night before.

Hume certainly hadn't.

He'd lain awake for hours, staring up at the darkness, his belly knotted, his mind churning. It was becoming too much now; his wife had turned into an obsession—his jealousy was spiraling out of control.

What was he turning into?

However, in the morning light, he'd regained control once more. There was plenty to keep him busy today, for he had to help the men shore up the castle gates—they had taken a hammering from one of the enemy's siege towers, the huge iron bars that held them in place creaking ominously while a huge oaken battering ram pounded on the other side.

Thinking of the battering ram brought Hume's mind back sharply to other matters—to the fantasy he often had of Fyfa spread out beneath him as he plunged into her. It had been a while since they'd coupled, yet he still recalled every detail of his wife's luscious body. He remembered the way her tight, hot quim had gripped him hard and milked his rod when he'd finally lost himself inside her.

Stop it. Hume clenched his jaw, wincing as he bit his cheek. The last thing he needed now was to start thinking about the honey pot between his wife's legs—a place he hadn't touched in far too long.

Across the table, Fyfa suddenly pushed aside her bannock and rose to her feet.

Hume's attention went to her untouched meal, and he frowned. It was unlike Fyfa to waste food.

"Where are ye off to?" he asked as she removed her apron and moved toward the door.

"I need to talk to the cooks," she replied, her tone airy. Fyfa deliberately didn't meet his eye.

"At this hour?"

"Aye."

Without a glance in his direction, his wife left their apartments, the door thudding shut behind her.

Muttering a curse under his breath, Hume pushed aside his own bannock and got up.

Where is she off to?

He'd had enough. He had to know, one way or the other—and if she had nothing to hide, then she wouldn't mind. Her secretive ways were driving him insane. It had gotten to the point that he didn't believe a word the woman said.

Was she meeting a lover?

He'd soon find out.

Crossing to the door, Hume let himself out into the corridor beyond.

The numerous tasks that awaited him today—including the gates—were suddenly forgotten; instead, he was focused on one thing only.

What he needed now was proof of his wife's infidelities—and today, he'd find it.

Turning left, he made his way to the service stairwell that led down to the kitchens. Fyfa should have gone this way. Entering the narrow stairs, he paused, ears straining. Aye, he could hear the soft pad of her footsteps descending below.

He followed her, glad for the worn leather boots on his feet that made his passage swift and silent. However, as he followed her, a sickly sensation rose within him.

Was this what he'd been reduced to—the sort of man who dogged his wife's steps intent on catching her out in a lie? Hume wasn't proud of his behavior, but he couldn't stop himself from following Fyfa. The queasiness in his belly increased with each step, yet he pushed himself on.

He had to know.

Moments later, he emerged into the smoky kitchens—where three of the younger cooks were laying into each other with wooden spoons, angry shouts reverberating against stone—and spied a flash of red hair disappearing into the stairwell on the opposite side of the long space.

Usually, Hume would have interceded in the brawl and sorted out the disagreement, but this morning, the cooks could have killed each other and he wouldn't have cared. This morning, he had other matters on his mind.

Cold rage washed over him then, dousing the nausea. *So, she came down here to talk to the cooks, did she?*

Hume crossed the kitchens in a few long strides, ignoring the angry howls, and dove up the stairs after Fyfa.

He'd known she was up to something—and his gut hadn't steered him wrong.

Closing the distance between them, he spied Fyfa up ahead. She alighted the steps quickly, her shoulders rounded, head bowed, as if she were deep in thought. She hadn't realized he was but a few yards behind her.

And then, Fyfa ducked right, into a store alcove.

Hume's heart started hammering like a war drum against his ribs.

Where the devil is she going?

Hume slowed his pace, his body coiled as he prepared himself for what he'd find in the alcove. His heart was pounding so loud he couldn't hear anything else; fury pumped through him. The nausea had returned, his stomach roiling now.

If he found a man waiting for her, he'd kill the bastard.

Stepping up to the entrance of the alcove, Hume's gaze swept the interior.

To his surprise, he saw that Fyfa was alone. His wife had her back to him as she crouched and pulled back some sacking, revealing a trap door beneath.

Hume stilled, his pulse still throbbing in his ears. Of course, the alcove was too open, too public. The lovers would meet somewhere hidden—somewhere they wouldn't be disturbed.

His breathing quickened while Fyfa opened the trap door and climbed down, disappearing from view.

She hadn't even looked back over her shoulder to ensure no one was walking by.

Hume clenched his jaw, pain darting through his ears. The woman was so eager to meet with her lover that she'd become imprudent. Dizziness swept over him—betrayal clenching in his chest. Swallowing, he reached out, bracing himself against the wall.

Moments passed while he stood there, staring at the closed trap door. Dread held him fast, rooting his feet to the ground. Now he'd come to it, he wasn't sure he could bear seeing Fyfa with a lover. Right now, he felt as if the sight might actually make his heart stop.

Drawing in a deep breath and then another, Hume gathered his courage.

He'd given the lovers enough time now, to allow them to put themselves into a compromising position. He couldn't leave it any longer.

Just get it over with, man.

Crossing to the trapdoor, he yanked it open and dropped through the hole, sliding down the iron ladder into the cellar below.

Hume's boots hit stone, the impact jarring his joints. Yet he paid the discomfort no mind. Already he was swiveling, his body coiled for the sight of his wife and her lover.

But, once again, Fyfa was alone.

She stood, like a frightened doe, a candle grasped in one hand, her blue eyes as wide as moons. Her pulse fluttered at the hollow of her neck.

Moments passed while they stared at each other, and then Hume's attention shifted to the cellar in which they stood. It wasn't what he'd expected. Instead of sacks of grain or barrels of ale and mead, he stood in what looked like a shrine. Flickering cressets lined the walls, and upon shelves sat neat stacks of colored candles, clay bottles, and drying bunches of herbs.

The floor was clear, except for a charcoal-drawn five-pointed star.

Hume's gaze settled upon that star, his skin prickling. And as he looked closer still, he saw that lumps of yellowed bone bearing strange markings had been scattered across it.

Heart bucking against his ribs, Hume looked his wife's way once more. And when he spoke, his voice came out in a croak. "What the hell is this?"

8

EXCUSES

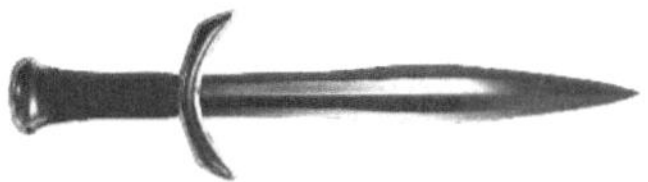

FYFA DIDN'T MOVE for a few moments.

He'd appeared from nowhere.

A heartbeat passed, and then another—and a sickly sensation washed over her.

Thrice-cursed idiot, she'd forgotten to ward the trapdoor on the way down. She'd never before forgotten, but this morning she'd been so distracted and worried, so wrapped up in her own thoughts, that she'd omitted to take her usual precautions.

Hume had followed her.

Why?

A chill seeped over Fyfa, drilling into her bones. Of course—he didn't trust her. He'd been hoping to catch her out. Canoodling with Captain Stewart most likely. And he had caught her out—but this clearly wasn't what he'd been expecting to see.

"What does it look like, Hume?" she said softly.

A nerve ticked in his jaw. "Don't answer me with a question, woman." His arm then swept in an arc around him. "This looks like" —his face twisted— "*witchcraft.*"

A beat of silence followed before Fyfa answered, "It is." Strangely, as she said those words, Fyfa felt something unknot deep within her chest.

For years, she'd kept her real identity secret. For years, she'd pretended to be someone she wasn't. And now, in an instant, the lie was being stripped away.

Aye, she saw horror light in her husband's eyes as she spoke, but at the same time, her own shoulders lowered.

She'd have kept who she was secret from Hume forever if she'd been able to—but fate had moved against them both.

Hume's gaze narrowed. "Ye are a *witch*?"

Fyfa nodded. The identity of her order was a well-kept secret. She'd sworn never to reveal its existence or location to outsiders—yet as she stared back at Hume, she realized she was ready to tell him everything. She couldn't stand the secrecy and subterfuge. Finally, she would be honest with him.

Hume had suffered greatly because of her. But perhaps the truth now could heal the rift between them. He was in shock, yet once he overcame that, he might understand.

However, her husband's face had gone hard, his big frame rigid.

"Ye never thought to discover such a thing about yer wife," she murmured, her fingers tightening around the candle she held. It was a deep-gold color. The hue represented ambition and knowledge—the perfect shade to burn at the heart of the pentagram while she cast the bones. Her telling bones still lay scattered where she had cast them the day before. "But surely, ye can see why I'd keep something like this secret?"

Hume's jaw tensed, his gaze shadowing. Yet he didn't speak.

"I'm a member of the Guardians of Alba," she said when the silence drew out between them once more. "An order of druidesses sworn to protect Scotland from invaders." She paused there, her gaze fusing with his before pushing on. It was best she said this directly, without bandying words. "And, aye, I was sent here to Stirling, to gather information on their behalf."

Hume went rigid, and when he finally spoke, his voice was rough. "It was all a lie ... ye never loved me?"

The raw hurt in his eyes cut her deep, and for a moment, Fyfa found it hard to draw breath. "I've always been fond of ye, Hume," she replied huskily, "despite all of the troubles we've had."

Goose-wit, that was the wrong thing to say.

His lip curled. "Fond," he growled. "Once again, ye refer to me as if I'm a dog, Fyfa ... not a husband."

Fyfa's heart started to race, and her palms grew damp. Panic wreathed up within her. "I really do care for ye, Hume."

The Goddesses strike her down, was that was the best she could manage?

"Ye've been living a lie," he shot back. "How can I believe a word ye tell me?"

"I swore an oath of secrecy to my order."

"Ye also made a vow to me on our wedding day." Reaching up, Hume dragged a hand through his short hair, leaving it in spiky disarray. "Ye are manipulative and scheming, Fyfa ... don't try to make excuses for yerself."

Fyfa flinched. Hume had never addressed her thus. "I did it for Scotland," she whispered. "But I'm sorry my actions have hurt ye ... that was the last thing I wanted."

Even if the words were true, they weren't enough. Even to her own ears, they sounded hollow, feeble. But Fyfa wasn't sure how to explain herself, how to make him understand. It seemed that every time she opened her mouth, she just made things worse.

"I too am loyal to Scotland," he replied, biting out the words. "But unlike ye, I don't use others to get what I want." His gaze swept over the interior of the cellar, over her witch ways that she'd collected so carefully over the years. This place was her refuge from the outside world, yet Hume gazed upon it as if he expected to see demons emerge from the shadows. "What manner of witchcraft do ye summon in here?"

"I'm a bandruì, Hume," she replied, weariness seeping into her tone. Crone's tears, she suddenly felt exhausted. "Please don't speak as if I'm some Satan worshipper. My order follows the old ways. We are at one with the seasons, the elements ... we see omens in the phases of the moon, the flight patterns of birds, and in the formations of clouds in the sky. We heal and cast the bones" —she motioned to the space behind her— "to divine the future. We are a part of this land." She paused then, struggling to keep her tone level. "And ye should use more respect when ye speak of us."

The distrust and disdain she now saw in Hume Comyn's eyes wounded her. It was a reminder of why the order kept itself secret and hidden.

Men had never understood the power of women.

But Hume's expression didn't soften. If anything, the distrust in his eyes deepened. He took a step toward her, and Fyfa stiffened. He didn't belong here—not in her secret place. "And that candle ye hold," he said, his tone roughening further. "What is its purpose?"

Fyfa swallowed. "I'm skilled in candle witching," she murmured. "Fire amplifies and releases energy … it transforms everything it comes in contact with."

"And those different colored candles." Hume's gaze had shifted to the shelves lining the pitted stone walls. "What are they for?"

Fyfa cleared her throat. His questioning made her nervous. She was sure there was a purpose to it—one that he would use against her. "The hue of a candle denotes its use. White for serenity, black for protection … green for prosperity."

"And red?"

Fyfa tensed. Here it was. "It encourages love, passion … and sensuality," she murmured.

Silence fell between them. Hume crossed to the shelving and picked up one of the red candles, holding it up to the light.

Fyfa started to sweat. She'd only ever used that candle once. It had burned down halfway, although the name she'd scratched into its side was still visible. She watched her husband's features tighten as he read his own name, his fingertip running over the etched words.

"Nothing between us was real." His voice was barely above a whisper. "Was it?"

"I only used the candle to ensure ye didn't turn me away that night," she replied softly. "I swear it, Hume." She took a step toward him. "Some things cannot be feigned. Surely, ye remember the passion that once existed between us? It would burn once more ... if ye gave it a chance."

He set the candle back down on the shelf and turned to her, his gaze steely. "Aye ... yet I now realize why."

"No, listen to me!" Panic flowered within Fyfa's breast. Curse it, the man was beyond listening to her. "Candle witching doesn't work that way ... it only amplifies what's already there." She paused then, searching for the right words to penetrate his hurt and anger. "Ye wanted me ... and I wanted ye ... I merely used the craft to break down any barriers between us."

Hume stared back at her. It was clear her explanation hadn't made the slightest difference. If anything, each word she uttered was building a wall between them.

"And has it helped, Fyfa?" he asked finally. "Has being wed to me given ye the information ye needed?"

"Aye," she murmured. "As steward, ye are privy to secrets and rumors that I wouldn't have access to otherwise." She dragged in a shaky breath. "I have discovered much to aid us over the years."

A beat of silence followed. The look on Hume's face made an ache rise in Fyfa's chest. Maiden's blood, he looked as if she'd just driven a blade into his heart.

However, when he spoke once more, his voice held a flinty edge to it. "But still, here we are ... with the enemy at our gates ... with starvation and ruin breathing down our necks."

Fyfa's chest constricted. "Aye, but without the aid of the Highlanders who have raided the English camp repeatedly, we would have fallen long before now. How do ye think help got here so quickly?" She paused then, letting her words sink in. "That woman who arrived here in late March and advised us of the English army's arrival, Nessa, wasn't my cousin, but a Guardian. Without her, we wouldn't have had warning."

Hume held her gaze. "But ye can't stop the enemy, can ye?"

Fyfa didn't break his stare. "Not this time, no," she admitted softly.

Hume stepped back from her then, his gaze sweeping over her sanctuary once more. "It's over, Fyfa," he said, each word falling heavily in the storeroom. "I thought our marriage was broken." His mouth twisted. "Yet I now see it was only ever mummery on yer part."

"Don't say such things, Hume." Fyfa's voice cracked. Her heart now fluttered like a trapped dove. She took another step toward him and raised a trembling hand. "Now ye know the truth, there are no barriers between us. I do want ye. Let me prove it to ye. Please."

"No." Hume's voice cut into her like an axe as he held up a hand to forestall her. He took a step back toward the iron ladder. "I don't wish ye to prove *anything* to me. It's too late for that. We are trapped together in this keep for now ... but I swear to ye ... if we get out of Stirling alive, I shall wash my hands of ye."

Fyfa watched Hume leave. She didn't try to stop him, didn't say a word. It really was over, she saw it in the depths of his moss-green eyes. He was wed to a woman he didn't know at all, and he wasn't about to forgive her for using him.

When he disappeared, Fyfa walked on stiff legs over to the pentagram and lowered herself to the cold stone floor. She was still clutching her golden candle, yet she couldn't even remember why she'd held it. All of a sudden, nothing in the world mattered.

A chill had settled over her with Hume's departure, one that drilled deep into the marrow of her bones.

He hates me now.

Aye, he probably did. But the hurt and disappointment she'd seen in his eyes wounded Fyfa even more. Hume hadn't had an easy life, and his experiences had made him wary of others. But in the early days of their relationship, he'd trusted her. She'd been his anchor in a world that had bruised him.

Until distrust crept in.

Fyfa heaved a deep sigh as she relived the disintegration of their marriage. It had been subtle at first. Fyfa was secretive about her daily routine and would often leave the keep to pass on details to one of her sisters visiting in town. Whenever Hume questioned her about her strange errands and disappearances, she'd keep her answers vague. After that, she'd sometimes caught Hume watching her with a veiled expression, as he waged a war with himself—between love and suspicion.

Finally, he'd seen her one afternoon, two years earlier, talking to a warrior at the market on Riverside. Fyfa had been standing close to him under the awning of a shop, her chin raised, her attention rapt. The man had melted into the shadows as Hume approached, and when her husband had demanded to know what she'd been talking to him about, her excuse was that she'd merely been discussing the situation with the English with a fellow MacKinnon—the clan she'd told him she belonged to.

It was a half-truth—for the man had been providing her with news from the border—yet Hume hadn't believed her.

It was then that Fyfa discovered her husband was capable of terrible jealousy. Angered by his reaction, Fyfa had responded badly.

They'd argued again later that eve, their voices echoing through the keep. However, the quarrel hadn't mended things between them—instead, they'd both lost their tempers and said things that could never be taken back.

Trust was irrevocably broken, and Hume hadn't shared her bed ever since.

And now he knew the truth—and despised her for it.

For a long while, Fyfa sat there on the cold storeroom floor, a strange numbness creeping over her.

She couldn't believe it: Hume was going to leave her.

Over the years, she'd wondered what would happen if he ever discovered the truth about her. She'd convinced herself that she'd be able to explain herself, and that his love for her would be enough.

But it wasn't.

Fyfa's belly hollowed out. She'd told him she was 'fond' of him—that she 'cared'. No wonder Hume had gotten angry. Those words were insipid, pale imitations of what he felt for her.

What was wrong with her? Why couldn't she give of herself? It was as if she'd given not just her loyalty but her heart and soul to the Guardians, to her cause, and had nothing else to give.

No wonder Hume wanted to leave her.

Nonetheless, it would be near impossible for him to annul their marriage. The church required proof that the union was 'invalid', usually because of an existing spouse or because husband and wife were too closely related. Neither of those things applied to Hume and Fyfa. So, instead, theirs would be a 'separation', in which they weren't required to live together and behave like husband and wife. However, in the eyes of the law, they would still be wed.

Fyfa swallowed hard as tears stung the back of her eyes. She'd failed Hume, failed her order—and failed herself. The role she'd worked so hard to establish and maintain was toppling down, like the walls of this castle when the English were through with them.

The English.

Drawing in a shaky breath, Fyfa's gaze shifted to the pentagram. Aye, that was why she'd come down here—to cast the bones to catch a glimpse of what the next few days might hold.

But now, she suddenly found it hard to care.

Her eyes burned, her vision blurring. Blinking hard, as she struggled to keep the tears at bay, Fyfa shifted, kneeling before the pentagram. With shaking hands, she lit the golden candle, placing it in the center of the five-pointed star.

Her chest and throat ached, and sorrow rose in a hot tide within her, yet she needed to focus on her mission, on the reason she'd been sent south.

She couldn't crumble now.

Still, her belly clenched as she scooped up the bones and weighed them in her hand. She wasn't in the right frame of mind to do this—she needed to calm herself, needed to clear her mind before she cast the bones.

They'd tell her nothing otherwise.

Fyfa closed her eyes, sucking in deep breaths and murmuring a calming charm under her breath. It took a while, but eventually, her pulse settled and her belly unknotted. She was ready.

Whispering to The Three, Fyfa opened her eyes and leaned forward, scattering the bones over the pentagram.

She watched them roll and tumble, waiting until they'd fallen into their final resting place before she leaned forward further to study them.

Fyfa's gaze narrowed. Candle witching was her greatest strength, although, like all her sisters, she'd been taught to read the bones. The skin on her forearms prickled as her gaze traveled over the pentagram. The bones were often vague in their telling, yet not so this morning.

Her frown deepened. Three symbols had fallen too close together for her liking: winter, the crone, and fire. They were in the last quarter of a Thunder moon—a time of storms—and those three bones flashed a warning.

"Blame, betrayal, and blood," she whispered to the shadows and the dancing flame at the heart of the pentagram. The end was close now. The very air in her sanctuary rippled with tension. "I just hope we're all ready for it."

9

A COMING STORM

"THOSE BASTARDS ARE building a giant trebuchet." Captain Stewart's voice carried across the ramparts.

A few feet away, Hume turned from where he'd been loading a stone into one of the catapults lining the wall. They had few of the weapons left, as over the past months, the English had destroyed them, one by one.

Hume stepped back from the catapult, nodding to the helmeted figure standing behind it. The guard loosed the weapon, and Hume turned to watch the stone fly from the walls. This missile found its mark, he noted with grim satisfaction, landing amongst the rows of archers who fired at the defenders, scattering them.

Ducking, as a volley of deadly yew arrows whistled overhead, Hume then turned to the captain, meeting his steely gaze. "Are ye sure?"

Cameron Stewart nodded. "It was hard to tell what they were up to ... until a day or two ago ... but now it's taking shape. Take a look for yerself."

Frowning, Hume moved back to the battlements, lowering himself to peer between two high merlons. It was risky to get this close, yet he wanted to see what had made Captain Stewart look so worried.

The challenge in the captain's voice—*look over the wall, if ye dare*—wasn't lost on Hume, yet he ignored it. A week had passed since Hume had learned Stewart wasn't Fyfa's lover after all. He hadn't appreciated the liberties the captain had taken with his wife in that hallway—but the captain's behavior paled to insignificance after Hume's discovery the following day.

His wife was a witch.

She'd only wed him in order to gain access to those who ruled Stirling.

He tried not to think about the reality of his marriage—for whenever he did, wrenching betrayal sucked the breath from him. All of it had been a lie.

Since discovering the truth about Fyfa, Hume had taken to avoiding his wife whenever possible.

Being up here on the walls, in the thick of things, was a welcome distraction.

Hume peered through the gap, blinking, in an attempt to sharpen his vision a little. He'd never been blessed with a hunter's eyesight. Of course, Fyfa had warned him that they were building something, and he'd shared her finding with Stewart the following day.

They'd all been expecting a new weapon of sorts—and even with his slightly blurred vision, there was no mistaking the massive contraption that reared up from below. Even the large row of mantlets—high wooden frames the enemy had built to protect themselves from the defenders—couldn't hide it.

His gaze alighted on the huge wooden beams that made up the frame of the beast. And as he watched, a great throwing arm swung into view, balanced by a monstrous counterweight.

Hume cursed.

Nearby, Stewart barked a laugh. "Aye, so ye've seen it."

"How the hell did they build this so fast?" Hume muttered.

"I'd say they've been working on it for a while," the captain replied, "there's been a frame up for the last few days ... but they likely built each piece separately. This is just the assembly."

Hume swallowed. And of course, that meant they were close to using it for the first time. "It looks powerful enough to bring down our curtain wall."

"Aye," Cameron Stewart replied, his voice hardening. "It's definitely time we had another talk to Sir William."

"Get down!"

Whoosh.

One of the many smaller trebuchets on the slopes beneath the castle released a volley of Greek fire—and the warning from one of the men came just in time for Hume. He threw himself to the ground, his belly hitting stone. Heat blistered his back as the flaming iron pot sailed over him—and hit the catapult he'd loaded earlier.

Screams rent the afternoon air.

The soldier manning the weapon staggered toward him, body aflame. His name was Lachlan—the oldest remaining member of the guard. Hume watched, horrified, as the Greek fire engulfed him. Tearing off the leather cloak about his shoulders, Hume launched himself off the ground and threw the cloak over the man. But it didn't smother the fire as he'd hoped.

"Drop to the ground and roll, Lachlan!" Stewart bellowed. However, the guard was beyond hearing him. His screams became blood-curdling.

Hume tried to get near him, to shove him down, yet the heat of the flames was too much.

Helpless, he could only watch as Lachlan Campbell stumbled to the stairs and threw himself down them.

Clack. Clack. Clack. The sound of weaving filled the women's solar, blending with the rumble of the continuing siege beyond. Outside the open windows, the sky was grey and the air heavy, warning of coming bad weather.

Fyfa glanced up from the pillowcase she'd been embroidering and stifled a sigh of frustration. It seemed so frivolous and empty, to be doing such tasks while the English launched missiles at their walls, yet Estelle enjoyed her company. The governor's wife grew lonely, cooped up in here like a princess in a tower. And despite that Fyfa would have preferred to be helping Boyd in the infirmary, or overseeing the running of the keep, she made sure she spent an hour or two with Estelle every day. She sometimes worried about her friend. Estelle Oliphant was a gentle soul who'd lived a sheltered life till now.

Even so, nervous energy seethed within Fyfa this afternoon. Her witching was little use to her at present. She wanted to be taking action, and yet locked away inside the castle, she had no choice but to wait the siege out like everyone else.

Shifting in her seat, Fyfa glanced over at where Estelle was hard at work upon a tapestry. With little else to do of late—for Sir William forbade her from venturing out without him—Lady Estelle had lost herself in her weaving.

The tapestry was taking form now, revealing a Highlander seated upon a stocky horse, the wind blowing his hair. The warrior held one arm aloft, upon which a hawk perched.

Fyfa took in the details. It was truly a bonny scene. The different hues of green and the windswept majesty of the landscape behind the warrior gave her a pang of homesickness for Assynt and the Wailing Widow Falls, where she'd grown up in the Highlands.

Many years had passed since she'd last seen it.

The twinge of homesickness deepened into longing then. She missed her mother and sisters. Loneliness had been her constant companion during the past week. She'd seen little of Hume, for he returned to their apartments late in the evening and rose before her in the mornings. He'd also started taking his meals in the kitchens, leaving Fyfa to dine alone.

Initially, after he'd discovered her true identity, she'd hoped he might have a change of heart. Aye, he was hurt and angry, yet he wasn't the sort of man to throw aside a marriage. But as the days drew out and he continued to avoid her, that hope died.

Hume was indeed done with her.

Forcing aside the sadness that descended upon her whenever she thought about her husband, Fyfa focused on the tapestry once more.

"It's a lovely drapery, Estelle ... ye truly have a talent."

Lady Oliphant glanced up from her work, a smile stretching her delicately-featured face. "It's one of my favorites," she admitted. "It reminds me of home." Her expression clouded then. "I miss the Highlands."

Fyfa favored her with a whimsical smile. "As do I."

"Will ye go to live at Inverlochy?" Estelle asked then. "Once the castle falls."

Fyfa tensed. She didn't like the fatalistic tone her friend was using, and yet it was hard to deny the facts. Although she hadn't had confirmation from Hume, she knew that scaffolding she'd spotted earlier was likely to be a weapon of some kind.

And the bones yielded only warnings these days.

"I suppose so," she hedged. "Although I haven't yet visited the castle."

Estelle inclined her head. "Why is that?"

Fyfa loosed another sigh. "Relations between Hume and his mother are ... distant. After she refused to attend our wedding, he hasn't had any contact with her."

Estelle nodded, although her gaze never left Fyfa's face. "I know things have been strained between ye and Hume for a while now," she said gently, "but ye appeared to be getting on better when ye joined us for supper?"

Fyfa's fingers clenched around the pillowcase she still held. Like most women, Estelle took note of such things. She'd confided in her friend a few months ago about the state of her marriage. "Aye, well ... looks can be deceiving," she murmured.

Estelle's blue eyes widened. "Has something happened?"

Fyfa's throat constricted, and she dropped her attention to her lap. She longed to spill all her secrets to her friend, and yet she couldn't. It was bad enough that Hume knew who she really was—she couldn't betray the order to Lady Oliphant as well.

"Ye can talk to me about it … if it helps," Estelle said after a pause. Rising from her loom, she crossed to Fyfa. She then lowered herself onto a stool before her, taking Fyfa's hands in hers.

The kindness in the woman's voice and the gentleness of her grasp made Fyfa want to weep. Swallowing hard, she forced herself to meet her friend's eye once more and cast her a tremulous smile. "I don't believe it would," she said huskily, "but I thank ye all the same."

Screaming intruded then—pure male agony.

Both women froze before their gazes cut to the open window.

The screaming continued.

"Mother Mary." Estelle let go of Fyfa's hands and crossed herself. Her face had gone chalk-white. "What's happening out there?"

Fyfa cast aside her embroidery and rose to her feet, crossing to the window. Peering outdoors, she wished this window looked out to the eastern walls. She had to know what was happening.

The terrible cries of agony stretched her nerves to breaking point.

And then, the screaming cut off as suddenly as it had begun, leaving the women's solar in eerie silence.

Fyfa muttered a very unladylike curse under her breath.

Turning, her gaze went to Lady Oliphant. Estelle stood a few feet away, one slender hand placed upon her breast. Her gaze was wide and frightened, and she swayed slightly on her feet.

Fyfa crossed to her and placed a steadying arm around Estelle's waist. "Ye should sit down," she murmured, guiding the governor's wife to a seat by the hearth.

"That sound." Estelle's voice was thin and held a tremble. "I've never heard the like."

Fyfa's mouth thinned. Neither had she. The scream and the chilling way it had abruptly ended made dread crawl across her skin.

What if that was Hume?

The thought made her breathing hitch, and her pulse started to hammer against her ribs. Hume spent his days helping to defend the castle alongside the garrison. It could have well been him. Fyfa broke out into a cold sweat. She needed to make sure her husband was unharmed, yet Hume wouldn't welcome her presence on the walls.

"I hate this," Estelle gasped then, choking out the words as her cold fingers clutched at Fyfa's. "William refuses to tell me how bad things are, but I'm not a fool. I *know*." Her gaze speared Fyfa's then, glittering with unshed tears. "Longshanks won't spare us if the castle falls ... will he?"

Fyfa's galloping heart sped up even further at these words. Her friend had voiced the fears of every soul inside this fortress. The Hammer's wrath was a thing of legend, and after such a difficult siege, he would surely want reckoning.

Not trusting herself to speak, Fyfa shook her head.

10

RAISE THE WHITE FLAG

"A GIANT TREBUCHET, ye say?" William Oliphant's greying brows drew together. "Have they used it yet?"

"No, Sir William," Stewart replied, his tone clipped. "If they had, ye'd know about it."

The governor's bearded jaw tensed, his blue eyes hardening as he surveyed the captain.

"If they use it, we're done for, Sir William," Hume added. "The trebuchet is easily thrice the size of any of their others … and it looks as if it can wield missiles of great weight."

The governor exhaled sharply before going to the window of his solar. Outdoors, it was a grey, humid day, the air heavy with the promise of rain. Smoke drifted by, and the pounding of lead balls and stone against the walls continued to shake the keep. "It's over … isn't it?" he murmured after a pause, turning to face them once more.

The haunted look in William Oliphant's eyes made Hume's chest tighten—distracting him from the mire of his own thoughts and the heaviness that sat like a yoke about his shoulders. It pained him to see the man who'd so bravely led the defense of Stirling lose hope. None of them wanted to believe it was over.

Hume Comyn's marriage was in ruins, and soon the mighty castle he'd proudly taken care of for years now would be as well. If he actually survived Stirling falling to the English, he'd have nothing left.

"Aye," Stewart murmured, his voice softening. "It's just a matter of time, Sir William."

Oliphant swore under his breath, the moment drawing out while he delayed the inevitable. Hume and Cameron exchanged glances then. It was a rare moment of camaraderie. Neither of them envied the governor this task. The man was damned, whatever decision he took now.

Long moments drew out, and all the while, the castle continued to shudder from the relentless assault. Eventually, Oliphant met Stewart's eye, and when he spoke, his voice was heavy with despair. "Raise the white flag."

Fyfa stared at her husband, the round of bannock she'd been shaping on the table before her forgotten. "He's surrendering?"

"Aye … Captain Stewart has just raised the white flag." Hume paused then. "The attack has stopped."

Fyfa tensed, her gaze going to the open window. He was right—earlier, the pounding of missiles had boomed through the castle, while now, an eerie quiet settled over the keep.

Swallowing, Fyfa turned back to her husband. He was trying his best to hide it, yet she could see from the way a nerve ticked in his cheek and the tense set of his shoulders that he was upset. "What now?" she whispered.

Hume crossed his arms over his broad chest. Her husband looked a bit worse for wear this afternoon. He'd lost the leather cloak he'd been wearing earlier, and soot covered the gambeson—a long-sleeved, quilted vest—he wore. Grime smudged his face, and he bore a shallow cut to his temple.

She'd heard about Lachlan Campbell, and how Hume had tried to save him, from one of the servants. She'd greeted the news with both sadness and relief. Campbell, like so many who'd fallen, had been a stout-hearted man—but it was only sheer good fortune that Hume had been spared.

"Now ... we wait," he replied, meeting her gaze. It felt as if this were the first time he'd looked at her directly since that awful morning in her sanctuary. Even now, his green eyes were veiled, wary. He was only talking to her out of necessity. "Longshanks will likely send someone soon ... to advise us of his terms."

Fyfa reached for a cloth, cleaning off her hands. To her consternation, she realized they were trembling. "Does Oliphant believe Longshanks will show us mercy?" she asked, struggling to keep her voice neutral. Right now, she didn't want to talk about that thrice-cursed Hammer or the defense of the castle. She wanted to talk about them—her and Hume—to ask if all hope really was lost.

But she didn't. The words seemed lodged in her throat.

"Aye." Hume's answer was clipped. "He believes that by surrendering now, he will save our lives."

Fyfa stilled, her gaze shifting back to meet her husband's. "And ye, Hume ... what do ye believe we should do?"

Hume's jaw tightened. "This was Sir William's decision ... but the man had no choice."

Disappointment soured Fyfa's mouth, distracting her from the unhappiness churning in her belly. Oliphant did have a choice—and he'd clearly made it. Where were their allies? Why hadn't others come to their aid now, when it truly mattered? For the past fortnight, Stirling had stood utterly alone. It was as if the warriors who had once rallied to their side had also lost hope.

Moments passed, and then Fyfa took a deep, fortifying breath and put down her cloth. She cautiously approached her husband. "Ye are bleeding, Hume. If ye take a seat by the fire, I shall dress that for ye."

Hume reached up, gently touching the cut to his temple. "It's nothing. I'll go to the infirmary and get the healer to take a look at it."

Fyfa made an irritated clicking sound with her tongue, even if his dismissal made her belly clench. "Nonsense ... Boyd has enough to deal with at present. It will only take me a moment to clean the wound for ye and apply some salve."

Their gazes locked then, tension filling the space between them. Fyfa swallowed the urge to tell him that despite what he thought, his well-being mattered to her.

Long moments passed, and then Hume moved across to the hearth, lowering himself onto a stool before it.

Fyfa let out a long exhale. Not daring to utter anything else, lest Hume took offense and left their solar, she poured a little vinegar into a cup and retrieved a clean cloth. She then approached him. "Lift yer chin a little," she murmured, as she dipped the cloth in vinegar.

Hume did as bid, yet his tension was palpable. His shoulders were rounded, his jaw clenched. He was allowing her to help him under sufferance.

Gently, Fyfa dabbed at the cut. It looked as if a shard of flying stone had caught him. The wound didn't need stitching, although it definitely required cleaning.

Hume didn't utter a word as she cleansed the injury.

The vinegar would sting like the devil, although he was stubbornly refusing to let it show. Sadness constricted Fyfa's chest then. She remembered a time when he'd protest like a bairn whenever she had to help him with an injury—back when he'd trusted her. What she would give to have those days back.

The wound had pieces of grit embedded in it, and as such, it took her a while to clean it properly. Afterward, Fyfa reached for a small clay pot of salve. The woodsy scent of mint and boneset wafted over her, a sharp reminder of Nessa—who'd shown her how to make the healing salve.

Longing joined the sadness wreathing up within Fyfa. How she missed her sisters. She could have done with a hug from them both at present. She felt fragile this afternoon—as if a strong gust of wind might shatter her.

Dipping her finger into the salve, Fyfa then applied a little to the wound. "Ye are lucky," she murmured. "A few inches to the right and it would have caught yer eye."

Hume merely grunted in reply, his gaze fixed upon the glowing lump of peat in the hearth. "Are we done?" he asked after a pause.

Fyfa drew back, wiping her hands. "Aye … it should heal without festering now."

Hume rose to his feet, towering above her. Their gazes met then, and a strange fluttering sensation rose in Fyfa's belly at the sudden intensity of his stare.

"What is it?" she murmured.

"Why did yer womb never quicken?" he asked, his voice low.

Fyfa tensed, caught off-guard by the question. An instant later, guilt crushed her ribs. Maiden's blood, she didn't want their conversation to take this turn, for it wouldn't lead anywhere good. She knew how much Hume had wanted bairns.

"Of course, I thought it was just fate that we lay together regularly for three years without ever making a bairn," Hume continued. "Yet I see things differently now." His gaze held her trapped, demanding the truth. "Did ye use witchery to prevent it?"

Fyfa's pulse started to race. Her first instinct was to lie, to insist that there were plenty of barren women—and yet there was something in his expression that prevented her. She'd hidden so much from Hume over the years, the only way she could make things right was if she was honest with him now. What did it matter anyway? He already thought the worst of her.

And yet, her belly roiled at admitting that she'd denied him a family.

"It wasn't witchery … exactly," she admitted softly. "Although I did take a draft of herbs each morning to prevent yer seed from quickening within me."

His face went rigid. "Why?"

"Because a Guardian of Alba's loyalty … her focus … must remain on protecting Scotland." She paused there, an ache rising in her chest. Her words sounded so hollow, so self-centered, and yet they were the truth. "How could I serve my order with bairns clinging to my skirt?"

11

THE WOLF'S BITE

HUME CROSSED THE outer-bailey, bending his head as sheets of rain drove across the castle. The bad weather that had been threatening for days, the wild summer storm, had finally arrived.

And with it, a messenger had arrived from the enemy camp.

Sir William Oliphant and Captain Stewart flanked Hume. The three men didn't speak as they headed toward the gates. Each man was likely lost in his own thoughts—Hume most certainly was. His head and belly hurt, and his mind was locked in a cycle he couldn't seem to break.

She never wanted bairns with me.

Hume's jaw clenched. The woman's duplicitous behavior knew no bounds. Not only had she used witching to bend him to her will, so she could spy on the goings-on in Stirling castle, but she'd deliberately taken steps to avoid her womb quickening. After being raised the only child in a lonely household with a viper-tongued mother, he'd always hoped to have a large family of his own.

In the early days, before things soured between him and Fyfa, he'd imagined what it would be like to teach a son how to use a sword and ride a horse. He'd envisaged a bonny daughter, with her mother's blue eyes and laughing smile, perched upon his lap as he told her a bedtime tale.

He'd once confided his hopes to Fyfa, years ago. What a fool she must have thought him.

Thunder boomed overhead, and a flash of lightning illuminated the purple sky, yanking Hume out of his brooding. This wasn't the right moment to be thinking about his lying wife. Instead, he needed to focus on the matter at hand.

Halting before the gates, Stewart exchanged looks with Hume and Oliphant. "Are ye ready?" he asked the governor.

Sir William's mouth thinned before he nodded.

"Open the gates," the captain called to the guards. "Let's see what Longshanks's terms are."

The guards' faces, slick with rain, were taut and worried under their domed iron helmets. This was the first time since the siege had begun that they'd opened the great oaken and iron gates of Stirling Castle. It took a while to lift the iron bars and remove the heavy barricades, but eventually, the heavy gates drew open. And all the while, the three men standing before the gates remained silent.

Hume bowed his head further against the wind and rain. Lightning flashed across the sky once more, and he tensed. It would be just his ill-luck if it struck him.

Perhaps it would be a mercy if it did. He was tired of suffering.

Fyfa crept back into his thoughts once more. He recalled the pain in her blue eyes and the imploring look upon her face earlier. His wife had regrets about the decisions she'd made—but it was too late.

Aye, Fyfa would always be his Achilles' heel. Her tender touch as she'd seen to the gash on his temple had only twisted the blade that felt lodged between his ribs. But things had gone too far. Everything about the woman was a falsehood. Was 'Fyfa' even her real name?

It would be sage to avoid conversing with his wife, and better if he had nothing to do with her at all, yet with the situation so dire at Stirling, he couldn't avoid it. Instead, he needed to wall himself off, retreat to a place where she couldn't hurt him.

The creak of the gates drawing apart intruded. Pushing thoughts of Fyfa aside, and trying to ignore the ache in his gut, Hume peered through the iron grid out into the rain-swept gloaming. The portcullis provided the last barrier between them and the enemy.

A lone rider stood on the narrow causeway that led down to the empty township below. The knight was a big man, faceless in a gleaming helm and chainmail, and wearing a distinctive white and blue striped surcoat decorated with small red birds. His gauntleted hands gripped the reins of a huge destrier.

"Good eve," the knight greeted them in French, his low, gravelly voice carrying into the outer-bailey. "I am Aymer de Valence, Edward's commander … and I bring word from the king."

"And what message does he have for me?" Oliphant replied in the same tongue. Few Scotsmen spoke English, and despite years of campaigning north of the border, only a handful of English soldiers learned Gaelic.

The governor had to raise his voice to be heard over the rumble of thunder and the howling wind.

Moments passed, and then the knight pushed up the visor of his helm, revealing penetrating brown eyes. "The king does not accept your surrender."

Hume's spine stiffened, while Stewart muttered a curse under his breath.

Sir William took a step closer to the portcullis. "Why not?"

De Valance stared back at him, his expression veiled. Only his eyes were visible. No doubt though, he was smirking under that helmet. "You've given us no end of trouble, Oliphant … it's time we made an example of you and your *rabble*."

Heat ignited in the pit of Hume's belly, a slow, coiling anger with fangs. Lord, how he hated these arrogant English dogs. How he wished to sink his dirk into this knight's throat.

"We see you have a new weapon," Oliphant replied, his voice remarkably calm. Unlike Hume, he appeared not to react to the knight's deliberately goading words.

"Does that have something to do with Longshanks's rejection of our surrender?"

A deep rumble drifted toward them, an amused laugh. "Aye, we were wondering if you were filling your braies over that," de Valence replied. "Edward's *Loup de Guerre* is a thing of beauty, is it not? Many of your countrymen—Scottish nobles who have bent the knee to Edward—have amassed here to see it at work."

Warwolf. The name made Hume's skin prickle, made cold sweat slick his palms. Why would his fellow Scots agree to watch such a spectacle? He glanced over at Oliphant to see the governor's expression hadn't changed.

Respect filtered through him. Despite everything, Sir William Oliphant had been the right man to lead the defense of Stirling Castle. Even now, in the jaws of defeat, he would not let them cow him.

"Is that all?" the governor finally asked. "Does Edward have any other message for us?"

A beat of silence followed. Lightning flashed once more, illuminating the gleaming armor that encased the knight's body. Seated there upon his armored steed, he looked like a fiend from hell.

"Aye," Aymer de Valence called, tightening the reins upon his destrier as it sidestepped, tossing its head in fear of the storm that boomed overhead. "The king advises you to prepare yourselves for the wolf's savage bite."

"Warwolf?" Fyfa's face was pale and drawn in the firelight. "What kind of name is that for a trebuchet?"

Hume shifted his weight, taking in the alarm in his wife's eyes. "One that's designed to strike fear into the hearts of the enemy."

After a lengthy meeting with Oliphant and Stewart, Hume had eventually returned to his apartments. It was growing late, and a storm still raged outdoors, hammering the wooden shutters and howling against the walls. He'd expected—and hoped—that Fyfa would have already retired for the evening. But instead, she sat by the fire, mending one of his lèines by candlelight, awaiting his return.

Hume had told himself he wouldn't speak to her again today, yet this conversation couldn't wait. Unfortunately, he bore ill-tidings.

"So that's it then?" Fyfa's hands tightened around the tunic, her mending forgotten.

"Aye." Hume glanced around the solar. How he could have done with a tankard of strong mead right now—anything to take the edge off the dread that cramped his guts.

"Did this knight, Sir Aymer, say anything else?"

Hume's mouth compressed. "Only that a few Scottish noblemen have gathered to watch Warwolf destroy the castle."

Fyfa's gaze narrowed, and she drew herself up in her chair. Warmth ignited within Hume—not anger, but something far more complex. Curse the woman, but he loved her fire, her spark. Even frightened, she was rebellious.

"Traitorous bastards," she growled. "They should be strung up by their cods for turning against us."

"Aye," Hume muttered. On that, they were completely in agreement. "No wonder the enemy camp has grown in size of late ... it's their Scottish visitors."

Fyfa cast her sewing aside and rose to her feet. She then started to pace the narrow space between the hearth and the table. "There must be something we can do ... something to foil them."

Hume shook his head. "We're out of resources, Fyfa. Longshanks has us by the throat." He paused then, his gaze narrowing. "Now's when ye tell me there's some kind of witchy spell ye can cast that will make everything all right."

Fyfa halted and swiveled to face him. Her shoulders had gone rigid. She'd most definitely caught the acerbity in his voice. "Ye think I can turn the lot of them into toads?" she asked, her tone cooling.

Hume raised an eyebrow, imagining a large croaking bullfrog with a lopsided golden crown hopping around uselessly. He'd enjoy crushing Longshanks under his boot. "If ye could, then ye'd be of some use to us," he replied. "Apart from sneaking around, spying, and luring fools into yer bed, what *are* ye capable of?"

Fyfa's beautifully molded lips pursed, and she thrust her chin out at him. "The Guardians of Alba have stood in the shadows for centuries," she bit out. "Ensuring the *men* who rule this land don't trip over their own feet. The Romans departed because of us, and the only reason this castle hasn't yet been taken is because of the assistance our allies have given ye."

"So ye say." He wanted to lash out, to hurt her as she'd wounded him. "But what about *ye*, Fyfa? What real help can ye give us in our hour of need?"

A brittle silence fell between them. Fyfa's eyes were narrowed, her jaw set. He could feel anger pulsing off her—the heat of it reached out and enveloped him.

The urge to reach for her then slammed into him—to haul her into his arms and kiss that furious mouth.

But Fyfa looked so vexed right now, she'd likely bite him.

He wouldn't care though; instead, he'd welcome the pain.

"I'm capable of inflicting a hex ... or even a curse ... if I wish to," she replied, her voice clipped. "But such witching comes at a price."

"And what's that?"

Fyfa placed her hands on her hips—a gesture that made her magnificent breasts jut arrogantly toward him. Hume's groin tightened, lust stirring once more.

"Firstly, it requires something ... hair or an item belonging to yer victim." She bit out the words. "Do ye happen to have a lock of Longshanks's hair in yer possession?"

Hume ignored the barb.

"And taking a life requires the sacrifice of another," Fyfa plowed on. "If I were to use witching to harm or kill the English king ... I would likely sicken ... or someone I love would die."

Another silence fell between them—this one charged.

Hume took a step forward, deliberately crowding her space. "The latter shouldn't bother ye, Fyfa," he murmured. "A woman like ye doesn't allow herself such weakness as *love*, surely?"

She certainly didn't love *him*—that was for certain.

Her gaze guttered. Her anger, which had been burning brightly till now, dimming. He'd struck deep.

"Do ye think me incapable of such feeling?" she asked, her voice barely above a whisper.

"Aye."

Fyfa's throat bobbed. "I never told ye of my origins, Hume."

"Aye, ye did. Ye are a MacKinnon of Skye." He paused then, his gaze narrowing. "Was that a lie too?"

She nodded. "The truth is that I have no family. I was a foundling ... left by my birth mother to die in the cold."

Hume went still. He hadn't expected this revelation. He wasn't sure what to say, but when he didn't reply, Fyfa continued. "Ye recall that strange birthmark upon my thigh? The druidess who heads our order ... believes it frightened my parents into abandoning me. They thought I was a changeling." Her gaze never left his. "I grew up surrounded by love though ... with a mother and many sisters. We aren't related by blood, but our bond is strong." She paused, swallowing. "So, ye see ... one of them would die if I ever did manage to kill The Hammer of the Scots."

Jealousy twisted within Hume. She cared about her fellow witches, and the woman who'd brought her up, yet she spoke as if he meant nothing to her. Hume had suspected as much, but the reality of it was a punch to the gut.

"Surely, it's a sacrifice ye should all be prepared to make," he ground out finally. "For Scotland."

12

CAST IT ALL ASIDE

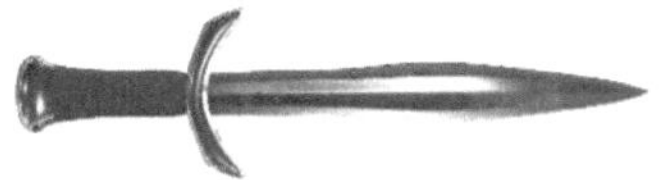

FYFA DIDN'T MOVE. Hume was deliberately goading her—she knew it, and yet she rose to the bait.

He stood close to her, their bodies just inches apart, his green eyes smoldering. His hands were clenched by his sides, yet he didn't reach for her—even if he looked as if he wanted to shake her till her teeth rattled.

But it didn't cow her. On the contrary, she now stood toe-to-toe with him, her right palm itching to slap him. She hadn't been looking for sympathy when she'd told him the price of using her witch-will to harm others, when she'd told him she was a foundling, but his callous response made fury cast a red haze over her vision. She deeply regretted keeping so many secrets from Hume and felt sick to her stomach at the thought of separating from him, yet he now infuriated her.

In many ways, anger felt better than sorrow, although it also quickened her senses. She was now aware of her husband in a way that put her on edge. The heat and strength of his body burned into her, despite that they weren't touching.

Frustration and longing boiled just beneath the surface, sucking the air from her lungs.

"Would it make ye happy, Hume," she said, finally, her voice strangely breathless, "if I went out there and threw myself at the enemy?" If he wasn't going to pull his punches, then neither would she. She leaned forward, angling her chin up further as she held his gaze.

"Granted, I wouldn't last long ... but would ye feel vindicated then?"

He stared back at her, his ruggedly handsome face going rigid. "No."

"What then? What can I do to appease ye?"

"Nothing."

Pain knifed through Fyfa's chest. "Ye don't mean that."

"I do ... I wish we'd never met."

"Liar!" Fyfa shoved him hard in the chest with the palm of her hand. "Ye can't deny everything!" Tears burned the back of her eyes then. Curse him, he'd pushed her too far. If he wanted to see her unravel, she would. "Aye, I kept my identity secret ... but the passion, the affection, wasn't feigned," she choked out. "It was the secrecy and yer jealousy that drove a wedge between us."

"Ye cast a spell over me," he countered, his voice cracking. "*Nothing* was real!"

"Ye just keep telling yerself that, ye great dolt," she snarled back. "If it makes ye feel better ... but admit it ... the true reason ye are angry is that despite everything, ye want me still. Ye want me and hate yerself for it!"

"I don't want ye, scheming witch!"

"Aye, ye do! I can see it in yer eyes, I can—"

Fyfa never finished her sentence, for Hume hauled her against him, his mouth cutting her off. The kiss was hard, bruising, and brief. After an instant, he hurled himself back from her as if scalded, but Fyfa went after him.

Reaching out, she gripped his gambeson with both fists and forced him to halt his retreat. "I don't want things to end this way between us," she gasped. "Tomorrow, everything will change. Who knows what Longshanks will do with us all once the castle falls ... this may be our last night alive. Do ye want to waste it in senseless bickering?"

Hume stared down at Fyfa. She could see the torment, the agony, in his eyes—and her chest constricted. She'd done this to him. She'd twisted him up inside.

"I know ye are angry and hurt, Hume," she gasped, "and ye have every reason … but please cast it all aside … just for one night."

A beat of silence passed between them, and then Hume made a noise deep in his throat—a sound that was something between a groan and a cry of anguish.

An instant later, his mouth crushed against hers once more.

Fyfa didn't hesitate. She let go of his gambeson and slid her hands up the broad expanse of his chest, the quilted fabric still damp from the rain that now lashed the keep and rattled the shutters. Her wrists linked around his neck, and she stood on tip-toe, her lips parting under his.

Maiden's blood, how she'd missed this. She drank him in. And in return, Hume devoured her.

He'd never kissed her like this—which such wildness, such unleashed ferocity. His mouth savaged hers, his tongue plunging into her mouth.

Heat exploded in the cradle of Fyfa's hips, and she melted against him, arms still locked around his neck. She kissed him back with the same roughness, and when she bit his bottom lip, he let out a feral growl, hauling her hard against him.

Hume then spun them around and walked her back so she slammed up against the wall. He bit her bottom lip too before soothing the sting with his tongue.

Fyfa gasped, wet heat pooling between her thighs. Dizziness descended upon her, and she clung to Hume's broad shoulders, welcoming the onslaught as his brutal kisses continued.

A moment later, Hume dragged his mouth from hers, leaving a column of fire down the line of her jaw, to her throat. Fyfa's eyes fluttered closed, her pulse galloping now. The feel of his lips, the rasp of his teeth, as he explored the column of her neck, made heat shiver through her, made her loins turn molten.

Eyes opening, she let her hands slide down over his gambeson, desperate for the feel of his skin underneath. Her palm slid over his heart—which beat as furiously as her own—and then she gripped the hem of the tunic, yanking it upward.

Breathing hard, Hume stepped back from her, grabbed his gambeson and the lèine beneath it, and yanked them over his head.

Firelight played across the sculpted muscles of his torso. Hunger twisted within Fyfa, her breathing coming in ragged pants now. Leaning forward, she buried her face in his neck, drawing the scent of him deep into her lungs. The tip of her tongue traced his hot skin, traveling down to the hollow of his throat, and then to his chest.

All the anger, the hurt—none of it mattered now. She would show him how much she'd missed him, how much she wanted him. Words weren't enough, and every time she'd tried to apologize to him, it just sounded hollow, just like more excuses.

But she could change all that tonight.

Down she went, her lips and tongue tasting him, lingering on the velvet musk and salt of his skin.

She could hear the rasp of Hume's breathing. He reached for her, yet she firmly pushed his hands aside.

Sinking down to her knees, her lips traced the plane of his belly to the waistband of his braies. The trews were loose, yet there was no mistaking the bulge within them. And when she pushed the braies down, his shaft sprang free.

"Fyfa!" he growled, reaching for her once more.

But she ignored him, her gaze riveted upon his magnificent erection. Long, thick, and curved, its swollen tip gleamed wetly. How she'd missed the sight of it over the past two years.

Giving a soft groan, as need slammed into her, Fyfa cupped his heavy bollocks with one hand, squeezing gently. She then bent her head and took his shaft into her mouth, as deeply as she could manage.

Hume's choked curse echoed through the solar, and a moment later, she felt his hands tangle in her hair— guiding her as she began to work him, sliding her mouth up and down his thick length before flicking her tongue over the tip of his rod.

"Oh God, Fyfa!"

Excitement thrilled through her at the hoarseness in his voice, the pleading. Aye, he wanted this as much as she did—he just didn't want to admit it. She could feel wetness slicking her thighs, an ache throbbing between them. It had been far too long.

Why had they denied each other this?

Fyfa intended to bring him over the brink, to let him spill his seed down her throat—in fact, she ached to do so—but Hume let go of her hair and stepped back, withdrawing his quivering rod from the heated cavern of her mouth.

Fyfa let out a cry of disappointment, but he was already hauling her to her feet and shoving her back up against the wall, his mouth slanting across hers once more.

Their kisses were frenzied as he yanked open the front of her kirtle, ripping the lèine beneath it, and slid the garments down over her shoulders. He then lowered his head to her breasts, suckling each one hard.

Gazing down, at where he pushed her breasts up and together as he feasted upon them, Fyfa realized she was making odd, mewing noises. Her nipples ached as he teased them with his lips, tongue, and teeth.

"Hume!" she gasped, writhing against him, reaching for him. "Please ... I need ye inside me."

Cursing again, he abandoned her breasts and hauled up her skirts around her hips, spreading her wide against the wall. His mouth then crashed down on hers for another searing kiss, and he drove into her.

Fyfa cried out against his lips. The shock of him, deep inside her, sent her tumbling over the edge. Her body quivered, molten pleasure rippling out from her womb. She trembled against him, clutching at his shoulders.

Gripping her hips hard, Hume withdrew, almost to the tip, before plunging into her once more. Fyfa clung to him, unable to do anything else.

Hume tore his mouth from hers then, his gaze fusing with hers. The intimacy of that look was almost too much, and yet Fyfa couldn't avert her gaze.

He rode her hard then, in powerful strokes that pushed her up the wall, her naked breasts bobbing with each thrust.

"Christ ... ye are beautiful," he gasped as he took her. "Ye are *everything*."

13

THE QUIET BEFORE THE STORM

IT TOOK FYFA a while to come back down to earth.

Clinging to Hume, their bodies both sweat-slicked and shuddering, she felt as if she'd just left the world for a short while. And during that time, she'd forgotten who she was.

The lust between them had been all-consuming and almost frightening in its intensity. Even now, she struggled to draw breath in the aftermath.

Likewise, Hume was breathing hard, his broad chest rising and falling sharply, as if he'd taken ten flights of stairs at a dead run.

They stayed like that a while, tangled together against the wall that divided the solar and the bed-chamber. Fyfa gradually became aware of her surroundings once more: the crackling of the hearth, the patter of the rain against the shutters, and the whistling of the wind against the keep.

Reality was returning, and although Fyfa tried to resist it, she couldn't. It was as inexorable as the tide. She couldn't fight it. Neither of them could.

Eventually, their breathing calmed and the sweat cooled on their bodies—and husband and wife looked at each other. Fyfa had been bracing herself for the moment their gazes would meet after the storm that had just swept over them. She had no idea how Hume would react in the aftermath.

However, his eyes gleamed with unshed tears, and she wasn't prepared for the sadness she saw in the depths of his gaze.

That look flayed her bare.

"Hume," she whispered, reaching up to cup his cheek. He looked broken, and she couldn't bear it. "Please ... all will be well."

His gaze guttered, and he swallowed hard. "Will it?" The rasp to her husband's voice betrayed the emotions he was trying hard to keep under control. "I think not."

Ye are everything.

Aye, she'd been lost in the midst of passion, yet she'd marked those words. She'd also marked the heartfelt way he'd said them. Hume Comyn was irrevocably, utterly, in love with her—and she'd broken his heart.

"I wish I could change the past," she said softly, her chest constricting. "I deeply regret keeping secrets from ye. If I could go back in time, I wouldn't—"

"Aye, but ye can't," he cut her off. Hume withdrew from her then, in a slow slide, and Fyfa felt the loss, the emptiness of not having him buried deep inside her. "This shouldn't have happened."

The ache in Fyfa's chest intensified. "Ye don't regret it, do ye?"

His gaze met hers, but he didn't reply. He didn't need to.

Gently, he set Fyfa down on the ground and stepped back from her before he relaced his braies.

Fyfa noted his hands were shaking.

"Hume," she whispered. "I—"

"No, Fyfa." His voice, soft yet firm, cut her off. "There's nothing to say."

"But, what just happened ... we need to—"

"It was a mistake," he rasped. Hume stooped then, scooping up his lèine from the floor before throwing his gambeson across the back of a nearby chair. "And it alters nothing between us."

Gripping his tunic in one hand, so tightly his knuckles had gone white, he made for the door.

Fyfa watched him go, her heart in her throat.

Out in the empty corridor, Hume knuckled away the traitorous tears that stung at his eyelids. He needed to get a grip on his emotions; he needed to get away from Fyfa. He then shrugged on his lèine and headed for the stairwell.

It was getting late—and he should be sleeping, readying himself for the final day of the siege. And it would be the last day, for Longshanks was impatient to show off his new weapon.

But sleep was the furthest thing from Hume's mind. What he really wanted was to turn on his heel, go back into the solar, and prostrate himself at his wife's feet.

He wasn't going to do that though.

Instead, he was going to keep from their apartments for the rest of the night.

By this time tomorrow, Stirling would have fallen—and if by some miracle they survived it, he'd send the traitorous woman on her way, back to her coven.

And then he'd attempt to pick up the broken pieces of his life.

Hume's mouth twisted. Who was he fooling? It was unlikely he'd ever manage that.

He took the stairs down to the vast entrance hall and went outside into the inner-bailey. Outdoors, the rain had eased to a drizzle. Thunder rumbled in the distance, and it sounded as if the storm had finally moved on. Boots crunching on wet pebbles, Hume strode to the walls, climbing the slick stairs to the ramparts.

It was silent up here, save for the humid wind carrying the odd splatter of rain that feathered against his skin. Down below, the fires of the English camp flickered gold in the darkness.

Hume made his way to the farthest point of the eastern wall, where he halted, staring out into space.

Up above, the clouds had parted to reveal a waxing gibbous moon. It glowed like a precious pearl against the black velvet curtain of night beyond, illuminating the walls in its hoary light. Hume folded his arms across his chest, trying to ignore the twisting pain there.

What had come over him tonight?

He'd acted like some kind of beast. One moment they'd been locked in an escalating argument, each seeking to wound the other, the next he'd rutted her like a randy goat. Fyfa had pushed him too far, had taunted him one too many times—and when things had escalated to that brutal kiss, he'd not been able to stop himself.

Hume was a man after all. Two years of longing, hurt, and frustration had exploded within him, and he'd lost his hard-won control.

Clenching his jaw so hard his back teeth started to ache, Hume glared out at the darkness. Curse him. Curse her. How was it possible to both love and loathe someone like this?

Because he did still love her, he realized with a dropping sensation in his gut. He'd never stop loving her.

Hume drew in a deep breath, seeking to quell the nausea that now swept over him. He'd just coupled with a witch. The thought that he'd wed a woman who whispered spells in her secret hiding place, lighting those candles and likely sacrificing animals upon that pentagram she'd etched on the floor—the very thought made his skin prickle with horror.

Had she bewitched him tonight? Hume went cold at the thought. He'd been ignorant of the fact she'd used witching to make him fall in love with her years earlier— why would he be able to sense it now?

What if none of it was real? His lust, his love, the aching cave in the center of his chest. What if Fyfa had manipulated it all?

Such thoughts made sweat bead on his brow, the sickly sensation increasing.

Christ's teeth, he felt as if he were going mad.

"Can't sleep either?"

A voice intruded then, followed by the slow tread of footfalls on stone. Jaw still clenched, Hume turned to where a dark figure approached, outlined against the night.

Moonlight gilded Cameron Stewart's swarthy face, although his eyes were cast in shadow.

"No," Hume replied, his tone terse. "Unsurprisingly."

Cameron was the last person, besides Fyfa, he wished to see right now. However, the captain of the guard either didn't mark his unwelcoming tone or didn't care. Stopping next to Hume, Stewart turned, his gaze sweeping to the glow of the English camp. "The quiet before the storm," he murmured. "My least favorite part of battle."

Hume grunted his agreement. He knew what the captain meant. He'd fought in one or two skirmishes over the years. Once the fighting started, nerves and fear vanished, swallowed up by survival instinct and battle rage. But the moments leading up to it were always terrifying.

Cameron Stewart's attention flicked from the view to the steward then, and Hume tensed as he felt the man scrutinize him. "Satan's cods ... ye look like someone just dragged ye through a hedge backward."

Hume snorted. He was sure he did—with his rumpled lèine, mussed hair, and swollen mouth, not to mention the pain that would be etched across his face.

His mouth flattened when he spied the captain's wry amusement. Even though he now realized Stewart hadn't been swiving his wife, the man still rubbed him up the wrong way.

He'd grown up with warriors like Stewart at Inverlochy Castle—men who'd never known a moment of self-doubt in their lives. Such warriors had made Hume's early years hard. He'd been a quiet and shy lad, and gangly before the years—and hard physical exercise—had filled him out. Like a pack of wolves, the lads he'd grown up with had singled Hume out as the weakest. From the day he turned thirteen, until he left Inverlochy at eighteen, Hume spent his days scrapping and watching his back.

As if sensing his rising ire, the captain grinned. "I don't know what ye are doing up here, Comyn ... if I had such a comely wife waiting in my bed, I wouldn't be."

A warning growl rumbled low in Hume's throat. He wondered if anyone would care if he tossed Cameron Stewart off the wall. They were done for anyway; Stirling no longer needed the brave captain to lead the guard.

"Ah, I see I've hit a nerve," Stewart murmured. "So there's trouble in paradise, is there?"

Hume dragged in a deep breath, in an attempt to quell his rising anger. Of course, the captain of Stirling guard remained unwed. Women were just a bit of fun for him. Cameron Stewart had no idea what it was like to suffer—and he also didn't have an inkling of what Hume was dealing with.

He was just about out of patience with him.

Silence fell between the two men, and perhaps the captain sensed Hume's despair, for his voice altered when he eventually spoke. "The beautiful ones always break hearts."

There was no sympathy in the man's voice, just a bitter edge that made Hume turn back to Stewart, his gaze settling upon his face. Perhaps he'd been wrong about the captain having no idea about suffering. Did he speak from experience? However, Stewart didn't offer any other comment, his expression impossible to read, and Hume turned away once more.

"I couldn't believe my luck when she started bestowing her smiles upon me," Hume admitted after a lengthy pause. He didn't know why he was admitting such to Cameron Stewart. But perhaps, since the pair of them might be dead come nightfall tomorrow, a sense of fatality loosened his tongue. "I should have realized then it would end in ruin."

Cameron snorted. "Aye … it's never a good idea for a man to feel grateful for a woman's affections." Again, bitterness laced his voice. "It's pathetic … and they always hate ye for it in the end."

Hume's mouth pursed. The captain's bluntness was like a kick to the cods in his current mood, and yet it occurred to Hume then that Cameron Stewart hadn't always been so confident with women.

"Fear not though." The captain's voice altered then, adopting a heartier tone as he slapped Hume on the shoulder. "Come tomorrow, ye'll have bigger problems to worry about."

14

THE SPECTACLE

THE CROWD AMASSED on the western edge of the camp mid-morning, the rumble of excited voices drifting across the sea of weather-stained tents.

Lamia Delamare joined them.

Despite that it was the height of summer, the storm of the night before had left the ground muddy. As such, she lifted her skirts and picked her way carefully through the tents. Her gaze went to the smoke-blackened curtain wall of Stirling Castle in the distance. The fortress still stood proud, its high battlements outlined against a pale blue sky.

A smile tightened Lamia's mouth, excitement curling in her belly. *Not for much longer.*

Up ahead loomed the great pavilion where Edward was holding court. The tent stood around a dozen yards from a giant wooden siege weapon, Edward's *Loup de Guerre*. The trebuchet was monstrous, towering high above the surrounding tents, and even dwarfing the large viewing platform that flanked it.

A group of giggling ladies-in-waiting sat there, dressed in their loveliest cotehardies. The fine fabric caught the light, making the court ladies look like a cluster of brightly colored butterflies. Catching sight of Lamia, one of them, Marion, waved, beckoning her to join them. Lamia ignored her. Instead, she continued toward the king's pavilion. She didn't want to view this from the stands with the other twittering ladies.

She didn't want to miss a word this morning and wished to see the expression on every face—Englishman and Scotsman alike—when the Warwolf released its wrath.

Lamia's anticipation increased, and she fought the urge to grin. Sensing her excitement, the small grass snake that was curled around her wrist, hidden from view by the bell-like sleeve of her cotehardie, tightened its grip.

"The day has finally come, Fantôme," she whispered to her familiar. This cursed siege had dragged on since spring, and like everyone in this camp, she couldn't wait to see it end.

And thanks to the *Loup de Guerre* it would—this very morning. For the last three months, she'd watched the giant trebuchet taking shape. The king had called in builders and an engineer from France, Jacques de Saint-Georges, as master of works.

And now, finally, Warwolf was ready.

Lamia entered the pavilion, which had the sides rolled up to allow those within a direct sight of the siege weapon and the walls of Stirling Castle in the distance. She then moved discreetly to where Edward's knights stood within, forming a line against the left wall. Only Aymer de Valence and Nicholas Harrington—the king's most trusted knights—and the king's son, Prince Edward, stood with the king. They were speaking to Edward at present, the rumble of their voices drowned out by the chatter inside the tent. Margaret, queen consort of England, sat next to her husband, her dainty hands folded across her swollen belly. Margaret still had three months to go before the babe was due and fortunately hadn't yet begun her 'lying in'.

This morning's spectacle was one none of them wished to miss.

Catching Lamia's eye, the queen flashed her a smile. Lamia grinned back, letting her excitement show. She and the queen were as close as sisters and shared most things—most, but not all. There were some secrets that Lamia held close to her breast.

And one of them was the ambition that simmered within her.

"Looking forward to this, I see, Lady Lamia?" An amused male voice made Lamia shift her attention from the queen to the knight standing a few feet away.

Philip de Eynsford's gaze met hers boldly.

Lamia's grin faded to a polite smile, and she greeted the knight with a nod. "Aye, Sir Philip ... as are ye, I wager."

The knight flashed her a smile of his own, revealing straight white teeth. "We *all* want to see what Warwolf is capable of."

Lamia inclined her head. "I wish I could have seen Oliphant's face last night ... when Sir Aymer told him there would be no surrender."

Lamia's attention flicked to Aymer de Valence. Big and broad, with a shaved head and ruggedly handsome features, the knight had recently replaced Hugh de Burgh in the role of commander. It was a pity Sir Aymer was wed, for the Earl of Pembroke was exactly the sort of man she wished to take as a husband: high-born, ruthless, and powerful.

Sir Philip huffed a laugh. "Aye, Sir Aymer said the man looked as if he was about to piss himself." He paused then and gave a wry shake of his head. "As if Edward was going to let him save face after the trouble he's given us."

Lamia's mouth pursed. *Indeed.*

She studied Sir Philip's face then, trying to decide what to make of him. Like Sir Aymer, this knight was also a relatively recent arrival to Stirling. After Edward's army had taken some heavy losses, they'd been in dire need of reinforcements. Sir Philip had arrived, just over a month earlier, with a small contingent of men-at-arms to devote to the siege.

And right from the day they'd met, Lamia had sensed his interest in her.

Clad in a glittering hauberk, the coif pulled down, with the crimson English surcoat atop it, Lamia had to admit de Eynsford cut a striking figure. Tall and lean with long peat-dark hair tied back at the nape of his neck, he had a strong jaw, chiseled features, and eyes the color of weathered oak.

Aye, he was comely—just the sort she wouldn't mind taking to her bed—but Lamia had done her research. Philip wasn't in the same class as Aymer, not even close. His castle at Eynsford, west of London, was a relatively humble one. He had some lands, but his family wasn't powerful. The king had only called upon him because he was desperate.

The de Eynsfords weren't destined for great things. It was a pity really, for Lamia was attracted to the man, yet Sir Philip's interest in her couldn't go anywhere.

Even so, the man had his uses.

Lamia stepped closer to Philip, her gaze shifting across the pavilion, to where a group of Scottish nobles stood. They were Edward's allies—men who had all bent the knee to the Scottish king—however, few of them were smiling this morning.

"Comyn 'The Red' looks as if he's about to swallow his own tongue," she murmured.

Sir Philip gave a soft laugh, his attention traveling to a tall man with fiery red hair and a beard to match. John 'The Red' Comyn noticed his stare and cut the knight a hard look. "Aye, if his scowl gets any deeper, it'll split his skull."

"And Robert Bruce also looks a bit grim this morn," Lamia observed. "I thought Edward had brought him to heel?"

Philip snorted. "From the looks on Robert and his brother's faces … I'd say they're here under sufferance."

Lamia smiled. Indeed, both Robert Bruce, Seventh Lord of Annandale and the Earl of Carrick, and Neil Bruce wore pinched expressions this morning. This was why she'd made a point of entering this pavilion, rather than taking a seat in the stands with the other court ladies. Every detail mattered to her—especially when it came to clan Bruce.

She hadn't forgotten her dream, just over three months earlier, in which she'd seen a muddy battlefield strewn with dead English soldiers. The whispered word, Fuimus—*we have been*, in Latin—had haunted her ever since. She'd discovered that it was the Bruce clan motto and had resolved to keep a close eye on them.

Lamia's jaw tensed then, and she swung her attention back to the king. *Curse you, Edward ... why couldn't you listen to your wife?* Sensing her shift in mood, her snake tightened its grip about her wrist.

The English king leaned back in his throne, long legs stretched out before him. Even though he was in his mid-sixties now, England's warrior king still looked as hale and hearty as ever. He wore a fine crimson surcoat edged in gold trim this morning, the hue matching the gleaming crown that sat upon his head. The king's long greying blond hair was unbound, falling over his broad shoulders. A neatly trimmed beard covered a strong jaw, and ice-blue eyes—a gaze that missed nothing—surveyed the amassed crowd as he spoke to Sir Aymer, Sir Nicholas, and the prince.

Lamia fought the urge to frown. The king was an astute man, and yet he'd refused to listen to Margaret's warnings about the Bruces. The queen knew of her favorite's special 'skills', although she'd wisely kept her knowledge from her husband. Edward likely wouldn't be happy to know a witch was his wife's lady companion. Instead, Margaret had been wily when she'd warned the king numerous times over the past months about rumors that clan Bruce had ambitions.

To make the story plausible, she'd told him Lamia had heard the tale from a Scotsman she'd met in Dunfermline over the winter. Lamia's 'lover' had revealed that the Bruces saw themselves as the true kings of Scotland. But Edward had dismissed Margaret's warning as nothing more than gossip.

And now he'd invited Robert Bruce and his brother to watch Stirling fall.

"What is it about the king that vexes you this morning?" Sir Philip de Eynsford's voice intruded once more, causing her to startle.

Glancing back at the knight, she saw that he was watching her with a speculative look.

"Nothing," she said lightly. "Why ever would you think that?"

"The groove between your pretty eyebrows for one thing, and the way your rosebud mouth pursed just then."

Lamia laughed, even if her pulse quickened. Curse her, she needed to be more careful, especially around men like Sir Philip. "I just wish he'd stop talking and give us the spectacle he promised."

Philip's lips parted as he readied himself to respond. However, he was forestalled by the wail of a horn and the flurry of drums. Upon the dais at the back of the tent, King Edward of England rose to his feet.

"Friends!" he boomed. "We are now ready … follow me."

The king led the way out of the tent, followed by the queen and the prince. Edward of Caernarfon had solicitously taken Margaret's arm. The king's commanders, Sir Aymer and Sir Nicholas, walked close behind, and then the other knights moved to join them.

Sir Philip offered Lamia his arm before favoring her with a courtly bow. "May I, Lady Lamia?"

Lamia smiled. She appreciated the man's gallantness, even if he was entirely too sharp for her liking. She then linked her arm through his. "Gladly, Sir Philip."

They walked outside, and the crowd formed a cluster a few yards back from the siege weapon. Lamia noted that a huge iron pot now nestled in the payload attached to a sling and the long beam—the throwing arm.

Her belly flip-flopped in nervous excitement.

"Come closer, one and all!" Edward boomed, his long legs eating up the ground as he paced before the trebuchet. "I give you … Warwolf!"

A great cheer went up from the stands and from the amassed crowd of men-at-arms who'd gathered to watch the display. The drums started to beat faster, the tempo increasing with each passing moment.

The king stopped then, swiveling around, his ice-blue gaze seizing upon the Scots who'd joined the watching crowd. Likewise, Lamia singled out the two Bruce brothers. The men stood side-by-side, their expressions inscrutable. Lamia's attention rested upon the Earl of Carrick. Robert Bruce was a big man with a strong-featured face and penetrating light-brown eyes. He wore his hair long—the heavy brown waves falling upon his shoulders—and had a short beard that covered a strong jaw.

"The governor of Stirling has offered his surrender to us," Edward continued, his voice carrying across the crowd. The excited chatter had died now, yet the drums beat on. "But I have refused him." He gestured to the weapon behind him. "I didn't spend three months building this beast, not to use it!"

Laughter followed this comment, although Lamia noted that Robert Bruce didn't join in. His jaw was tense as he stared back at the English king, the only sign that he wasn't enjoying the show so far.

"Now all of you will mark what happens when you stand in my way," Edward concluded. He turned then, nodding to the helmeted man standing beside the trebuchet holding a flaming torch aloft. "Light the Greek fire!"

The soldier nodded and moved forward, thrusting the torch into the massive iron pot. It burst into flames with a roar.

The drums raced now, eagerness rippling through the air.

Edward drew his longsword, walked to the siege weapon, and swung the blade, severing the rope that held the payload in place.

With a whoosh, the throwing arm launched skyward.

A gasp went up from the watching crowd, even from the Scots, at the show of strength.

Lamia's breath caught, her gaze following the flaming missile. It soared high and then crashed against Stirling's eastern curtain wall. An instant later, she watched the castle's outer defense crumble.

Cheering erupted, and Edward swaggered away from Warwolf, a grin plastered across his face. A moment later, a cluster of musicians under the stands struck up a merry tune upon lyres and bone whistles, and a carnival atmosphere ensued.

Edward strolled across to Robert Bruce and slapped him on the back. They stood just a few feet away, and so Lamia heard every word that now passed between them.

"I'm glad you came today, Rob," he murmured. "Your father was a good friend … and I'm sorry that he's gone." Lamia listened with interest. Indeed, she'd heard that Robert Bruce the elder had fought with Edward in the Holy Land. Edward then flashed Robert a grin. "I hope you took note of what just happened here," Edward concluded. "Far better to have me as a friend than an enemy."

15

THE WAIT

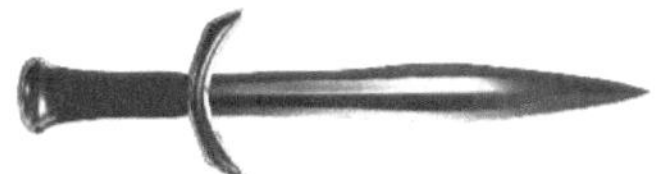

FYFA DIDN'T LINGER in the steward's apartments once the sun rose. It felt odd to stand in the solar she'd shared with her husband for the past five years and know that this was the last morning she'd spend time here.

None of it seemed real.

The morning had dawned, warm and breezy. The air felt light after the storm of the night before had swept away the tension. However, another charge now hung in the air. Even inside the solar, Fyfa could taste it.

Another storm was about to hit Stirling—one none of them would weather.

Jaw clenched, Fyfa strapped a dirk—one of Hume's—around her waist. She didn't usually go about her day armed, yet having a blade at her side eased her tension, just a little.

She had no idea what would happen to them once the castle fell, but she wouldn't let herself be raped. A sickly chill feathered through Fyfa at the thought.

I'll take the dirk to my own breast before that happens.

She took nothing else with her from the apartments. She'd been unable to face any food this morning. Making her way down the narrow corridor to the service stairwell, Fyfa caught the muffled sound of sobbing emanating from behind closed doors. Some of the female servants had locked themselves away in their chambers while they waited for the end to come.

Fyfa scowled. If she thought that would help, she'd have done the same. Nonetheless, the English soldiers would merely break down the doors once they took the castle.

Making her way downstairs, she went to her sanctuary one last time. Stepping off the ladder, she looked around, taking in the neatly stacked shelves of candles and baskets of herbs. Her throat tightened, and her gaze blurred. How she would miss this place.

Pushing her grief aside, Fyfa deftly collected a few items that she would carry with her. A lump of smoky quartz—a cairn stone of persuasion—salt to ward off evil, and a small black candle for strength and protection. She tucked the items away in pouches upon her belt.

Fyfa then lingered a few moments. Her gaze swept over the familiar interior and all the treasures she'd have to leave behind. She couldn't believe she'd likely never see this place again.

With a shake of her head, she then climbed up the ladder to the alcove, closed the trapdoor, and warded it shut. Even if she would soon no longer reside in Stirling Castle, she didn't want anyone else intruding upon her sanctuary.

Going outside into the outer-bailey, Fyfa tried to calm the restlessness that churned within her. The waiting was stretching her nerves to breaking point. She didn't want to be cooped up indoors, listening to the screams of hysterical servants when the end came, and yet they'd all been instructed to keep away from the eastern walls this morning.

Head bowed, Fyfa walked to the small knot garden that led off the inner-bailey. The garden sat on the northern side of the keep and so would be relatively protected from the attack.

The space was, unsurprisingly, deserted this morning. It was an irony that the roses, despite the heavy rains of the night before, were some of the loveliest she'd ever seen bloom here. Their scent drifted across the rows of neatly manicured hedges.

Fyfa walked to the center of the garden, as she often did when entering this space, and stopped before the statue there. A kelpie's head reared up, his mane flying, his mouth open. Kelpies—or water-horses—were part of Scottish folklore. Hume had told her that his grandfather had sculpted it, and the kelpie had always fascinated Fyfa.

The mythical beast was wild, dangerous, and free. It symbolized Scotland and was a reminder of everything she and her sisters fought for.

Aye, her life was in tatters. The castle was about to fall, and her marriage was a disaster—but she still had her purpose: to help defend Scotland from invaders. She needed to ignore the wrenching sensation in her gut and the unhappiness that threatened to smother her.

It was easier in thought than in practice though. The situation with Hume had tied her in knots.

After he'd left her the night before, she'd wept. Everything had just gotten too much. Her coupling with Hume had been so passionate, so raw, that it had left her destroyed in its aftermath. She'd wanted to offer him a heartfelt apology, to beg him to let them start again, but he hadn't let her.

The sadness in his eyes had been too much for her to bear.

She'd waited up for him in the solar, yet he'd never returned to their apartments. She wondered where he was now. Would she see him before the castle fell?

Stop this, Fyfa, she chided herself, turning away from the kelpie statue. She had to push her misery aside and remember why she was here. *Ye need to focus.*

Aye, she was a Guardian of Alba, an ancient order formed to protect this land from invaders. Her hands had been tied of late, for she'd been locked inside Stirling's walls, but things were about to change. The situation was dire, but that was even more of a reason to concentrate.

Fyfa circuited the perimeter of the garden, deep in thought. It had been two weeks since Colina had sent that missive—and the High Bandruì's words whispered to her once more this morning.

Beware of Lamia Delamare, the witch at the Hammer's side. She knows who we are. Nessa has left the camp. Gain what news ye can.

Foreboding crawled down Fyfa's spine. That witch was an added complication they didn't need. There was so much at stake now, especially since the order knew who would lead Scotland to freedom.

Robert the Bruce will save us.

The reminder calmed the rapid thud of Fyfa's heart and eased the heaviness in her belly.

Aye, she wouldn't despair, not while she believed in Colina's prophecy. The Bruce had to be protected, and the Guardians would already have taken steps to do so. Fyfa wanted to do her part. If she actually managed to survive the fall of Stirling and didn't end up rotting away in an English dungeon, she would return swiftly to Assynt and see how she could help.

She wondered then, if Robert Bruce was amongst the Scots who'd gathered in the English camp below Stirling.

Tension coiled in Fyfa's belly at the thought. *Surely not.*

The sudden impact of something big hitting the castle caused the ground beneath Fyfa's feet to buck. She staggered and fell, the pebbles on the path digging into her knees.

She gasped an oath, scrambling to her feet.

Shouting followed, drifting across the keep.

Heart pounding in her ears, Fyfa raced from the knot garden, her feet flying across the inner-bailey. However, she skidded to a halt when her gaze alighted upon the eastern walls—or where the massive curtain wall should have been.

There was now nothing but a haze of acrid smoke and a blurred view across the English camp.

Fyfa stared, blinking as her eyes started watering from the smoke. *Greek fire.* She'd heard this giant trebuchet, Warwolf, was powerful, yet she'd thought it would take a few strikes at least before it managed to breach their defenses. How had they brought down an entire wall so easily?

"Fyfa!" Hume appeared at her side, his face covered in dust and soot. "What are ye doing out here?" He took hold of her arm with the intent of steering her back toward the keep. "Ye need to get inside."

"What's the point in that?" She shook him off, her gaze still riveted upon the devastation. "I'm no safer indoors if that weapon strikes again."

Her gaze swept the eastern edge of the inner-bailey, where men were shouting and running. Panic filled the air. Captain Stewart was bellowing at the men in an attempt to restore order. It was chaos. She swiveled then, meeting her husband's eye. She hadn't seen him since the aftermath of their coupling, and in other circumstances, such direct eye contact would have been awkward.

But not now—not when Stirling's curtain wall was breached.

"How many men were up on the wall when it fell?" she asked, dreading the answer.

"None," he said, biting out the word. "We knew they'd strike there this morning, so Stewart ordered everyone off."

Relief rushed through Fyfa, causing her knees to wobble.

Thank The Three.

"What now?" she asked, coughing as smoke caught in her throat.

Hume's mouth flattened, deep grooves appearing on either side of it. She'd never seen him look so grim.

"There's nothing we can do," he replied roughly, "except wait and hope they accept our surrender."

The occupants of Stirling Castle gathered in the outer-bailey, watching as the portcullis lifted. Just over one hundred souls remained, including servants and what was left of the garrison. Faces ashen, jaws tense, they waited.

Silence fell, except for the ominous creaking of the heavy iron gate lifting, its sharp teeth outlined against the blue sky beyond.

Standing at her husband's side, Fyfa swallowed hard.

She could see them waiting on the causeway leading up to the gates—knights on horseback and a number of men-at-arms—their helms and chainmail glinting dully in the sunlight.

She'd been in Stirling twice before when the English had taken it—for the castle had been gained and lost a few times over the past years—but this surrender felt different to the others.

The siege had lasted long enough to make The Hammer's anger grow sharp and mean. What would he do to them all?

As she looked on, Sir William Oliphant moved forward to stand before the servants and what remained of Stirling's garrison. Lady Estelle went to join him, yet he waved her back, bidding her to remain at Captain Stewart's side.

The portcullis had now raised. Nothing lay between them and the enemy.

The clip-clop of hooves echoed against stone as two knights rode forward, faceless in their gleaming helms, upon armored destriers. One of them wore a blue and white surcoat.

Watching them, a shudder passed through Fyfa before hate clenched her belly. How dare the English defile this place again?

The knights reined their mounts in just outside the gates, and when the one in the distinctive surcoat spoke, his voice carried across the now silent outer-bailey, "Edward of England now accepts your surrender, Sir William."

"Aye," the governor replied, his voice hard-edged. Fyfa couldn't see his face, although his shoulders had gone rigid. "And what are his terms?"

"He will discuss them when you are face to face," the knight replied, his voice flat. "But for now, you are to all throw down your weapons and leave this fortress on foot."

A beat of silence followed, and then Oliphant nodded. He turned, his face haggard, his eyes blazing. "Do as he bids," he ordered roughly.

Cameron Stewart muttered a curse. Fyfa went rigid, her fingers clenching around the scabbard of her dirk. She didn't want to part with it.

"Fyfa." Hume's voice held a warning note as he unbuckled his dirk and dropped it to the ground. Around them, there were more muffled oaths as the guards reluctantly obeyed the command.

Slowly, his movements jerky, Captain Stewart joined them.

Fyfa shifted her attention to her husband, their gazes fusing.

"Do it," Hume commanded, his tone hardening.

Teeth clenched, she started unbuckling her dirk, even if her will fought the act.

Behind them, one of the serving lasses whimpered, while one of the cooks to Fyfa's left—a widow named Moira—started weeping, the raw sound cutting through the air. Fyfa swallowed hard. The woman's sobs were hard to bear. Moira hadn't been right since she'd lost her husband early in the siege. She wept now as if all hope was lost.

A few feet away from the weeping woman stood a lad. He clenched his thin hands around the hilt of a sword that was far too big for him to wield.

"Craig," Hume spoke up then, his voice both gentle and firm. "Drop that. Yer mother needs ye."

The lad glanced at Hume, his face going taut. However, the steward stared back, unwavering, and Craig eventually lowered his gaze. An instant later, the boy dropped his sword to the ground and went to Moira's side, putting an arm around her sobbing form. "It's all right, ma," he murmured, his voice catching. "I'm here."

Watching them, Fyfa fought the crushing despair and grief that clawed at her breast. "This is wrong," she said, forcing the words out between clenched teeth, as she let her weapon fall to her feet. "All of it."

"Aye," Hume agreed softly. "But this isn't the time for heroics."

16

A BENEVOLENT OVERLORD

THE ESCORT OF knights and men-at-arms brought the defenders of Stirling Castle before their king without delay.

It felt strange, to walk through the empty cobbled streets of Stirling town, past the rubble of buildings and the barred shutters of the windows. After months cooped inside the fortress, it was easy to forget that there was a world beyond.

Even so, the tension in Hume's chest wound tighter with each step.

He'd liked seeing the defiance in Fyfa's eyes, as she'd stood there, debating whether or not to keep her dirk—but the truth was, rebelling against fate was useless now. Despite everything, his wife's fiery Scottish pride was something he'd always adored about her. He was still reeling after the night before, after so foolishly losing control, yet circumstances had cleared his head and focused his thoughts.

He'd told her they would separate—and they would—but not before he did his utmost to keep her safe.

Hume's hands fisted at his sides. Not that he could do much right now.

The best he could manage was ensure that Fyfa remained with him for the moment and kept quiet. They'd been defeated—and it was wise to be patient and wait to see what Longshanks would decide.

His wife walked to his left, her gaze narrowed as she took in the damaged state of the town. It was eerily silent: none of the residents had dared return to their homes while the siege continued.

They walked on, leaving the town behind and turning east, taking the road into the English camp. Soldiers gathered on the roadside to watch them. Some of them hooted and catcalled, shouting out insults. Most of the insults were in English, a tongue he didn't understand, although one or two were in French, and those he *did* grasp. Humiliation started to pulse like a hot coal in Hume's belly.

"Shit-eating bastards," Cameron Stewart muttered under his breath. The captain walked to Hume's right, and when Hume glanced his way, he saw the man's lean face was set in hard lines, his gaze burning. "I should have known they'd crow."

"Merdaille!" One of the men shouted.

Scum.

The heat spread up Hume's chest. God's teeth, he wished he had a dirk in his hand. Maybe he'd been too quick to give up his dagger after all. Eyes fixed ahead, at where Oliphant led the group of Scots, arm-in-arm with his wife, Estelle, Hume deliberately didn't look Fyfa's way.

He didn't want to see the rage on her face—the same fury that writhed inside him.

They didn't waste time taking the captives before the king.

It was just as well—better not to draw out the agony.

Fyfa spoke the French tongue well and hadn't missed the insults those English soldiers had shouted at them on the way in. Her jaw was now set, especially when she saw the crowd awaiting them before a great open-sided pavilion. These folk were more finely dressed than the rabble at the gates to the camp, the gathering of nobles a patchwork of brightly colored surcoats. Among them, Fyfa spied the clan sashes of Scotsmen. Her mouth soured.

Traitors.

However, her attention didn't linger on the Scotsmen who'd come to see Stirling fall, for—like everyone else around her—her gaze traveled to the tall, crowned figure, who stepped forward to greet them.

Thrice-cursed bastard. The Hammer was every bit as imposing as she remembered. He carried his sixty-odd winters extremely well and moved with a wolf-like, stalking gait as he approached Oliphant.

Even from a distance, Fyfa spied his distinctive, icy stare.

"It was quite a show, was it not, Sir William?" The Hammer greeted the governor of Stirling in French. He then flashed him a smile.

The arrogance in the man's voice made Fyfa clench her fists by her sides so hard that her fingernails bit into her palms.

"Aye … you have a bit of rebuilding work to do," William Oliphant replied. To the man's credit, his tone was steady. If being brought before the English king bothered him, he wasn't showing it.

Longshanks laughed at that—a warm sound that carried over the crowd. Around him, the crowd tittered. "Aye, but it was worth it." The king gestured to the monstrous wooden trebuchet behind him. "Just to see Warwolf in action."

"Impressive indeed," Oliphant replied. Once again, his voice was carefully neutral.

The English king's mirth faded, his gaze sharpening when it returned to the governor's face. "You did a fine job of defending Stirling, Oliphant … something I'm sure history will make mention of … but I'm pleased to see that you understand when you're defeated."

Oliphant said nothing.

The Hammer reached up, scratching his bearded jaw as he continued to eye Sir William. "I have given some thought to what to do with the defenders of Stirling," he murmured, "and must admit that my first instinct was to have the lot of you beheaded."

A chill rippled through Fyfa at this. She cut Hume a glance, to see that he was staring at the English king. His jaw bunched, tension emanating off him. He looked like he wanted to lunge at The Hammer and rip his throat out.

Fyfa's lips thinned, even if she appreciated her husband's sentiment. *Too late for that now, Hume.*

Next to her husband, Captain Stewart looked just as murderous—Cameron had gone white about the mouth, his gaze hooded.

"But then," Longshanks continued, gesturing to the crowd behind him. "I have a number of your countrymen here ... as my guests ... and I don't want too much ill-feeling. I wish you all to think of me as your 'benevolent overlord'. Kneel to my rule, and you will all keep your heads." A collective sigh of relief whispered through the crowd of Scots. Yet it died away when the Hammer's cool gaze snapped back to Oliphant. "However, I must make an example out of one of you ... especially after all the trouble you've put me through over the past months."

Oliphant's spine went rigid, even as his wife started to tremble beside him. Wordlessly, he put an arm about Estelle's shoulders.

"You disappointed me, Sir William." The English king's voice hardened. "I gave you your freedom once before, if you remember, and you pledged your loyalty to me." The Hammer paused there, letting his words carry across the crowd. "But you have broken your pledge ... and such a man cannot be trusted." His mouth twisted. "You are now my prisoner ... and will be incarcerated in the Tower of London until I see fit to release you." His head inclined then. "Yet I must warn you ... I don't foresee that day ever coming."

"No, please, don't do this! I beg you." Estelle Oliphant's voice cut through the warm morning air. She tried to free herself from her husband's grasp, to throw herself at the king's feet and plead for mercy, yet Oliphant held her tightly. "My husband doesn't deserve such treatment."

"Enough of this, Lady Oliphant," Longshanks drawled. "Your husband deserves much worse." He shot the governor an irritated look as Estelle's wails followed, a mournful, keening sound that rent Fyfa's breast. "Please calm your wife ... before my merciful mood passes."

The Hammer stepped back then, his gaze sweeping over the crowd behind the governor of Stirling. "The rest of you have your freedom. However, I must insist that you stay on for my celebratory banquet."

"Misbegotten cur! He enjoyed every moment of that!"

"Of course he did ... he's been waiting months for it."

Hume stood inside his cousin's pavilion, watching as John 'The Red' Comyn paced the space, his hands clenching and unclenching at his sides.

Fyfa had joined them, although she stood silently in the corner, her fingers wrapped around a restorative cup of wine.

"Filthy whoreson, I'd like to get my hands around his throat," John snarled.

"We all would," Hume replied, wishing his cousin would lower his voice. They were speaking in Gaelic, for even though they were surrounded by Scots in this corner of the camp, they were still in the midst of the enemy—and John's booming voice carried. Hume also wished John would temper his language a little around his wife.

He glanced over his shoulder at Fyfa, to see that her gaze blazed with the same fire he saw in his cousin's eyes.

Stifling a sigh, Hume turned back to John. Of course, Fyfa and John had always shared the same passionate hate for the English. She'd jumped at the chance to thwart the English during their last occupation and had helped John conspire against them. They'd managed to take Stirling back while Longshanks was off hunting William Wallace. Hume liked the enemy no better, yet he was less vocal about expressing his views. Even so, his cousin was here at Edward of England's calling.

He might be nearly foaming at the mouth, yet he'd bent the knee to the English king.

"I'm surprised to see ye here, John," Hume said after a pause. "I didn't expect ye to yield again."

John Comyn ceased his pacing, whirling his big frame to fix his younger cousin in a gimlet stare. "I had no choice," he ground out. "It sticks in my craw, yet once the Bruce agreed to come, I had to follow." He paused then, his gaze shadowing. "And I wanted to be here when the castle fell … to ensure ye'd both be safe."

"And yet, if Longshanks had decided to take our heads, ye wouldn't have been able to do anything about it," Hume pointed out.

"I would have," John replied, his jaw setting in that stubbornness that had always both frustrated and impressed Hume. "Worry not, lad … I would have spoken up if it had come to that."

Hume stared back at him. John Comyn was fiercely loyal to his kin, but his words may not have been enough to save them.

"So what happens now, John?" Fyfa asked, her voice quiet yet flint-edged. "Are we *really* free to leave after that damned banquet?"

John glanced her way, a deep groove appearing between his bushy red brows. "Aye, it appears so."

"Surely, we don't all have to break bread with him?" Hume asked, a chill slithering down his neck. He'd rather have supped with the devil.

His cousin's scowl deepened. "Aye, I'm afraid so, lad … even Lady Oliphant must. How else can Longshanks rub his victory in our faces?"

17

BEWARE OF THE WITCH

FYFA STEPPED OUTSIDE, her gaze scanning the collection of pavilions that formed the semi-circle of Scottish tents. Her countrymen had set up camp at one end of The Hammer's inner perimeter—a space that looked as if it had been enlarged to accommodate them. A chain of supply wagons formed a barricade around the king's 'inner circle', keeping the noisy and dirty army at arm's length.

And keeping us trapped inside with him.

The observation made Fyfa frown. Save Sir William, The Hammer had given the rest of the defenders their freedom. However, while they resided inside his camp, all of them were his prisoners.

That fact wasn't lost upon the Scots either. The crowd amassed in the clearing before her was subdued, on edge. Many of the faces of those who'd defended and lost Stirling Castle were pinched and pale. Like Fyfa, they were all probably wondering if they could trust the English king.

Could they sleep easy while they were here—or would The Hammer send his men to cut their throats after nightfall?

There were many of them packed into the ring of Scottish pavilions. The nobles—of which John Comyn was one—resided in large tents in the outer ring while the servants and soldiers tried to make themselves comfortable in the clearing at its heart. Despite the warm day, hearths had been lit, and women tried to distract themselves by preparing bannocks.

Fyfa inhaled the sweet, nutty aroma of oats cooking on iron griddles—it was a familiar smell yet one that didn't settle her.

Instead, she muttered an oath under her breath, her gaze sweeping up to Stirling Castle and the ruins of its once-mighty curtain wall. A keen sense of loss swamped her, the sensation so strong that she caught her breath. That fortress had been her home for years. She couldn't believe that she was being forced to leave it—especially in such circumstances.

The news that they were to dine with the king and his retainers the following eve had made bile sting the back of her throat. She imagined it would be hard to choke down food—even if it was a fine meal—while watching that warmongering bastard lounging a few yards away.

The Hammer would gloat, supremely arrogant and confident in the knowledge he'd beaten them.

"Not forever, ye haven't," Fyfa murmured aloud. "It's not done yet, Longshanks." She moved away from the Comyn pavilion then, circuiting the edge of the clearing. Hume and John had left her alone while they went off to meet with the other Scottish noblemen. Fyfa had wanted to go with them, for Robert Bruce would be joining the discussion, but John had brushed her request off, muttering that this was to be a 'men's' discussion and 'not fit for delicate female ears'.

He and Hume had left her silently fuming in the tent. However, she hadn't stayed indoors long.

Robert the Bruce is here, in Stirling.

Once she'd gotten over the initial shock, and anger that he'd capitulated with The Hammer's demands, Fyfa's mind had started to churn. The man likely had no idea of the danger he was in—she needed to do her utmost to protect him.

As she walked, Fyfa eyeballed the fluttering banners of the English inner circle just yards away. "So, we aren't prisoners here?" she muttered to herself. "Let's see if that's truly the case."

She would see for herself if The Hammer's word was good.

Like her countrymen and women, she felt caged in the heart of this vast English encampment. She too itched to depart, but this precious opportunity was too good to waste. Her decision to stray from the Scottish perimeter wasn't just an act of defiance. Her mother and sisters would be hungry for information about the English campaign, and Colina's warning about the witch that lurked here also spurred her on.

Fyfa's mouth thinned as she pondered her decision. She wasn't sure if taking a walk amongst the enemy would achieve anything except get her arrested. However, she had to try.

She was edging around the crowd, and making for the English tents beyond, when she passed Captain Stewart. He was standing by one of the hearths, his gaze unfocused as he stared at the flames.

His expression made Fyfa's step falter; she'd never thought to see the arrogant captain of Stirling guard wear such a desolate look.

Feeling her gaze upon him, Cameron Stewart glanced up. "Fyfa," he greeted her, his voice flat. "Where are ye going?"

"To explore." She cast him a thin smile. "I want to test out the theory that we are indeed free."

He snorted. "I wouldn't, if I were ye."

"Why not? None of us are English captives … supposedly."

Stewart inclined his head. "Does Hume know ye are out looking for trouble?"

Fyfa frowned. "No, and I'd thank ye to say nothing to him about this."

Their gazes fused, and then the captain shrugged. A shadow hung over him this afternoon, a heaviness, and she could tell he was having trouble even focusing on her. "Be it on yer head then," he murmured. "However, I'd counsel ye to remain within the inner perimeter. It's not safe out there for a Scottish lass amongst those randy

English soldiers. Most of them won't have had a woman in months."

Fyfa raised her chin, eyeballing him. She wasn't goose-witted—she didn't need warning.

Without another word, she marched off, spine stiff.

She realized then that she didn't trust the captain not to tell Hume he'd seen her leave their tents, the moment he spied her husband again. She had little time to explore and needed to make the most of it.

Emerging from the ring of Scottish pavilions, she crossed a stretch of trampled grass and edged around the great carcass of Warwolf. It sat poised, a cauldron of unlit Greek fire in its payload, ready to attack once more.

Fyfa's gaze narrowed. How she wished she had access to a naked flame right now—she'd have loved to use witching to set this monstrosity alight and watch it burn.

She glanced around her, noting the clusters of chain-mail-clad men nearby, drinking and laughing.

Aye, perhaps such a move wouldn't be prudent.

Pulling the woolen shawl she'd donned before leaving John's tent closer around her shoulders, she hurried on, past the large open-sided pavilion, which was currently empty, and into the heart of the English tents.

And all the while, her gaze scanned her surroundings, taking in every detail. After months of being cooped up inside Stirling Castle, able only to cast the bones and pray to The Three for assistance, it felt good to take action once more.

The witch is in here somewhere.

The fine hair on the back of Fyfa's neck prickled. How she wished she could seek the woman out—yet there was a fine line between boldness and folly, one she wasn't yet prepared to cross.

She did her best to be unobtrusive, yet Fyfa knew she was starting to attract looks. Her fiery hair, unbound as always, drew attention. Earlier in the day, she'd noted how the English ladies in the crowd behind the king wore their hair in demure braids and buns, some of them with fine nets over their crowning glory. Fyfa, like most low-born Highland lasses, preferred to let her hair tumble free. Lady Oliphant had tried more than once to get her to tame her hair into braids, yet Fyfa had always resisted. Nonetheless, she wished she'd tamed it before venturing in here. It was tempting to raise her shawl over her head, yet now that a group of knights, gathered drinking around a central hearth, were watching her, it would only draw even more attention her way.

She wondered then if one of them was Hugh de Burgh, the English commander whom Nessa had seduced. The knight was bound to be in here somewhere.

She could approach the knights and indulge in some harmless flirting to find out, yet such an act might get her into trouble.

No, it was best she kept walking—best she brazen this out and keep her eyes open. Drawing herself up, Fyfa raised her chin high and marched on.

The tinkling of female laughter reached her then— and a few yards distant, a group of women emerged from one of the pavilions. This tent was bigger than many of the others and draped with red and gold Plantagenet banners.

Fyfa's breath caught at the sight of the ladies, as she took in the shimmering fabric of their cotehardies and the intricate dressing of their hair. The group of women traveled upon a scented cloud; Fyfa breathed in the perfume of rose, lavender, and other, more exotic, scents she couldn't place.

These women were so different to her. She suddenly felt out of place in her plain pine-green kirtle with matching shawl, and her untamed hair.

The women all spied her at around the same time. Like a flock of sheep startled by the sight of a wolf, they huddled together, peering at her with unabashed fascination.

However, rather than wilting under their stares, Fyfa gazed back.

"What is *she* doing in here?" One of the women— pretty with dark-blonde hair—asked in French, her haughty voice ringing across the inner perimeter. "I thought the Scottish rabble were supposed to keep to their own tents.”

“Hush, Philippa, there’s no need to be rude,” the small, dark-haired, and plump woman next to her murmured. She then cast Fyfa a curious look. “I’m Lady Marion de Aldeburgh,” she introduced herself with a smile. “And you?”

“I doubt she even speaks French,” the haughty one—Philippa—replied.

“I think you’ll find that many Scots do.” Another woman spoke up then. She had a husky voice, laced with amusement.

Fyfa’s gaze settled upon the lady who had just spoken. She was striking, her slender form encased in a silver-grey cotehardie that matched her eyes. She had flaxen hair piled high upon her head, a style that emphasized her swanlike neck—and she watched Fyfa keenly.

“That’s right,” Fyfa said finally, finding her tongue. “I do speak French.”

“And who *are* you?” Lady Philippa demanded, her voice sharpening.

“I am Fyfa Comyn … wife to the Steward of Stirling Castle.”

“The *former* steward, don’t you mean?” One of the other women piped up. Her comment caused a titter of laugher. However, neither Marion nor the striking blonde woman in grey joined in.

“You shouldn’t be in here, you know,” Marion murmured, casting a glance over at the fire, where the group of knights was watching them all with unabashed interest. “Not without an escort.”

“I was just stretching my legs,” Fyfa replied with an airy gesture. “As far as I’m aware, I’m not a captive here?”

“Of course you aren’t,” Marion replied, her round face turning a charming shade of pink. She then cast a glance at the flaxen-haired beauty next to her. “Shall we invite her to take a turn with us around the perimeter?”

The woman favored her friend with a cool smile. "Oui, bien sûr." She nodded to Fyfa then. "Will you join us, Lady Comyn?"

Fyfa nodded, relief fluttering through her. She would definitely attract less attention if she strolled through the English perimeter with these women. And, if she was clever, she could also learn things from them.

The flock of ladies-in-waiting moved around the large clearing before the pavilions, and Fyfa fell in next to them, walking alongside the flaxen-haired lady.

And as soon as she stepped close to the woman, a strange prickling sensation rose upon her skin.

An unusual smell reached her then, the faint whiff of hot iron and musk. Fyfa's pulse accelerated. The scent was foreign, and yet at the same time recognizable. It called to her witch-will, made her fingertips tingle and her blood heat.

It's her.

Fyfa cut the court lady a quick look and immediately regretted it. The woman's pale gaze snared hers. "What's your clan name, Lady Comyn?" she asked lightly.

"MacKinnon," Fyfa replied without hesitation. It was the same name she'd given when she'd started work in the kitchens of Stirling Castle years earlier. It was a lie, of course, for a Guardian of Alba had no clan—she needed no clan. "Why do you wish to know?"

The lady-in-waiting's gaze searched her face, and it was with great difficulty that Fyfa resisted the urge to look away. "There's something familiar about you," the woman replied with a half-smile. "I wonder if we have met before?"

"I don't think that's possible," Fyfa answered, even as her heart started to hammer wildly against her ribs. She wasn't the type to be cowed by another woman, yet there was something about this one that set her nerves on edge.

A pause fell before Fyfa cleared her throat. "Since you know my name, can I ask yours?" she asked casually.

Those pale eyes held her fast. "Lady Lamia," she replied.

Fyfa's belly knotted, and it was a struggle to keep her expression neutral.

Beware of Lamia Delamare.

A prickling sensation now marched across her skin like an army of ants.

"You should be wary here," Lamia said then, nodding to where some of the knights were still eyeing them. "Marion is right ... a woman as eye-catching as you really shouldn't take a walk in here unescorted."

Fyfa saw that, indeed, a few of the men were watching her hungrily.

A cold sweat beaded her skin, and nervousness tightened her belly. She suddenly wished she had Hume's steadying presence at her side. She'd taken his stalwart protection for granted over the years. However, she was now aware of how safe he'd made her feel.

Ignoring her discomfort, Fyfa forced a smile and met Lamia's eye once more. "Aye, but I'm safe enough with you all, am I not?"

In response, the lady merely smiled.

Dizziness swept over Fyfa. Aye, this excursion had been an act of rebellion, and possibly ill-advised, yet her risk had paid off.

I've found my witch.

18

MY RESPONSIBILITY

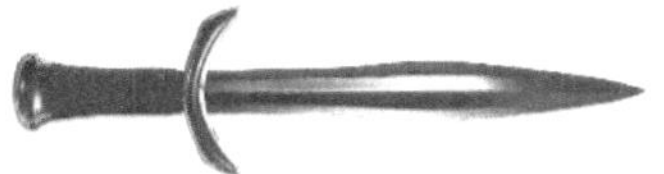

LAMIA WATCHED FYFA Comyn leave the cluster of English pavilions, her gaze tracking her.

Fantôme tightened her grip around Lamia's wrist, demanding answers. However, Lamia had none to give.

She'd been surprised to see the bold Scotswoman walking through the inner perimeter. Fyfa's flame hair made it impossible for her to pass unnoticed. It tumbled over her shoulders and down her back in a 'come hither' fashion that had caused the knights to gawk, Philip de Eynsford and Aymer de Valence among them.

Everything about the woman screamed sensuality, from her bold walk to her curvaceous figure. Fyfa's vibrancy made Lamia's jaw clench. She was usually confident in her appeal; few women overshadowed her. Yet this Scotswoman, in her plain kirtle and humble woolen shawl, somehow had.

She hadn't liked the way Sir Philip, especially, gawked at her. Although she had dismissed the knight as a potential husband, she liked knowing that he wanted her.

She didn't appreciate him ogling Fyfa Comyn.

But beyond the irritation that the woman's beauty turned de Eynsford into a gaping fool, there was something about Fyfa that had alerted Lamia's instincts. She was wedded, the wife of the former steward of Stirling, and had revealed her clan name without hesitation, and yet for an instant, Lamia was sure she'd noted the scent of pine and freshly turned earth when the woman had stepped up next to her.

It was a familiar smell, yet one she hadn't detected for a few months now—not since a Scottish witch by the name of Nessa had resided within the camp.

The woman had turned up one evening, while the English marched to Stirling, and had used witching to gain access to both the outer and inner perimeters. She'd brought a wind with her that had smelled of pinewood and peat. Nessa had been the lover of Hugh de Burgh, King Edward's former right-hand. Everyone had thought—Lamia included—the Scotswoman had followed him from Dunfermline because she'd been besotted by the knight. But when Lamia had eventually consulted her scrying bowl, she'd discovered the Nessa was part of a powerful coven.

One that Lamia feared could potentially thwart England's Scottish campaign.

Neither Nessa nor Sir Hugh remained at Stirling. The knight had been gravely injured at the beginning of the English campaign, and when it became clear that he'd never walk again without a limp, the king had sent him home to the Welsh borders. He'd left one morning with his squire and Nessa riding behind him—and Lamia hadn't set eyes on any of them again.

It had vexed her that she'd missed her chance with Hugh de Burgh—for even though he'd been forced to retire from military life, he was a powerful Marcher Lord. She'd had her sights set on him—before that Scottish witch had drawn his eye.

But it angered her even more that she hadn't had the opportunity to learn more about the mysterious Nessa, and her coven, before she disappeared.

Lamia continued to watch Fyfa until she vanished behind one of the pavilions, before her mouth pursed.

Was this woman one of them?

Her instincts warned her not to underestimate this woman as she had Nessa. Fyfa Comyn wasn't clad in blue, yet that scent was quite distinctive.

Fantôme squeezed her wrist once more, warning Lamia of what was at stake.

Edward's Scottish visitors would only remain here another day or two, and she had something important to accomplish before they departed.

Lamia's chest tightened. She had to do something about Robert Bruce—the leader of his people and likely the one who would cause trouble—while she still had access to him.

"How I wish I looked like that." Marion's voice intruded then, jerking Lamia from her thoughts. She glanced over to see that the court lady was gazing at where Fyfa had disappeared. "Maybe then, one of the king's knights would glance my way."

Lamia's gaze narrowed, irritation darting through her. Marion was the only one of Margaret's ladies-in-waiting who didn't usually get on her nerves—but such a simpering comment caused her irritation to rise nonetheless.

Lamia Delamare wasn't like the other court ladies. Aye, she wished for a powerful husband—and she intended to find one—but Lamia had aspirations beyond a husband and children. Edward of England had made history today, the victor of a long siege upon 'The Brooch of Scotland'. But why was it only men who did the great deeds? The great women of history, such as Boudicca of the Iceni, were always shamed and defeated in the end.

Lamia wanted to taste victory. She wanted to achieve greatness, and she would, even if the monks, the scribes who recorded history, would likely never record her deeds.

The king wouldn't listen to Margaret's warning about the Bruces, so she would have to take matters into her own hands.

"Most men are tiresome bores, Marion," she admonished her friend, cutting the knights a cool look. The men had returned to their tankards of ale, yet Sir Philip was now watching her.

Lamia ignored him, shifting her attention back to Marion. "And lusting after a woman and wanting her for a wife are not the same thing."

Marion's chestnut-brown eyes widened. She was a small, dowdy creature, and even that fine plum-red cotehardie she wore couldn't turn her into the jewel she longed to be. However, she was a kind soul—and had more wits about her than Philippa and the rest of them.

Lamia hooked her arm through Marion's then, steering her back toward the pavilion where the queen consort's ladies-in-waiting spent their afternoons, embroidering, sewing, weaving, and gossiping. "Come, fret not, Marion," she murmured. "One day, you will find yourself a husband ... but I'd counsel you to look for a man who is worthy of you."

The sight of Hume, striding toward her as she re-entered the Scottish encampment, made Fyfa's breathing quicken. The look on his face told her that he knew where she'd just been. Her step faltered, and she drew to a halt, letting him approach.

"Stewart tells me ye have just been for a walk in the English camp," he greeted her with a scowl. "What possessed ye?"

Fyfa drew herself up and cast an irritated look at where Stewart stood with his men. He wasn't looking her way. Instead, he was downing a tankard of ale. Someone had cracked open a barrel, and the men were filling up their cups. However, despite that all of them had lived through the fall of Stirling, none of them wore celebratory expressions. Some of the men were muttering amongst themselves. The subdued, nervous air of earlier had shifted into a rumble of discontent and simmering anger.

Her gaze narrowed as she eyeballed Stewart. *Traitor.* As she'd thought, he hadn't been able to keep his mouth shut.

"I was curious," she replied, forcing herself to keep her tone light. "I wanted to take a look inside the English perimeter."

"Ye could have gotten yerself into trouble." Hume took a firm grip on her arm and steered her back toward his cousin's pavilion.

Impatience flared within Fyfa. "Let go of me, Hume," she said between clenched teeth. They were attracting a few pointed looks. But Hume didn't seem to care—and he didn't release his hold on her arm.

Instead, he escorted her into the tent and only released her when they were inside. Fyfa was relieved to see they were alone; John hadn't yet returned from visiting the other Scottish nobles. She didn't want Hume's cousin to witness the tension between them.

Jaw clenched, she rounded upon her husband. His expression had hooded, although it was preferable to the infinite sadness she'd seen in his eyes the night before. "I'd appreciate it if ye ceased pulling me around like that." She met his eye, challenging him. "After all, ye no longer want me as yer wife. What does it matter to ye where I go ... or what I do?"

Hume stared back at her, his features growing taut. He then folded his arms over his broad chest. "Until I see ye safely delivered back to yer *coven*, ye are still my responsibility," he replied, his tone cooling. "And that means I expressly forbid ye from taking a stroll anywhere except our encampment. Christ's bones, we're surrounded by wolves here!"

Fyfa drew herself up, her nostrils flaring. She hadn't missed the distaste he'd used when he'd said the word 'coven'. "Aye, but ye know I'm a Guardian of Alba," she replied, glaring at him. "It's our duty to protect this land. I'm of no use to them cowering away in this tent."

His gaze narrowed. "And ye help them by taking a stroll amongst the enemy?"

"I was hoping I might learn something useful."

"And did ye?"

For the second time in as many days, Fyfa's palm itched to slap him. Instead, she took a step toward him and raised her chin.

"I discovered something of great importance, *actually*," she replied through gritted teeth. "There is another witch here … one of the English queen's ladies-in-waiting, in fact."

That floored him. Hume's lips parted, his gaze widening. A moment later, he found his tongue. "What?"

Drawing in a deep breath, Fyfa folded her arms across her chest. "Do ye remember that day when ye caught me with a message … the one I threw in the fire?"

His features tightened, and a blush tinged his cheekbones. "Of course I do."

Was Fyfa imagining it or did she see shame shadow his gaze?

"Well, that wasn't a love-note as ye believed, but a message delivered by crow from the head of my order," Fyfa continued. "It was a warning that Longshanks has a witch at his side … a woman called Lamia Delamare. I didn't think I'd actually get to cross paths with her when I took my walk this afternoon … but I believe I did."

Hume frowned, and Fyfa could tell he was attempting to make sense of her words. Of course, she hadn't told him about the High Bandruì's vision. But it was now time she did. She had little left to lose, and she'd already realized that Hume wasn't going to betray her secrets to anyone. He could have done so many times, both to the Oliphants and his cousin, but hadn't.

Drawing in a deep breath, Fyfa dragged a hand down her face. "There's more I haven't told ye, Hume."

Her husband scowled. "Aye? Why aren't I surprised?"

Ignoring the jibe, Fyfa pressed on. "In the spring, the head of my order had a vision come to her … in a dream," she began, "and in it, she saw a battlefield with the English defeated against the Scots and one banner flying high in the wind." She paused there. "A red lion against a sea of gold."

Hume's eyes snapped wide. "That's Robert Bruce's banner," he murmured.

Fyfa nodded, impressed that he knew his clan banners so intimately. He was a quiet man, but he missed little.

"Aye," she replied. "William Wallace has disappeared … and our High Bandruì believes his time has ended. Instead, Robert Bruce will be the savior of Scotland."

Hume blinked, slowly shaking his head as he took this in. "The savior of Scotland?" he asked, incredulous.

Fyfa nodded once more, even as her pulse accelerated. She was aware of how far-fetched this must sound to a pragmatic man like Hume Comyn. He already knew who she was, but news about there being another witch nearby, and about Robert Bruce's destiny, was quite a bit to digest. She tensed, bracing herself for her husband's disbelief, his scorn. No doubt, once he considered her words, he'd find the things she'd just revealed preposterous.

Long moments passed, and yet she saw no such sign upon Hume's face. Instead, he was watching her with a look of consternation, his eyes narrowed as if he were deep in thought. "Ye have a lot of faith in yer leader," Hume murmured eventually. "How can ye be so sure?"

"I trust Colina's divination … she is the most powerful druidess our order has seen in generations." Fyfa frowned then. "However, when she cast the bones after her dream, they offered her a warning. A shadow lies over the Bruce … he needs our protection if he is to fulfill his destiny." Her gaze fused with Hume's then. "We must watch over him while he remains within the English camp. This is a dangerous place for him to be at present."

And for us all, she added silently.

"Do ye think that witch, Lamia, might be a threat to him?"

"I don't know … but Colina warned me about her for a reason."

"Could she also have discovered that the Bruce is one day fated to defeat the English?"

A chill washed over Fyfa as she pondered her husband's question. She certainly hoped not. "I don't know," she admitted. "But it's certainly a possibility." She paused then, cocking her head. "Do ye actually believe me, Hume?"

A humorless smile stretched his lips, and Fyfa found herself focusing on his mouth. She recalled what it tasted like, and how passionate his kisses had been. Had he actually taken her just the night before? It seemed like days ago now.

She kicked herself then for letting her thoughts drift to such things.

"Aye," he replied, stepping back and raking a hand through his short hair. The gesture left it tousled, and Fyfa quelled the urge to step forward and smooth it. "There's no way ye could have made up such a wild tale." His features tightened then. "Now we must decide what to do about it."

A knot of tension released within Fyfa's chest. "Are ye offering to help?"

"Aye," he replied gruffly.

A smile creased Fyfa's lips then, warmth flooding through her. He was a good man, her husband, if he could overlook everything between them, albeit for a short while, and assist her. "Well, in that case," she murmured. "I think we should pay the Bruce a visit."

19

I WILL HEED YER WARNING

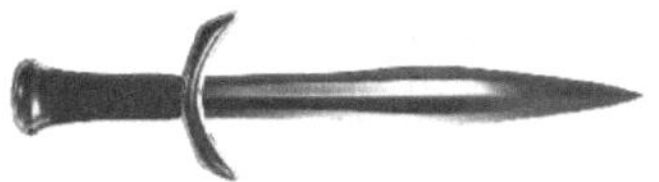

"WE MUST BE wary, Hume," Fyfa murmured as she and her husband approached the Bruce pavilion. "It's not advised to warn someone about their future ... it can turn the will of the goddesses against ye."

Hume cut her a look. "I've already assured ye, I won't. Just as long he believes our tale."

Fyfa met his eye, her belly clenching. Hume had suggested that they fabricate a story of how she'd overheard two of Edward's knights discussing the Scottish nobles. It was certainly more believable, and far less risky, than telling him the truth.

"Come," Hume replied briskly. "Let's see how this goes."

They closed the last few yards to the Bruce tent. Around them, the light was fading as the long twilight drew out. Few of the residents of Stirling castle were relaxed enough this eve to lay out sheepskins and try and get some rest. Instead, a large group of men—Cameron Stewart among them—were still drinking around the fire. Drunken, belligerent voices drifted over the clearing, and Fyfa frowned. The simmering discontent grew. Although she understood her countrymen's frustration, she hoped none of them would do anything foolish while they were in their cups.

However, Fyfa couldn't focus on Stewart and the others right now. She had to find a way to warn Robert Bruce, without making him suspicious.

Reaching the tent, she and Hume ducked inside.

The two Bruce brothers were seated together, talking quietly. Both of them looked up at Hume and Fyfa's entrance.

The bigger of the two men frowned, his gaze sweeping over the newcomers before it settled upon Hume. "Aren't ye John Comyn's cousin? I saw ye with him earlier."

Hume halted before bowing his head respectfully. "Good eve, Robert. Aye, I'm Hume … the former steward of Stirling, and this is my wife, Fyfa."

The Bruce's younger brother, Neil, favored them with a tight smile. "Bad business this … although I'm relieved Edward spared yer lives."

Fyfa stiffened. She supposed she should be grateful for that—although she wasn't about to thank that thrice-cursed bastard for anything.

"How can we help ye?" Robert asked. He had a serious face and a wary gaze, hinting that he wasn't someone who trusted easily. He was clearly wondering why John Comyn's cousin was paying him a visit. Fyfa was relieved to see he was guarded. Robert Bruce's path would be much easier if he was suspicious of most folk. He was younger than she'd expected, no older than thirty winters—the same age as both her and Hume.

"I apologize for intruding on yer privacy this eve," Hume replied, "but my wife learned something today that we believe ye should be warned of."

Robert Bruce's dark brows drew together. "Go on."

"She was taking a walk within the English pavilions when she overheard two of Edward's knights discussing ye."

The Earl of Carrick's expression grew grim, while next to him, his brother tensed. "Continue."

"They were questioning why Longshanks had bothered to invite ye here at all … for it's clear ye are 'a scheming bastard who has been plotting behind our backs'."

Hume paused there, and Fyfa's palms grew damp. She'd warned Hume not to embellish the lie too much or the Bruce would grow suspicious.

She recalled the things John Comyn had told her over the years. He'd said that Robert Bruce was cunning and ambitious. However, John had never gotten along with Robert—and relations between the two men had worsened ever since a meeting of a council of the magnates at Peebles five years earlier. The discussion had deteriorated until 'The Red' had lost his temper with Bruce and seized him by the throat. John had once told her that the Earl of Carrick had ambitions and believed the Bruces were the true heirs to the Scottish throne.

Fyfa cleared her throat then, before picking up the story, as she and Hume had agreed. "One of the knights muttered that ye have ambitions to rule Scotland one day … and his friend agreed before adding that Edward of England is aware that ye aren't a man to be trusted. He invited ye here for that very reason … to observe ye." Fyfa halted then, noticing the hard glint of Robert Bruce's eyes and the deeply furrowed brow of Neil beside him. "They agreed that Edward will dispose of ye, the moment he suspects any disloyalty … ye should be wary."

Silence followed her tale, although it was Neil who spoke first. "I don't believe it," he growled, with a shake of his head. "Surely, Longshanks wouldn't break his word?"

Robert cut him a sharp look. "Wouldn't he? Ye heard what he said to me this morning … it was as good as a threat."

The brothers' gazes fused, a silent look passing between them. Fyfa wondered what Robert thought of the allegations. Nonetheless, she'd marked that he hadn't responded to them. Did that mean that he did have ambitions? Considering Colina's vision, it would certainly make sense.

The brothers' stare drew out. Eventually, Neil's jaw tightened before he nodded.

Robert turned back to Fyfa. "I thank ye for bringing the news to my attention … although I do ask myself what ye were doing wandering amongst the English tents?"

"I have already asked my wife that," Hume replied before Fyfa had the chance. "Unfortunately, she's far too nosey by half."

Fyfa gritted her teeth. She glanced over at Hume, irritation surging through her when he shot her an indulgent look. She could have sworn she saw a glint in his light-brown eyes.

"Aye, I'd counsel ye to be more careful in future, Lady Comyn," The Bruce agreed, his expression grim now. "However, I'm grateful to ye … and I will indeed heed yer warning."

Lamia Delamare entered her pavilion, letting the tent flap drop behind her. Releasing a sigh of relief, she crossed to the neatly made bed and let Fantôme slide free of her sleeve. The small white grass snake slithered out onto the coverlet.

"I thought that supper would never end," she murmured. The king had been in the mood to celebrate. He planned to hold a banquet the following eve, yet had decided to make merry this eve as well with his kin and retainers.

Lamia had spent the evening fending off Prince Edward's wandering hands. The young man had drunk far too much, and as the eve wore on, he'd focused his amorous attentions upon the queen consort's favorite.

Glancing around her, Lamia saw that the servants had tidied up her pavilion and replaced the candles. Unlike the other ladies-in-waiting, who all shared lodgings, Margaret had given her a tent to herself.

Of course, the queen knew Lamia needed privacy. Nonetheless, Margaret had no idea of what her best friend was planning.

As much as she wished for her husband's victory over the Scots, the queen wouldn't have condoned it.

"Come, Fantôme." Lamia crossed to her leather trunk, opened it, and dug out a wooden box. "We have work to do."

The snake coiled before lifting its head to watch her, a tiny forked tongue darting out.

Lamia brought the box to the bed and seated herself next to her familiar. Then, drawing a small key from a chain around her neck, she unlocked it. The contents of this box were precious to her—essential elements for witching. She always kept it locked, for she couldn't risk a snooping servant stumbling upon them. Her obsidian scrying bowl and a number of witch ways lay within: feathers, crystals, and candles, as well as stoppered vials and pots.

Lamia carefully drew out three vials, each with a different colored stopper. "Which tincture should I use, Fantôme?" she whispered. "Belladonna, Hemlock, or Wolfsbane?" She picked up the green stoppered vial. "Belladonna is deadly, but it works slower than some poisons." She put down the vial, her hand hovering over the one beside it. "While Hemlock, although equally deadly, does have a taste that might give it away when added to wine." She paused then, her gaze shifting to the third vial, the one with the red stopper. "But Wolfsbane is the most formidable of them all, and it works swiftly too." Her mouth pursed. "Perhaps a little too swiftly for my purpose."

Studying the vials, Lamia thought to her past uses of them—for there had been two individuals she'd poisoned over the years. The first was a snooping servant who'd found her cache of books on witchcraft back in France. The woman had to be silenced, and a few drops of Belladonna to her morning broth had done the trick. The second had been one of Edward's knights in London. The man had cornered her in a palace corridor one afternoon, pushed her up against the wall, and taken what he wanted. Two drops of Wolfsbane in his wine the following night had given her the vengeance she'd sought.

Lamia glanced over at Fantôme. "Ye think the Belladonna will work best?" She picked up the green vial once more. "Aye, I believe ye are right … he will leave the banquet with a terrible headache, dry mouth and throat, and will die later in his tent."

Placing the two other vials back in the box, she picked up a lump of clear quartz. For this to go smoothly, she would need a strong working, to allow her to move undetected and without arousing suspicion during the banquet.

What about that witch?

Lamia tensed then, her fingers closing over the smooth, clear crystal she held. "Fyfa Comyn could be a problem, Fantôme," she murmured. "I was overconfident with Nessa … and it cost me … but I will not make the same mistake twice." She glanced at where her familiar watched her steadily, the snake's pinprick eyes flat and unwavering. "Aye, that is sage advice … I will add Belladonna to her wine as well."

"What were ye two doing with Bruce?" John Comyn asked. He swirled the wine around his pewter goblet, watching Fyfa and Hume over the rim.

Hume tensed. Of course, as they'd emerged from Robert Bruce's pavilion, they'd crossed paths with his cousin. John had spent the afternoon talking to his friends, Neil Campbell and James Douglas. Hume had initially drunk with them, although as the afternoon wore on, he'd gotten tired of the endless talk of politics and ventured outdoors—which was when he learned his wife had been off exploring.

"He offered to share some wine with us," Hume replied after a pause, hoping the lie didn't show on his face. He didn't like holding back from his cousin, yet he knew there was little love lost between John and Robert, and Hume was wary of confiding in him. "He wished to ask us about how we'd all fared during the siege."

"Did he?" A muscle in John's bearded jaw tightened. He slugged back the dregs of his goblet and reached for the jug of wine upon the trestle table between them. Hume noted his cousin's red cheeks and wondered just how much wine he'd consumed during the day. Outside the pavilion, he could hear raucous, belligerent voices. Most of the men gathered around the fire were now well into their cups.

"Aye," Fyfa replied, flashing John a smile. "Robert was gracious. He wished to congratulate Hume on how long we managed to withstand the assault."

"I've had to listen to Campbell and Douglas singing the Bruce's praises all afternoon," John growled, flashing Fyfa an irritated look. "Don't ye start."

"Why not?" Fyfa replied, arching an eyebrow. "He seemed perfectly charming to me."

A burning sensation lanced across Hume's chest at these words. Curse him, why did Fyfa's comment make his body go rigid with jealousy. He'd realized, after the discoveries of the past fortnight, that her secrecy had nothing to do with a lack of fidelity. However, his wife's naturally flirtatious temperament and her careless words caused every insecurity he'd ever had to surface. She had lied to him after all—he'd be an idiot to ever trust her again.

And yet, this afternoon, they'd worked together—and he'd enjoyed it. For a few moments, as they'd entered Robert Bruce's tent side-by-side, he'd been able to forget that it was over between them.

Hume's fingers tightened around the stem of his own goblet, yet the mouthful he'd just taken suddenly tasted like vinegar.

But it was over. The day after tomorrow, he and Fyfa would set off north. He would escort her back to her coven, and then he would do his best to forget she'd ever been his wife.

Hume reached up, rubbing at the burning under his breast bone. The problem was that he'd never be able to forget Fyfa. This woman was etched into his bones, his soul—and he'd miss her till his dying breath.

20

NO GOING BACK

BEDTIME WAS AWKWARD. It had been a long while since Fyfa shared a bed with her husband—yet they couldn't sleep apart now or John would start asking difficult questions.

Questions neither of them wished to answer.

Hume's cousin had prepared a private space for them, a pile of sheepskins and blankets behind a hanging in one corner of his pavilion. It was a cramped space, and nervousness fluttered in Fyfa's belly when she crawled into it and pulled one of the blankets over her.

Outdoors it was a mild night—although rough male shouting drifted through the walls of the tent. Defeat and drink weren't a good combination. The anger that had been bubbling away like a cauldron of stew upon a hearth all day now exploded.

Fyfa tensed. She understood their frustration, but the last thing any of them needed at the moment was to rouse the ire of Longshanks.

Her worries were reflected on Hume's face when he pushed back the curtain and entered their cramped bower. Light from the candles burning in the main space of the tent filtered through the gap in the curtain, illuminating his frown.

"What's going on out there?" she greeted him.

"Stewart just picked a fight with one of the king's knights," Hume replied, pulling a face. "Unfortunately for him ... he ended up brawling with five of them and lost. He's going to have two black eyes come morning."

"And the rest of the men?"

"Their blood is up … but John and the others have managed to calm them." Hume's gaze traveled over the narrow cot they were expected to share before his mouth thinned. He didn't need to tell her he was unhappy about sharing a bed with her—it was written all over his face.

Fyfa had removed her kirtle and washed before going to bed. However, she still wore her ankle-length lèine. Gone were the days when she would sleep naked with her husband.

Turning away from her, Hume stripped off his lèine and his gambeson and heeled off his boots. Fyfa watched the muscles of his back flex and recalled what his skin had felt like under her fingertips the night before.

She then banished the thought.

Hume climbed into bed, still wearing his braies, while Fyfa shifted to the edge of the cot. Her back ended up pressed against the side of the tent, in an attempt to give him as much space as possible.

Now that he lay next to her, she could feel the tension vibrating off her husband's strong body. And she knew it had little to do with this evening's brawling.

Instead, it had everything to do with her.

Hume lay upon his back, his profile outlined in the dim light of their bower. He appeared to be staring up at the roof, as if he wished to be anywhere but here, with her.

"Thank ye for listening to me today, Hume," she whispered, breaking the awkward silence between them. "And for helping me warn Robert Bruce."

"I'm as patriotic as ye," he replied quietly. "And I'll do what I can to keep Scotland free of English overlords."

"I know," she murmured. "I've never doubted yer love for our land."

He inclined his head to her then, his gaze glinting. "Haven't ye?" His features hardened. "That'll be why ye kept lying to me for so long, is it?"

The words stung, yet Fyfa weathered the rebuke. She knew she'd earned it. "Ye deserved better," she admitted after a pause.

He stared at her for a long moment before his gaze shifted back to the roof of the tent once more. Silence lay heavily between them.

Long moments passed, and a lump rose in Fyfa's throat. It hit her then, with the force of a sledgehammer to the chest, that she didn't want to lose Hume Comyn.

She'd told him she was fond of him, that she cared for him, but her feelings ran far deeper than that. The fierce sensation that now clawed at her breast felt as if it risked rending it.

Hume was as important to her as any cause. Her blinkered attitude had cost her dearly, and soon she'd lose the person who meant most to her in the world. Her loyalty to her order had turned her blind. For some reason, she'd always believed there was only room in her heart for her mother and sisters, and for their shared mission. Although Guardians of Alba did take lovers, few of them wed or had families. It was a distraction from what was truly important.

Fyfa had gone into her union with Hume determined not to let him into her heart—but she'd ultimately failed.

Dizziness swept over her then.

I love him.

Fyfa swallowed hard. *Goose-witted woman, of course ye love him.* Why on earth had it taken her so long to admit it to herself?

"So, it really is over between us?" she asked huskily, breaking the tense silence.

A beat passed, and when Hume replied, there was a rough edge to his voice, giving away the turmoil within. She'd wounded him deeply, and there was no going back from that. "Aye," he whispered. "But fear not, Fyfa, I'll see ye safely home."

Home.

The Wailing Widow Falls of Assynt had once been her haven, yet it hadn't been for years.

Tears stung the back of Fyfa's eyes. This man was her home.

"Would it help if I told ye I dearly wished for us to start afresh?" she said, her voice wobbling now. Curse her, she was going to start weeping in a moment.

"No," he rasped after a pause. "I can't have ye near me, Fyfa … don't ye understand? Not after all the lies."

A brittle hush fell between them.

Fyfa's pulse started to pound in her ears. This was it, her last chance to mend things between them. Maybe if she revealed that she loved him, he would have a change of heart. Perhaps then he'd be open to reconciliation?

However, the words wouldn't come. She'd taken things too far—Hume would think she was trying to manipulate him, use him as she had from the start. And she felt too brittle at present to weather his scorn.

And so, she took the coward's path. "Not everything was a lie, Hume," Fyfa finally whispered, her throat aching, a tear trickling down her cheek. "And even if ye no longer want me, please remember that."

"Can I come in, Estelle?" Fyfa poked her head into the tent, her gaze alighting upon the pale figure sitting upon a stool in the corner. "Or do ye wish to be left alone?"

Lady Oliphant glanced up. She'd been staring into the flames of the small brazier that burned before her. Estelle's delicately featured face looked haggard and tired this morning, her eyes bloodshot and puffy. She then attempted to smile and failed. "No, I'd welcome yer company … please come in, Fyfa … take a seat with me."

Fyfa nodded and moved across to the stool next to her friend before lowering herself onto it.

The sides of the pavilion billowed and snapped. A brisk yet warm wind had sprung up this morning, bringing the sweet smell of summer.

Summer. With everything that had occurred of late, Fyfa had barely noticed the passing of the season. Spring had sped by in a blur, and suddenly they were almost in August. She wasn't sure where the time had gone.

"I brought ye a honey-cake," Fyfa said, passing Estelle a small cloth-wrapped package. "The English cooks are preparing this eve's banquet, and Queen Margaret had them send some cakes over to us."

"That is kind of her," Estelle said absently. She placed the still-wrapped cake upon her lap but made no move to eat it.

Fyfa clenched her jaw. She didn't care what the queen consort's motives were for sending them cakes, it couldn't make up for the fact that Stirling was now in English hands. The Plantagenet banner flew high over the keep this morning—and the sight of it had made fury pulse through her.

Nonetheless, she didn't voice her ire to Estelle. Her friend was still reeling from her husband's sentencing.

"How are ye faring?" she asked after a pause, her gaze searching Estelle's ravaged face.

The older woman's mouth lifted at the edges, although her eyes remained filled with sorrow. "I'm still breathing, so things can't be that bad."

Fyfa favored her with a tight smile. Estelle still hadn't lost her wry sense of humor. "Have they let ye see Sir William?"

Estelle nodded. "Yesterday eve." She paused then, her throat bobbing. "They will let me see him once more, to farewell him, the day after tomorrow."

Silence fell between the two women, and then Fyfa reached out, placing her hand over Estelle's. Lady Oliphant's fingers were ice-cold, as if it were the depths of winter instead of the height of summer. "I'm sorry … I wish I could do something to prevent this."

Estelle nodded. "Thank ye." She then managed a brittle smile. "All hope isn't lost though … my husband is alive, at least."

Fyfa squeezed her hand. "Aye, and perhaps, with the passing of the months, Longshanks will soften toward him."

The women fell silent then, while Fyfa struggled for the right words. It was a bitter irony that this couple, who had always been so happy, had been torn apart by circumstances beyond their control, while the rift between Fyfa and Hume had been caused from within.

There really was no justice in the world.

Fyfa had passed a largely sleepless night. She'd lain in the darkness, listening to the slow whisper of her husband's breathing and the rumble of his cousin's snoring in the bed nearby, while she stared up at the shadowed roof of the tent. Tears had flowed silently down her cheeks, running into her ears and wetting her hair. But she hadn't brushed them away. Sadness had crushed her ribs in a vice. It still did.

"Where will all the residents of Stirling go?" Estelle asked finally, turning her attention upon Fyfa. "The castle was their home."

Fyfa huffed a sigh. "They shall return to their clans, I imagine." She frowned then. "There was some brawling last night between some of our men and the English. Did ye hear it?"

Estelle nodded, her expression tightening.

"They've quietened down now that they've all sobered up," Fyfa assured her. "Defeat is galling for men who held out so long against their enemy. At least Longshanks's banquet will be over tonight." Fyfa paused then, clearing her throat. "And where will ye go, Estelle?"

"To the Highlands," Lady Oliphant replied softly, her gaze settling upon the flickering flames of the brazier. "William has asked me to return to his family seat, Kellie Castle, and so I will do as he bids." She glanced up, giving Fyfa a searching look. "Are things better between ye and Hume?"

Fyfa forced a smile before nodding.

Relief lit in Estelle's eyes. "It will be good for ye and Hume to start afresh at Inverlochy ... far from all of this."

Fyfa swallowed. Her friend's words were like pins digging into her flesh, yet Estelle had no idea. She meant well and believed that whatever troubles Hume and Fyfa had, they could be resolved. She had no idea of the

double life Fyfa had been living or the fact that Hume
had finally discovered the truth. No, Estelle was ignorant
of these facts, but Fyfa wasn't going to ruin her hopes for
them. Instead, she merely forced another smile. "Aye,"
she murmured.

21

ON EDGE

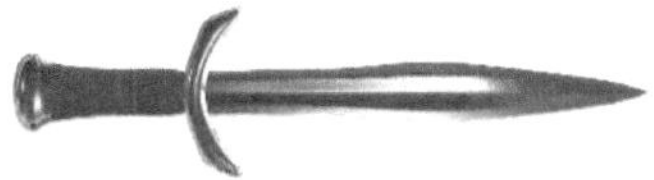

"WHAT'S AFOOT WITH ye and Fyfa these days?"

His cousin's question made the mouthful of salted beef Hume was eating stick in his throat. He coughed and reached for the cup of ale before him and took a large gulp. Eyes smarting, he straightened up to see John was watching him under hooded lids. "I don't know what ye mean," Hume rasped.

They were alone, for Fyfa had gone off to see Estelle Oliphant.

"I've got eyes, lad," John replied, his ruddy brows crashing together. "I can see things are ... strained. What have ye done to mess things up?"

Hume scowled. He'd always liked his cousin—he was one of the few of his kin who'd treated him decently. But John's insistence in continually calling him 'lad' when he was a man of thirty winters—and his hints over the years that Fyfa could have done a lot better—galled.

"What makes ye think it's my fault?" he growled.

His cousin's eyes glinted, and Hume realized he'd walked straight into a trap. John had said that to goad him into speaking plainly. "Aye, so there *is* a problem, after all."

"Aye, and I'd prefer not to speak of it."

"Has that bonny wife of yers been sharing her honeypot with other men?"

Hume suppressed the urge to flinch. He hadn't seen 'The Red' in a year or two and had forgotten just how blunt the man could be. Although he'd foolishly suspected Fyfa of taking a lover—and had nearly been driven mad with jealousy at the thought—he didn't like his cousin thinking such of her.

Although their marriage was over, he still felt protective of Fyfa. Aye, she'd lied to him, wed him only because his position offered her the opportunity to spy on the comings and goings of Stirling Castle, yet he wouldn't throw her to the wolves.

He had to protect her honor.

"No," he said gruffly, "and I'd appreciate it if ye didn't say such things about my wife."

John huffed a laugh. "Ye know I've always liked Fyfa … I've never forgotten the help she gave me when we took back Stirling three years ago. A bonny face is one thing … but the lass has spirit and courage."

Hume's belly twisted. He knew that—and having John rub his face in it wasn't helping. Sharing a bed with her the night before had been torture. The scent of her skin, the whisper of her breathing. He'd slept badly, especially when he realized she wasn't sleeping at all. Fyfa's breathing had caught once or twice, and he'd wondered if she was weeping.

"However," his cousin continued, his voice adopting a tone that made Hume's hackles rise. "Ye reached too high when ye chose that one for a bride." John shook his head, censure in his eyes. "Ye should have done as I did, and choose a plainer wife."

Hume's mouth thinned. His cousin's wife, Joan, hadn't been blessed with beauty and could be a bit humorless at times. If he didn't know any different, he'd have thought John was letting bitterness get the better of him.

"So, what are ye saying?" Hume abandoned the bread and salted beef he'd been eating for his noon meal, fixing John with a narrow-eyed stare. "That Fyfa's too good for me?" He was tired of folk whispering behind his back. It didn't help of course, that he too secretly had questioned why Fyfa had chosen him.

John's eyes widened, before his mouth quirked. "Not at all … ye are a man of principle, Hume … and such individuals are rare." He shook his head then. "But wedding a beautiful woman is both a blessing and a curse ... she has made ye unhappy, hasn't she, lad?"

His cousin's words hung between them in the tent.

The knots in Hume's belly tightened. Lord, how pathetic his cousin made him feel, like some useless castrated fazart who couldn't handle his wild, beautiful wife. Anger ignited then, spreading through his abdomen and up his chest in a hot wave.

He didn't want his cousin's pity.

He didn't want his wife's apologies.

Instead, he itched to take a sword in hand and slash his way through the English camp. He hated feeling like this, as if his life were unraveling before his eyes and he was powerless to stop it.

Longshanks had Stirling, and Hume would soon separate from Fyfa. Right now, it felt as if nothing would ever be right with the world again.

Hume's fingers tightened around his cup of ale. "Aye," he admitted roughly. "Although, I've played my part, John. Fyfa can't be held accountable for my own failings."

Fyfa was on edge when she left Estelle Oliphant's pavilion. Stepping outside, she inhaled the warm air, scented with wood smoke and frying bannock, and let the wind caress her face. Estelle's grief hung over her, lingering even when she exited the tent. Fyfa couldn't begin to imagine what it would feel like to see her husband put in chains.

Soon, Sir William would be taken south, from Scotland, and locked in the Tower of London.

What if Hume had also been taken prisoner?

Queasiness flooded through her. She couldn't have borne it. Thank The Three, he'd been spared.

Standing there, her gaze swept over the circle of tightly packed pavilions and the clearing beyond. Things were quiet today, especially after the ruckus of the night before. A group of Scotsmen were still sleeping off all the ale they'd consumed by the smoking hearths. She spied Cameron Stewart then.

The man's face was a mess—covered in purpling bruises and lacerations. Indeed, he did sport two black eyes. Unlike some of the others, he wasn't sleeping. Instead, he sat before one of the fires, glowering at the embers.

Fyfa frowned. Although Stewart had advised Oliphant to consider negotiation with the enemy, he seemed to have taken the fall of Stirling hardest of all: almost as if he took on personal responsibility for their defeat. No one had laid the blame at his feet—for the captain had done a valiant job of rallying the garrison over the past months—but observing the ruin of his handsome face, she realized that there was more to Cameron Stewart than she'd thought. For years, she'd dismissed him as a warrior of supreme arrogance, the kind of man that shrugged of life's disappointments.

Yet she now understood that wasn't so.

Fyfa's gaze traveled up to the fortress above them, her chest constricting when she saw both the Saint George's Cross and the Plantagenet banner fluttering from the top of the keep now.

Her jaw clenched, and she tore her gaze away. Such a sight was a punch in the eye.

Moving away from Estelle's tent, she walked to the Bruce pavilion. There wasn't anyone watching her at present, and there was no sign of either of the Bruces.

She had to work fast.

Halting before the threshold, Fyfa dug into one of the pouches at her waist, grabbing a handful of salt. Casting a glance around her to ensure she still wasn't being observed, she then casually scattered a line of salt before the entrance to the tent.

Salt to ward, honey to beckon—that was the rule.

She had no idea if Lamia Delamare knew of Robert Bruce's destiny, yet she wasn't taking any chances. If the witch tried to work a hex or a curse upon the Bruce, the line of salt would thwart her.

It was a temporary solution at best though, and she would need to scatter more salt across the threshold later in the day. However, once she left this camp, what protection she'd given Robert Bruce would disappear. He'd assured her he'd leave Stirling as soon as possible, and she hoped he would.

Moving away from the Bruce tent, Fyfa dusted the salt off her hands.

Sensing movement to her left, she glanced to the Comyn pavilion, to see Hume emerge. Her husband paused, his attention sweeping the clearing as hers had, before his gaze came to rest upon her.

And for a moment, the pair of them merely stared at each other. And then Hume advanced on her. Watching him approach, Fyfa's belly fluttered. Things had altered between them of late—now, whenever her husband was near, Fyfa found it difficult to concentrate.

Hume wore a shuttered look upon his face when he stopped before her. "How is Lady Oliphant faring?" he asked.

Fyfa sighed. "As well as can be expected." She paused there. "I couldn't have borne it, if ye had been taken prisoner too, Hume."

He stared down at her, a shadow moving through those moss-green eyes. "Aye, well," he said roughly. "Longshanks barely glanced my way when we were brought before him ... I doubt he even remembered me. It was Sir William he wanted to make an example of." Hume fell silent then, his gaze remaining upon her.

The sudden intensity of it made Fyfa's belly feel as if a cluster of frantic moths had taken up residence there.

"Ye did well yesterday with the Bruce." Hume stepped closer and lowered his voice. "I believe he heeded ye."

Fyfa stilled, warmth spreading through her. Despite everything, Hume was still her ally in this—he believed in what she was doing.

"Thank ye," she murmured. "We work well together, don't we?"

The corners of his mouth lifted into a soft smile. "Is there anything else we should be doing?" he asked then. "We have warned Bruce ... but what of that witch?"

"Lamia Delamare is still a potential threat," she replied. "There are a few precautions I must take, just in case she knows about Robert Bruce."

Hume frowned. "Such as?"

Fyfa smiled. "I've just warded the threshold of the Bruce pavilion with salt ... but I will need a private space where I can do some candle witching." She glanced over at the Comyn tent. "Is John still in there?"

"No, he went to talk to the Campbells. He should be with them awhile."

Fyfa nodded. "Good." She flashed him another smile. "Ye can assist me ... if ye like?"

22

CELEBRATING VICTORY

FYFA TOOK A seat at the long banquet table to the merry sound of flutes and harps. Banners and bunting fluttered in the wind, and the rich aroma of roasted meats drifted across the camp. Around her, at the tables that had been set out in a square under the large open-sided pavilion, finely dressed men and women took their seats.

Next to Fyfa, Hume muttered an oath under his breath before casting her a pained look. "Longshanks intends to crow like a cockerel this eve, doesn't he?"

"Aye," Fyfa murmured, her attention returning to the liveried pages who were now bringing in platters of roast duck. "But ye have to admit, the bastard knows how to celebrate in style."

Hume snorted a humorless laugh in response. "With any luck, he'll choke on *that* ..." He gestured to the massive platter of roast swan that two pages carried to the table, placing it on the table before the two huge carven chairs reserved for the king and queen.

Edward and Margaret hadn't yet made their entrance.

Fyfa prayed The Three would heed her husband's words. However, a heaviness settled over her when she spied a young man who bore a close resemblance to the king saunter into the pavilion and take a seat to the right of the king's chair. Prince Edward had close-cropped dark-blond hair and the same ice-blue eyes as his father. Of course, one could cut off the serpent's head, but the beast would just grow another. Even if the king were to drop dead tonight, his son would take his place.

Adjusting herself upon the bench seat, where she sat between Hume to her left and John to her right, Fyfa's gaze traveled down the tables, marking each individual who attended this evening's banquet.

As always, the long twilight drew out, although flaming torches had been lit and erected around the edge of the pavilion. The rolled-up sides allowed the warm wind to whisper through the tent and gave all of them a clear view of the Warwolf, outlined against the darkening sky.

Fyfa's mouth thinned. Of course, The Hammer had decided to hold the victory banquet here for a reason.

The music grew loud then, joined by trumpeting horns that drowned out the rise and fall of voices.

Everyone seated in the pavilion rose to their feet as a man and woman, clad in flowing red and gold, entered.

It galled Fyfa to show The Hammer any sign of respect, and when she glanced at Hume's face, she saw from his glower that he felt the same way. However, there were a number of guards in hauberks, longswords strapped to their hips, standing nearby. They closely watched the Scots, seated at one of the long tables.

Fyfa drew in a deep breath and let her ire settle. *Better to save rebellion for another day.*

She watched the couple approach the table, surprise flickering within her at the sight of Queen Margaret's swollen belly. She hadn't expected Edward to allow his wife, heavy with bairn, to join him on campaign. Her surprise increased when she noted the solicitous way he helped his wife to her seat, waiting until she was comfortable before taking his own place. She frowned. Such gallant behavior didn't sit with the memory she had of this man at all. The last time he'd taken Stirling, he hadn't brought his wife with him.

Once Edward had lowered himself into his seat, his golden crown gleaming in the torchlight, he nodded to his guests, and they sat back down. The music died away, a weighty, expectant silence replacing it.

"Greetings, all," Edward addressed them, his low yet powerful voice carrying across the pavilion. His gaze shifted then to the line of Scots seated to his left. "And to our Scottish allies."

Allies? Fyfa clenched her jaw, while next to her, she felt Hume shift on the bench seat. She didn't need to look her husband's way to know that the word also galled. Of course, The Hammer knew that—she saw the way his pale blue eyes glinted and the half-smile upon his face.

And there was no mistaking the challenge in his voice either.

The king's attention shifted then and settled upon one individual in particular. Fyfa's own gaze flicked left to where Robert Bruce sat next to Hume. He stared back at Edward, his strong-featured face inscrutable, his stare unwavering.

Fyfa's skin prickled.

There it was—the sign her order had been looking for.

Edward of England knew that Robert Bruce, Seventh Lord of Annandale and Earl of Carrick, was a threat to his campaign. Shifting her focus back to the king, Fyfa saw the glint in The Hammer's eyes.

Indeed, Robert Bruce needed to watch his back. The Hammer was wary of him.

An instant later, the English king shifted his attention from Robert Bruce, his gaze sweeping the interior of the pavilion. "Eat, drink, and make merry," he said, a wide smile splitting his face. "Let us celebrate the Plantagenet banner flying high over Stirling tonight."

Once again, Hume shifted next to Fyfa. She could feel the resentment vibrating off him. Without thinking, she reached across and placed a hand upon his thigh.

She'd meant the gesture to be a calming one, yet her husband's leg went rigid under her touch.

Hurt washing through her in a hot tide, Fyfa yanked her hand back as if scalded. Although circumstances had caused her and Hume to work together, she had to remember that their marriage was over. He didn't want her touching him.

Grief compressed her chest, followed by a pang of sadness. Thrice-cursed goose-wit, she'd ruined the best thing that had ever happened to her.

The music erupted once more, the melody of the harp and flute filling the pavilion. More page boys appeared, bearing platters of pies, breads, and an array of roasted and braised vegetables.

If Fyfa hadn't felt sick to her stomach with unhappiness and nerves, her mouth would have watered at such a sight. For months, they'd survived on plain fare. Indeed, she'd never seen such a spread. Surely, the English camp's supplies had been running low too— Edward must have sent for provisions from south of the border in anticipation of his victory.

Of course, he'd known his giant trebuchet would ensure the fall of Stirling in the end, and he'd had time to plan for the occasion.

She noted then that a handful of ladies-in-waiting had risen to their feet. Some of them carried platters of pewter goblets aloft, which they set out before each guest, while others trailed behind them with ewers of wine to fill the goblets.

Fyfa glimpsed Lamia Delamare among the court ladies doling out goblets.

It was strange, for she'd almost forgotten about her when she'd sat down inside this pavilion—despite that she'd spent most of the afternoon working warding spells. Hume had joined her, his eyes wide as she lit the black candle she'd brought with her from Stirling and whispered ancient words, and a wind—laced with the scent of pine and earth—gusted through the pavilion. To his credit, he hadn't interrupted her though. And when she'd finally concluded the witching, he hadn't questioned her.

Even now, Fyfa found it hard to focus on Lamia. She wore a silver-green cotehardie that shimmered in the torchlight. But whenever she tried to stare at the woman, her gaze kept wanting to slide away.

Fyfa's breathing slowed, understanding dawning. *She's using misdirection.* It was a clever trick indeed, more subtle than applying a glamor to cloak her identity. 'Misdirection' meant that Lamia could wander in plain sight without anyone actually seeing her.

It was a struggle for Fyfa to remain focused on her. She kept glancing away and then losing her train of thought.

Reaching into a pouch at her waist, she drew out her cairn stone—a lump of smoky quartz that she and her sisters often used in their witching. Clenching it tightly, she then whispered a charm under her breath.

"What are ye doing?" Hume murmured in her ear. The whisper of his breath against her skin made Fyfa's eyes widen, awareness feathering through her. Curse him, the man was distracting her.

She glanced his way, even as the cairn stone began to warm against her palm.

"Lamia is here," she whispered, her gaze fusing with his. "Do ye spy her?"

Hume frowned, his attention straying to the surrounding banquet. Guests were helping themselves to slices of roast meat, while court ladies handed out and filled goblets with rich French wine. "No," he replied.

Fyfa swallowed. "She's deliberately hidden herself … but I see her."

His brows crashed together as he surveyed the pavilion once more. "Where is she?"

"Just three feet from us now, handing out goblets," Fyfa replied between gritted teeth. "Act normally … pretend nothing is amiss."

He obeyed her, favoring her with a tight smile. "Would ye like some duck, wife?"

"Aye, thank ye," Fyfa replied, struggling to keep her tone light.

An instant later, a familiar scent—hot iron and musk—wafted over her. It was light yet recognizable. She wondered if she was the only one who could smell it.

A slender hand appeared then, placing two goblets before them.

Fyfa didn't look up, didn't give the slightest indication that she knew the identity of the woman. She couldn't give herself away.

Even so, the fine hair on the back of her arms prickled, and the cairn stone suddenly pulsed red-hot against her palm.

A warning.

Fyfa's heart started to hammer against her breastbone. *What's she up to?*

"Wine?" Another lady-in-waiting had appeared. It was Marion, the small dark-haired lady Fyfa recognized from the day before. As then, she favored Fyfa with a warm smile.

Stiffly, Fyfa nodded before managing a smile in return.

Marion filled Fyfa's goblet before moving on to Hume's.

Fyfa's gaze fixed upon the goblet before her. The cairn stone was burning so hotly against her palm now, it felt as if it were scorching her skin.

Surely, the wine wasn't poisoned? Marion was pouring the same wine for everyone at the table.

Not the wine ... the goblet.

An oily chill slithered through Fyfa's belly.

Of course—Lamia was handing out goblets and could select which ones she passed to each guest.

Fyfa drew in a deep, steadying breath. She'd heed the cairn stone's warning. Her goblet was most definitely poisoned. She glanced left at where Hume was reaching for his goblet. Her hand struck out, and she grabbed his forearm. She didn't care this time when he stiffened under her touch. "Don't drink the wine," she hissed. "And warn Bruce not to either."

23

THE POISONED GOBLET

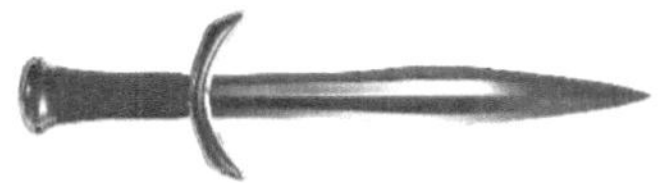

SWEAT TRICKLED DOWN Fyfa's back, between her shoulder blades.

She couldn't believe Lamia Delamare would be so bold as to make an attempt on Robert Bruce's life in such a public place. But she was.

And she was also trying to kill *her*.

Fyfa's pulse now thundered in her eyes.

She knows who I am.

Hume, The Three bless him, didn't question her. The urgency in her voice and the death-grip she now had on his arm made the seriousness of her command clear.

Without another word to her, he leaned to Robert Bruce and whispered something to him.

Fyfa glanced their way to see the Earl of Carrick stiffen. His gaze went to the goblet Marion had just filled before his features tensed. He then glanced her way and nodded.

Relief slammed into Fyfa, weakness flooding through her limbs. She'd worried that the Bruce wouldn't heed her, yet he did. A little of the panic that clawed its way up her chest and throat drew back.

She'd foil Lamia Delamare yet.

Her attention shifted then, farther down the table, to where Lamia had just finished handing out goblets and was now gliding back to the opposite side of the pavilion. Once again, it was difficult to keep focused on her, but Fyfa's fingers clenched around her cairn stone as it continued to burn against her palm. The heat galvanized her. Her gaze tracked Lamia while she handed the empty tray to a page and then took her seat next to Queen Margaret.

And at that moment, the misdirection charm lifted. The court lady murmured something to the queen consort, and the women laughed together.

"Do ye see her now, Hume?" Fyfa asked between gritted teeth. "She's sitting next to the queen."

"Aye," he murmured. "The blonde woman in the silver-green dress?"

Fyfa nodded. She shifted her attention away from Lamia then. It was best not to stare, not to draw the woman's suspicion that she knew what she'd done. Instead, Fyfa glanced back at her husband. He was watching her, his jaw set.

"So, it's the wine?" he asked.

"No … the goblet. I don't know whether she's poisoned yers or his brother's … but mine is, and I strongly suspect Robert Bruce's is too." Indeed, her spine tingled in warning whenever she let her gaze settle upon her goblet.

A nerve flickered in Hume's cheek. "How did ye—"

"What are ye two whispering about?" John Comyn's hearty voice intruded then. He'd been talking to one of the other Scottish nobles seated next to him this eve. However, his cousin and Fyfa's furtive behavior had caught his eye.

Fyfa flashed John a smile, hoping it didn't appear too brittle. "Can't a husband and wife share a few secrets?" she replied, deliberately injecting a saucy note into her voice.

'The Red' cocked an eyebrow, his gaze roaming over her face and then Hume's. "Aye."

"We're just talking about what the future holds, cousin," Hume added, his tone also falsely bright. "I was warning Fyfa about my mother."

John pulled a face. "Maureen Comyn isn't a woman easily charmed."

Fyfa forced herself to smile once more. "I'm sure I can bring her around."

John laughed. "Well, ye can try lass ... I wish ye luck."

He turned back to his previous conversation then, and Fyfa let out a shaky breath. She cast Hume a grateful look, aware that her heart was still galloping. Crone's tears, this banquet was taking a toll on her nerves.

"What now?" Hume asked, leaning close to her once more, his eyes bright.

Her gaze fused with his. "Now, we watch and wait."

Hume nodded before he reached out and sliced some duck from the platter a page boy had just set before them. He served them both before handing Fyfa some bread. "Best make a show of eating," he murmured, "or folk will grow suspicious."

Fyfa nodded, even if her stomach felt tied in knots.

He was right, of course.

Forcing herself to take a mouthful of duck, she glanced left at where Robert Bruce was talking to his brother. He'd begun his meal yet hadn't touched his wine.

Fyfa let out a shaky breath. *Thank the Goddesses*.

She noted then that the duck was delicious. She'd never eaten such beautifully roasted meat—and it was a pity that her host, and her current circumstances, meant she couldn't enjoy it.

The meal drew out, and Fyfa ate slowly, sharing a few words with John, while Hume conversed with Robert Bruce for a while.

And as the music continued to play, and bowls of rich custard were brought to the table, she noted that the King of England kept glancing across at Robert Bruce. Eventually, Longshanks rose to his feet, motioning for the musicians to halt, mid-tune.

Silence settled over the pavilion. Outside it was almost dark, and moths fluttered around the flaming torches.

"It is time for a toast." The Hammer's voice carried across the tables in French. He then raised his jewel-encrusted goblet high. "To an enduring alliance between the English and the Scots."

The mouthful of duck Fyfa had been chewing turned to ash. With difficulty, she swallowed it down. She didn't glance at her husband, although she could feel his tension, his silent outrage.

"To an alliance!" The words rippled across the table, although Fyfa noted that no one seated near her spoke. The banqueters then all lifted their goblets to their lips.

All but Fyfa, Hume, and the Bruce.

Edward of England's ice-blue gaze traveled across to Robert Bruce once more, and this time a groove formed between the king's eyebrows.

"Robert," he called out. "Is there something wrong with the wine?"

Fyfa's belly lurched. *Mother's milk ... no.*

Bruce met the king's eye. "Not at all, Your Highness," he replied in the same tongue, his tone neutral. "I'm just not in the mood for it, this eve."

Longshanks sank back down into his carven chair, while beside him, Margaret shot her husband a questioning look. However, the king ignored her—his gaze remaining fixed upon the Scottish lord.

"It's poor form ... to refuse a toast," he replied, shifting his attention to Robert's brother. "Isn't it, Neil?"

Neil Bruce frowned before casting his brother a warning look. However, the Earl of Carrick's attention remained fixed upon the king.

"It's not my intention to offend, Your Highness." His voice was a low rumble.

Edward of England's brows drew together. "And yet, you still refuse to touch the wine ... a king could easily take offense."

"Just drink the wine, Rob," Neil muttered under his breath.

The Bruce's broad shoulders tensed. Everyone inside the pavilion had ceased eating and drinking, their gazes trained on the Seventh Lord of Annandale. Moments passed, and then Robert's mouth thinned.

"Are you so easily upset, *Edward*?"

A brittle silence followed, and when The Hammer broke it, his voice was cool and laced with clipped anger.

"No, Rob … but I will be if you continue to refuse my hospitality."

Robert Bruce's brow furrowed, while his brother muttered something else to him.

Watching them, Fyfa broke out in a cold sweat.

An instant later, Robert gave a curt nod and reached for his goblet.

Fyfa's heart leaped into her throat.

Without hesitating further, or thinking about the repercussions, she jumped to her feet. "No, Bruce!" she shouted before continuing in French. "You cannot let him bully you like this!"

Gasps rippled around the pavilion. She glanced at her husband to see that Hume wore a stunned look; he stared at her, poleaxed, as if she'd just ripped off all her clothes and was dancing naked upon the table. But he made no move to quiet her.

Rounding on Robert Bruce, Fyfa pointed an accusing finger at him. "Will you let the English king unman you?"

The Bruce's brown eyes widened. "What?" he growled.

Fyfa hoped her gaze held enough panic to warn him that she was merely trying to help.

"You are a Scot nobleman," she continued, stabbing her finger at him. "You have already debased yourself by kneeling before Longshanks … and now you permit him to shame you before your peers. Enough!"

With that, she reached past Hume and knocked the goblet out of the Bruce's hand. The pewter vessel sailed high, blood-red liquid arcing into the air, before it landed on one of the fine mats that had been laid out over the floor of the pavilion for this banquet.

More gasps, hissed whispers, and muttered oaths filled the tent.

"Fyfa!" John Comyn growled from beside her. "Have ye lost yer wits, lass?"

"Get that madwoman out of my sight!" Edward of England's voice boomed through the murmurs of outrage. Fyfa glanced his way to see the king had gone white about the mouth, his blue eyes as hard as shards of ice. "Before I slit her throat!"

"Enough, wife." Hume's tone was urgent as he rose to his feet, clamped an iron hand around Fyfa's arm, and towed her away from the table. "Time to go."

Fyfa didn't resist. Battle fury pulsed through her in waves. Only self-preservation permitted her from turning her wrath upon The Hammer. But, as they left the tent and chaos in their wake, she chanced a glance back.

Robert Bruce and John Comyn were now exchanging angry words, their voices drowned out by the roar of voices around them, while Edward of England lunged to his feet and bellowed for quiet.

However, Fyfa's gaze didn't remain on them—instead, she looked to the flaxen-haired woman dressed in shimmering silver-green, who sat at Queen Margaret's side. Margaret watched the uproar, a bemused expression upon her pretty face, while her lady-in-waiting stared at Fyfa, her pale eyes blazing with fury.

One look at Lamia, and Fyfa had confirmation her suspicions had been right: she'd just foiled a murder plot.

Hume didn't utter a word as he towed his wife through the English camp and back to the circle of Scottish tents. On the way back to the Comyn pavilion, they passed by their countrymen and women, who were gathered for a simple supper around the hearths. Unlike the rumble of mutiny the evening before, there was a resigned air among the Scots tonight. They were all tired after the previous night, Longshanks hadn't broken his word, yet—and tomorrow at dawn, they'd all be leaving.

"That went fast, Comyn," one of the men called out, bitterness lacing his voice. "Wasn't Longshanks's company to yer liking?"

Hume ignored him and the rumble of rude comments that followed. He hadn't wanted to attend the banquet, although it was just as well he had.

If Fyfa's instinct was right—she'd just saved Robert Bruce's life.

They entered the tent, where the light of a single brazier illuminated the shadowy space, and Hume dropped Fyfa's arm, turning to her.

Their gazes fused, and Hume's breathing caught.

She was a warrior standing there, her lovely features taut, her blue eyes gleaming. A faint blush stained her high cheekbones, and her breast rose and fell sharply as if she still struggled to contain her outrage.

He drank her in. "Ye were brilliant, Fyfa," he said huskily. He reached out then, took her by the shoulders, and hauled her against him for a bruising kiss.

He couldn't help himself—the woman set his blood aflame. Her bravery, as reckless as it was, had made him proud to stand at her side.

Fyfa kissed him back, a groan rising in her throat, as his tongue parted her lips and drove into her mouth. She reached up, her fingers digging into his scalp, urging him on.

When they broke apart, both of them were breathless. They stared at each other once more, and Hume felt something subtle shift between them—a thawing of sorts. His lips parted, and he was just about to speak when the flap opened and a broad-shouldered figure ducked into the tent.

John Comyn had joined them—and he wore a grim expression upon his face.

24

I WILL SEE IT DONE

'THE RED' STRAIGHTENED up to his full height inside the pavilion, his gaze sweeping from Hume to Fyfa. "Well, ye certainly know how to ruin a party, lass," he muttered.

John went to a low table by his bed and poured himself a cup of ale. Then he lifted it to his lips and gulped it down thirstily. He wiped the foam off his mustache with the back of his hand and turned back to Fyfa. There was a glint in his eye that told her he was struggling between pride and outrage at her behavior. "Ye can't stay here," he announced. "Not after making such a scene."

Fyfa huffed. "We're leaving at first light tomorrow."

"That's not soon enough."

Hume scowled. "Should we go now?"

John nodded. "Longshanks still looked mightily vexed when I left ... and he's not a man lightly crossed. Ye said some inflammatory things. He has killed men for less." He slammed down his cup and headed toward the exit. "Come ... I shall give ye one of my men's horses."

A short while later, the trio led a heavy bay gelding toward the gates of the English camp. The moon, almost full now, soared overhead, casting a hoary light over the sea of tents and the bulk of Stirling Castle in the distance, its walls outlined against a star-sprinkled blanket.

The guards at the gates cast a jaundiced eye over the Scots as they approached.

"Let me handle this," John mumbled.

Fyfa nodded. She'd said enough this evening, and truthfully, was feeling jittery in the aftermath. Once the fire in her blood had dimmed, she'd realized Hume's cousin was right—they needed to get out of this camp before The Hammer had time to dwell on the things she'd said.

She didn't regret a word of them—yet she didn't wish to linger here and find out if Longshanks was the kind to let such insults pass.

He likely wasn't.

And Lamia was likely still fuming about being thwarted. It was definitely time to leave.

"A bit late for setting out, isn't it?" One of the guards greeted them in rough French. "The king wishes his Scottish guests to remain here till tomorrow."

"Aye, but I've spoken to him and explained that my cousin and his wife must leave tonight," John replied in the same tongue. "They have a long ride ahead of them ... and the woman is 'with child'. She's been feeling unwell ... and needs to be surrounded by her kin at such a time."

Fyfa tensed as the guard's insolent gaze raked over her. She leaned against Hume, doing her best to look poorly.

"She appears well enough to me," the guard murmured, not bothering to hide the appreciation in his voice.

"Edward has given us leave to depart this eve," Hume cut in, placing a protective arm around Fyfa's shoulders. "He wishes for a strong alliance between the Scots and the English ... for us to trust each other. Would ye disappoint him?"

The guard met Hume's eye, his heavy jaw bunching. Then, after a moment, he gave a snort. "What do I care?" he grumbled. "I'm out here on guard all night while everyone else is making merry." The man then stepped back and waved them on.

Leading the horse forward, Hume helped Fyfa up before turning to his cousin. "Thank ye, Red," he murmured, shifting to Gaelic. "I won't forget this."

His cousin grunted. "Just ride swift to Inverlochy," he replied. "And I will join ye both there later." He then passed Hume a dirk, sheathed in a leather scabbard. "Take this ... ye shouldn't travel unarmed."

Lamia strode through the camp, hands clenched by her side. She'd just come from the Scottish tents, where she'd discovered that Fyfa Comyn had fled.

Fury knotted under her ribcage, beating like a war drum.

"Curse that bitch," she muttered under her breath. "She's ruined everything!"

Fantôme tightened her grip around Lamia's wrist, counseling her to stay calm, but Lamia was too vexed to heed her familiar.

Her plan had been water-tight. Everything had gone as she'd wished. She'd dropped Belladonna into the goblets of Fyfa Comyn and Robert Bruce, and wrapped herself in a misdirection charm that meant that no one noticed the identity of the lady who handed out the goblets.

But somehow, Fyfa had seen through her guise.

Storming up to the king's pavilion, she ducked inside.

The king was still up, seated upon a large chair, while his son and his knights surrounded him. Sir Philip de Eynsford was among them. His oak-brown gaze snapped up in surprise at Lamia's entrance.

The conversation in the pavilion died, and the king frowned.

Lamia straightened up, letting the tent flap fall closed behind her. In usual circumstances, she'd never have dared intrude like this—but tonight was different.

Tonight she was desperate, and something had to be done.

"That woman who insulted you, Sire," she began, breathlessly. "She's gone ... Fyfa Comyn and her husband have just fled the camp."

Edward's lanky frame tensed, his fingers tightening around the stem of the goblet he held. "What?" he growled.

"The Scottish tents are aflame with the news, Sire," Lamia pressed on. "They're all saying that Hume and Fyfa Comyn have ridden off to start a rebellion." That wasn't true, but Lamia needed Edward to heed her and take action as he should have after Fyfa Comyn insulted him.

If he'd moved swiftly, the woman wouldn't have been able to slip away.

Prince Edward snorted at this news, while Sir Aymer rolled his eyes, and Sir Nicholas favored her with an indulgent smile. However, Philip de Eynsford had gone still, his gaze never shifting from her.

"I don't remember Hume Comyn as a rabble-rouser," the king said.

"Aye," Sir Aymer agreed, scratching his shaven jaw. "He appears a dour man with little to say."

"No, he's left that to his shrew-tongued wife," Edward growled.

Lamia observed the king's face keenly, spying the ire that still burned in his ice-blue eyes.

"They are both a danger to this campaign, sire," Lamia spoke up once more. "You can't let such an insult pass unpunished ... or for news of it to circulate Scotland."

This was the first time she'd been so outspoken in front of the king. Until now, she'd held her tongue around Edward and his knights—for women, even the queen consort, weren't encouraged to participate in political discussions.

However, this eve, she was out of patience.

She risked truly vexing the king by being so bold, yet she wanted Fyfa dead. Once again, a member of that mysterious coven had thwarted her.

The king stared back at her, his bearded jaw tensing.

Long moments passed, and then he nodded. "Aye, Lady Lamia, you are a trifle overwrought tonight ... yet you have a point." His gaze shifted to Sir Philip, who'd been watching the exchange without voicing a comment.

"Fetch me *The Blade*," Edward murmured.

The king was alone in the reception area of his grand pavilion, nursing a goblet of wine that he had no taste for this eve, when a lean figure swathed in smoke-grey entered the tent.

"You called for me, Your Highness?" The man's voice was low and slightly accented.

"Aye, Hassan ... take a seat."

The hooded figure walked to a stool and lowered himself onto it. The long cloak he wore fell back, revealing the glint of the various blades he wore strapped to his person.

The shadowed face, hawkish and arrogant, watched him, dark eyes veiled. "Who is it this time?"

A smile lifted the corners of Edward's mouth. Hassan al-Aziz Muhammad, also known as 'alnasl'—*The Blade*—had worked for him for years now but hadn't had a mission in months. It was an irony really that he had this man's loyalty, for the Saracen had once been one of the Hashashin—a powerful order of assassins in the Holy Land. One of whom had tried to kill him.

It had happened in Acre many years earlier. One of the Hashashin had stabbed him, but Edward had managed to fight him off, grab his dagger, and stab his would-be-killer in the head, finishing him. The assassin's blade had been poisoned, and it was only due to the quick thinking of Eleanor, his first wife, and his skilled surgeon that Edward survived the attack.

However, the incident had brought the lethal skill of the Hashashin to Edward's notice, and when he returned to England to take up the crown, he'd brought back a sixteen-year-old assassin with him, luring him with the promise of riches. Hassan had been young, but deadly, even then.

The Blade had served him loyally ever since and was now wealthier than a baron. Nonetheless, Edward preferred to keep his assassin out of sight of the other men. There was something about the Saracen that made his knights nervous.

"Two Scots … Hume Comyn and his wife, Fyfa," Edward replied. "I've heard that they are likely heading for Inverlochy Castle … near Fort William in the Highlands." He paused there, letting Hassan take these details in. "You're to intercept the couple before they reach their destination and deal with them in the usual manner."

The Blade nodded, his shadowed features unchanging. "I will see it done, Sire."

25

NEVER A RIGHT TIME

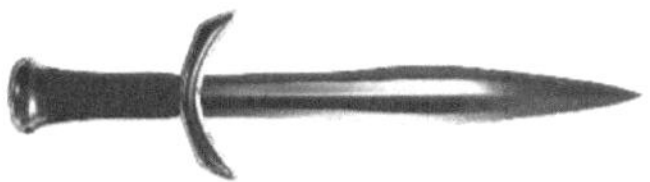

THEY RODE THROUGH the night, under the silver light of the moon.

The feel of the moonlight on her face calmed Fyfa, and her pulse slowed. Yet she could feel her witch-will awaken, curling within her, as it always did when the healing light caressed her skin.

Hume guided the gelding north, over bare hills and through wooded valleys. They followed the road, which was safer to use at night, the thud of the horse's hooves on the hard-packed dirt a steady rhythm as the night wore on.

Fyfa sat perched before her husband. At first, she'd sat there rigid and tense, but the farther they got from Stirling, the more she relaxed against the hard wall of Hume's chest. The cage of his powerful arms on either side of her, as he gripped the reins, made her feel protected.

Hume had always looked after her.

She sank further against him then, the heat of his body enveloping her. This eve had been surprising for many reasons. When he'd dragged her back to their tent, she'd expected him to rail at her, to tell her she was an utter lackwit for drawing such attention to herself.

But instead, he'd complimented Fyfa before pulling her into his arms for a searing kiss.

Her lips tingled as she recalled his passion, the tremor in his big body as he'd pulled her close. And when they'd broken apart, the air had been charged between them.

John's arrival had prevented Hume from speaking further, yet Fyfa had seen the change in her husband's face as they'd stared at each other—it was as if a veil had lifted between them.

She wanted to kiss him again, to tell him what lay in her heart—yet now, just like earlier in the tent, wasn't the right time.

They spoke little as they rode, preferring instead to keep their senses focused on their surroundings. John was worried Longshanks might send men after them, to haul them back to Stirling and face his wrath.

Fyfa's pulse accelerated at the thought. No, she wouldn't be able to relax until they reached the Highlands.

They stopped to rest once or twice during the night, watering their horse at one of the many burns they passed on the way—and once the first light of dawn brushed the eastern sky, Hume urged the gelding off the road.

"We should travel cross-country now," he murmured, speaking for the first time in hours. "Just in case Longshanks has sent anyone after us."

"Do ye really think he'd bother?" Fyfa replied huskily.

"After the insults ye flung at him ... aye."

Fyfa couldn't help it: a rueful smile stretched her lips. She wished that her sisters, Nessa and Breanna, could have witnessed the scene at the banquet. Breanna especially would have cheered her on. Her sister was the real warrior among them.

"I hope Robert Bruce does actually leave Stirling with the dawn," she said after a pause. "His life is still in danger ... especially if he remains at the camp."

"I don't think he'll linger," Hume replied. "The shock on his face when ye knocked his wine from his hand was something to behold."

Fyfa huffed a laugh. "I had to get his attention ... he was about to take a sip from that poisoned goblet to appease Longshanks."

"And ye are sure it was poisoned?"

"Aye," she said softly. "My mother and sisters need to know that Lamia Delamare has made an attempt on Robert Bruce's life."

Silence fell between them then, and when Hume broke it, his voice held a subdued edge. "I will take ye to them directly … where exactly in the Highlands are they?"

"Assynt … it's in the northwest … around four days ride north of Fort William," she replied, her throat constricted. Aye, she wished to return to her order, to warn them what had happened, but Hume's words reminded her that their marriage was over.

"I know it," he replied, all business now.

He said nothing more, and an ache rose under Fyfa's ribs. There were so many things she wanted to say to this man. But to do that, she needed to face her fears, dredge up her courage, and tell him outright how she felt— before he walked out of her life forever.

How odd, she'd been courageous at the banquet, even braved the ire of The Hammer himself for her cause, yet when it came to matters of the heart, she quailed.

Coward, she chided herself inwardly. Fyfa swallowed hard—since she'd realized the truth about how she felt about Hume Comyn, she had given him a weapon against her. Aye, she'd married him for the cause, not for love, but her feelings had changed over the years. And once he knew how desperately she loved him, he could take his revenge on her.

It was terrifying to know that he wielded so much power over her, but as they rode north, while a blushing sunrise stained the sky, Fyfa knew she didn't want to live without her husband.

They eventually rested above a waterfall. It wasn't hard to find, for its rumble gradually grew louder as they followed a burn northward. The trees drew back, revealing a foaming column of water that tumbled over lichen-covered rocks. Fyfa took in the column of water with a pang of longing. It was a much smaller cascade than that of the Wailing Widow Falls, although the waterfall reminded her of her mother and sisters to the north.

Riding up to the top, where a flat area sat under a stand of pines, they dismounted from the horse. Fyfa stretched out her stiff hips and back before she dug into her pouch and took out the last handful of her precious salt. She then sprinkled it in a semi-circle around the spot by the water's edge where they would rest, murmuring under her breath as she did so.

Hume, who was unsaddling the gelding, turned to her. "What are ye doing?"

"Just casting a protection charm," she replied. "There isn't enough salt to keep harm out entirely ... but we should have some warning if anyone approaches."

He nodded. "Aye, it doesn't hurt to be careful." There was a hesitant edge to his voice—almost as if he wasn't sure what to say to her now that they'd halted their flight from Stirling.

Fyfa stepped over the salt she'd sprinkled and lowered herself down onto a flat stone by the water's edge, while Hume turned back to their horse. She watched him remove the gelding's saddle. He rubbed the horse down with a twist of grass before tying it to a nearby pine on a long tether, so the beast could graze a little.

Hume tended to the horse carefully, checking its hooves and legs for any sign of heat or injury—the gelding still had a long way to carry them. They couldn't risk it foundering. Of course, focusing on the horse meant that he didn't have to converse with her.

Despite the moment they'd had in John's tent, there was still a reserve between them.

Fyfa yawned, blinking in an attempt to remove some of the grittiness from her eyes. She wanted to talk to Hume, to lay her soul bare to him, yet fatigue had made her head feel as if it were stuffed with wool. She didn't want to make a mess of things, to say the wrong thing. The way she felt right now, the words were likely to come out all jumbled. Perhaps it was better to wait until she was rested.

Hume turned to her, his brow furrowing. "Ye are exhausted," he observed. "Lie down for a spell. Get some sleep."

Fyfa put her hand over her mouth in an effort to stifle another yawn. "What about ye?" she asked. "Surely, ye must be ready to drop also?"

His mouth curved into a wry smile. "Aye … but someone has to keep watch. Go on, get some rest."

"Will ye wake me after a spell?" she asked before laying out her cloak and stretching out upon it. Fatigue weighed upon her, like a heavy pair of hands pressing on her shoulders. She did need to sleep, but when she woke, she would speak plainly to her husband. "That way, I can take my turn at watch."

"Aye."

Fyfa mumbled something in answer, but already, as she sank into the hard ground, sleep was claiming her, pulling her under.

Hassan reached out, his fingertips tracing the crescent in the soft peaty soil: a fresh hoof-print. A smile lifted the corners of his mouth. It was as he'd guessed—his targets had left the highway and now traveled cross-country.

They were being prudent, *as if they are worried someone is coming after them.*

The Blade rose to his feet, dusting the dirt off his fingers. No doubt they imagined Edward of England might send some of his men to haul them back to Stirling. However, they would not expect 'alnasl'—the king's secret weapon.

The half-smile still lingering, Hassan crossed to the sleek courser behind him and vaulted up onto the horse's back. He rode the swiftest steed in the king's stable and would be gaining on his quarry with each furlong.

He'd catch up with them long before they reached their destination.

Gathering up the reins, Hassan urged the stallion into a canter, and into the wooded valley that stretched out before him. The sun had risen some time ago, and the summer sky was a soft blue. For once, there wasn't a sting in the air—for in Scotland, even in summer, one never forgot the cold.

Hassan pushed back his deep cowl, letting the warm air feather his face.

A faint longing wreathed up within him then, for the hot, dry air of Acre and the endless blue sky. It had been over thirty years, but there were still times when he missed his homeland. He could still remember the scent of night-blooming jasmine, the aroma of spices in the markets, and the calls to prayer five times a day. He'd been barely a man when he'd departed the Holy Land with the prince who would soon become the King of England, and he was now in his forty-seventh year—yet even after all this time, he still struggled to call England home.

And Scotland was even more foreign to him. This northern land was wild and beautiful, yet the last winter had frozen him to the marrow. He'd be relieved when they returned to the relatively milder climes of London.

The thunder of his courser's hooves split the morning's peace, and *The Blade* leaned forward, urging his horse into a gallop. It had been too long since Edward had called for him—and he was eager to spill some blood.

Fyfa awoke with a headache. Groaning, she sat up and rubbed her eyes, blinking as she struggled to reorient herself. "What time is it?" she mumbled.

"Just after noon," Hume replied. He was sitting on a flat rock, looking out across where the river spilled over the top of the falls. "We should move on soon."

Fyfa muttered a curse. "Ye have let me sleep too long," she muttered. "Ye need to rest too."

Hume huffed a laugh, although there was a trace of awkwardness in his manner. "I'll sleep when we reach Crianlarich … if we ride hard, we'll make it by nightfall."

Fyfa rolled her neck and shoulders, in an attempt to ease the ache in her temples. She'd slept heavily, and her neck muscles felt as hard as boards.

"Here." Hume handed her a stale piece of bannock. His cousin had given him a small round of oaten griddle cake before they'd set off. "Get this down, and we'll be on our way."

Fyfa nodded, taking the bannock from him. Their fingers brushed as she did so, and a frisson of heat rippled up her arm.

It was a reminder of the kiss they'd shared before leaving Stirling, a reminder of all the things that were unvoiced between them. Nearby, their mount cropped at grass, its tail swishing at the midges that were assaulting it.

Fyfa took a small bite of bannock and chewed quickly. Swallowing, she reached for a skin of ale and took a gulp. "Hume," she said softly, catching his attention once more. "I thank ye for taking me back to Assynt … I know it's out of yer way."

"It's fine," he said, picking up a flat stone and throwing it into the swiftly flowing river. "I know how important yer cause is to ye … and contrary to what ye might think … I believe in it too."

Fyfa swallowed another mouthful of bannock. "I know ye do." She paused then, awkwardness constricting her chest. She couldn't put this off any longer. "Hume … I need ye to know something."

Hume glanced her way, his features tightening. "Is this the moment for this?" he asked quietly. His gaze was wary—he knew that a frank conversation had been looming yet clearly didn't want to have it.

"There will never be a right time," she answered, setting aside the remains of her bannock. Crone's tears, she just needed to spit this out. "But, I must tell ye … before my courage fails me … how sorry I am. For everything." She paused there, her pulse now racing, sweat beading her skin. "I can't take any of it back—the lies, the secrets—but I beg ye to find it within ye to forgive me … can ye?"

A nerve ticked in her husband's cheek. "It's all right, Fyfa," he said softly. "We both had our parts to play. I too owe ye an apology. Sometimes things just aren't meant to be."

But Fyfa barely heard him. She was so worked up now and frustrated that the words seemed to be coming out all wrong. They were clumsy and insufficient. She'd never had trouble expressing herself in the past, yet when it came to expressing what lay in her heart to her husband, it was as if her wits had scattered.

"Back in Stirling, I told ye that I cared for ye, that I was fond of ye … but the truth is that I *love* ye, Hume." Fyfa broke off. Her breathing was coming in gasps, her heart bucking against her ribs like a wild thing. "And the thought of being parted from ye … of living on without ye … makes me want to give up. None of it matters, Hume … if ye no longer want me."

Hume stared at her, his lips parting in shock. Her admission had clearly felled him.

Fyfa's vision blurred. The Goddesses save her, she couldn't bear this. It felt as if her chest was being ripped asunder. Was this what love really was—agony?

Hume cleared his throat then as he readied himself to answer—and Fyfa braced herself for his response. If he rejected her, she would beg. She had no pride left. None at all.

However, at that moment, her witch-will surged hotly in her blood, a sudden gust of unseasonably cool wind buffeting them.

Hume's expression changed, his shoulders tensing as he glanced around him. "What—"

"Get down!" Fyfa shouted—just as a knife arced through the air from the trees, straight toward her husband.

26

OVER THE FALLS

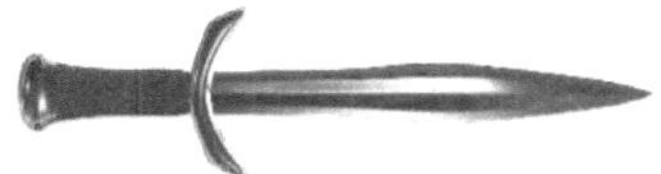

HUME FLUNG HIMSELF forward, narrowly missing having a knife-blade embed in his throat.

However, his reprieve was brief—for a moment later, a lithe figure clad in smoke-grey hurtled from the undergrowth toward him.

Fyfa caught the glint of steel in the noon sun, and her scream echoed across the riverbank, rising high above the roar of the waterfall. "Hume!"

But her husband was already readying himself. Yanking the dirk John had given him free of its sheath, he rolled off the flat stone he'd been sitting on, just avoiding a deadly swipe from a wickedly curved blade.

Fyfa froze, icy terror sweeping through her. Who the devil was this?

The sound of ripping material followed as the attacker's knife caught on the sleeve of Hume's lèine. Once again, he'd moved out of the way just in time. But watching how his attacker moved—the lethal grace, the glint of dark eyes within a deeply shadowed hood—Fyfa knew Hume would die if something wasn't done.

Hume and his attacker had both rolled to their feet now and were swiping at each other, steel flashing. To her surprise, her husband wielded a dirk with some skill, and despite that he was a big man, he was quick on his feet. The two men circled each other, and Hume's attacker wasn't finding it easy to slip under his guard. But to her horror, Fyfa saw the grey-clad figure now wielded *two* of those curved knives, and he was gradually pushing Hume back toward the river edge.

She had to move fast.

Darting to the river, she plunged her hand into the icy water. And then she started to whisper a 'sain'—an ancient rhyme.

> "Ward from evil,
> Shield from malice,
> Defend from harm,
> Maiden,
> Mother,
> Crone,
> Heed my charm."

Witching surged through her once more—like molten ore through her veins. She felt it draw at her, like a fast outgoing tide, yet she resisted the pull. She wouldn't let it drain her—not when Hume needed her.

Grasping a handful of water, she leaped forward and flung it at the attacker.

The action brought with it another gust of wind—laced with the scent of pine and rich, dark earth. However, this one was much more violent than the first. It hit Hume's assailant, shoved him sideways, and would have knocked him off his feet, if the man hadn't been as nimble as a goat.

He stumbled and righted himself, lunging toward Hume, knife-blades flashing. Hume ducked, falling onto one knee as he drove his dirk-blade up, embedding it to the hilt in the side of his attacker's chest.

The man gave a wheeze of surprise, staggering—yet he continued to go after Hume. He didn't even try to yank the dirk free, such was his single-minded purpose.

A curved blade narrowly missed taking off Hume's ear as her husband reeled back.

The wind gusted again, catching the attacker up in its clutches and shoving him backward. The man's hood blew back—revealing hawkish features, angry dark eyes, and dark-tanned skin. Teeth bared, he fought the wind, yet it had him in a strangle hold.

Fyfa whispered the sain once more, the words tearing at her throat. Her body now shook from the effort it was taking to keep the attacker from breaking free.

With a shout of rage, the grey-clad figure reeled backward into the rapids.

Fyfa watched, her breath catching in her throat as he struggled to get back to the riverbank. However, the river current caught him in its clutches and carried him over the edge of the falls.

Sinking to her knees, Fyfa remained staring at the point he'd disappeared. The wind died to a whisper, taking the rich scent of witching with it.

"Fyfa!" Hume rushed to her, gathering her in his arms as she crumpled. "Are ye hurt?"

"No," she gasped. "Just weak."

Hume drew her to her feet, his embrace tightening around her. "Ye saved my life, lass," he mumbled against her hair.

"Ye were doing a fine job of defending yerself," she replied, struggling to catch her breath. "But that man's a killer."

"Aye," he agreed, his tone turning hard. "Longshanks's lackey, I'd wager."

"Do ye think he'll have drowned?"

Still holding her, Hume turned, his gaze shifting to the edge of the falls. "Hopefully ... and I'd like to think my dirk-blade pierced something vital." His expression turned severe then. "But I'd rather not wait around here to find out." His gaze met hers. "Can ye walk?"

Fyfa nodded, pushing herself back from him. She felt like a newborn lamb, for strong witching like this drained a bandruì to the core, but she could stand unassisted, and she could mount the horse if he helped her. "Aye," she rasped. "Let's get away from here."

They rode from the waterfall as if pursued by Satan himself, their gelding's hooves churning up the soil behind them. The terrain was rough here—a wooded, mountainous area—and it slowed their path down.

Still, with each furlong he put between them and the knife-wielding cut-throat, a little of the tension knotted within Hume uncoiled.

The bastard had a dirk in his chest and had just been sent over the edge of a waterfall. If he hadn't dashed his skull to pieces on the rocks below, he would likely have drowned or bled out from his wound.

Hume didn't think they'd be seeing him again—but even so, he pushed the gelding hard, the back of his neck prickling.

He'd never seen a man fight like that—even all his years training with Cameron Stewart and his men couldn't prepare him. He'd held his attacker off for a spell yet had known with a cold chill to the belly that it was just a reprieve. The bastard had wielded those curved blades with alarming precision.

The prickling sensation at the back of Hume's neck increased, crawling down his spine now.

Edward of England wanted him and Fyfa dead.

His cousin had been right—they'd been wise to move on quickly. Only John's caution had saved them.

Hume rode with one hand gripping the reins, while his free arm wrapped around Fyfa. She'd slumped against his chest, her face buried in the hollow of his neck.

The witchcraft she'd wielded back at the waterfall had exhausted her. She hadn't been able to mount the gelding without Hume's assistance.

Tenderness swept through him.

God's teeth, the woman was fierce. In the space of a day, she'd insulted the English king and then spat in the eye of one of his men.

And she'd saved Hume's life.

I love ye, Hume.

Those words, spoken just before the attack, haunted him. The huskiness of her voice, the plea in her sea-blue eyes, had caused a deep wrenching ache within him. Fyfa's admission had nearly broken her, and he'd yet to respond to it.

However, he would.

They reached Crianlarich as the twilight sky started to darken from blue to indigo and the first stars twinkled into existence. Nestled near the banks of the River Fillan and surrounded by tawny peaks—Ben More the largest of them—the village was known as the 'Gateway to the Highlands'. Scrubby pines surrounded the hamlet, which consisted of little more than a scattering of squat, white-washed cottages with sod roofs.

There was only one tavern in the village, a low-slung cottage with two long wings stretching back to the stables. And to Fyfa's relief, they had a room free. It was the last one, the tavern owner proudly told her—as he showed Fyfa to the back of the complex, while Hume busied himself with stabling their mount—for there were plenty of merchants and traders on the road this time of year.

The room he showed her was small and dark, although the bedding on the decent-sized bed looked clean enough, and lumps of pine burned on a small hearth in the corner giving it a cozy feel.

"Will ye be taking supper in the common room this eve?" the squat man asked, his gaze roving over Fyfa with a boldness she didn't appreciate.

"No," she replied. "My *husband* and I will take our supper here … and can we also have hot water, soap, and drying cloths brought to us?"

"Aye, lass." The tavern owner didn't appear put off by her pointed tone. He continued to run his gaze appreciatively over her before unabashedly gawking at her bosom. "I'll get one of my daughters to bring ye hot water now then."

"Thank ye," Fyfa replied between gritted teeth.

Relieved when the creepy wee man left the room, she stripped off her cloak and hung it up behind the door. She'd just taken off her shoes when there came a knock on the door.

"Hot water, soap, and cloths for ye," came a cheerful female voice.

"That was fast," Fyfa murmured. She let the lass in, favoring her with a grateful smile as she bustled over to a table in the corner and set the items down.

"Supper is boiled mutton and turnip stew," the young woman informed her cheerfully. "Shall I bring some up now?"

"Aye, thank ye," Fyfa replied, her belly growling.

The lass's eyes widened. "Ye really are hungry."

Fyfa's mouth quirked. "Aye."

The lass left, and Fyfa quickly stripped off her clothes and bathed. The soap was lovely, scented with lavender, and Fyfa took the opportunity to wash her hair as well.

She was seated on the edge of the bed, bare feet curled up under her as she combed out her wet hair with her fingers, when another knock sounded at the door. "It's me, Fyfa." Hume's deep voice reached her. "Can I come in?"

"Of course ye can," she called back. "This is yer room too … ye paid good silver for it." They were fortunate that Hume carried a purse of pennies with him, and that the English hadn't confiscated it after Stirling had fallen.

The door opened, and Hume stepped inside. As always, his presence seemed to fill the room. Nervousness fluttered within Fyfa. That cut-throat had interrupted them after she'd finished pouring her heart out to Hume back at the waterfalls. He hadn't yet responded, although she sensed the moment was coming.

Her palms grew damp at the thought.

However, Hume wasn't focused on her at present. Instead, his gaze narrowed as it swept over the space. "Is this what a silver penny buys these days?"

"It was the last room they had ... I suppose we should be grateful for that. Supper is on its way." Fyfa motioned to the still steaming bowl of water on the nearby table. "And ye should make the most of the water while it's still hot."

Hume's expression lightened. "Aye," he murmured. "I stink of horse."

Actually, Fyfa didn't agree. She'd traveled most of the afternoon with her face pressed up against the base of his neck. Hume Comyn smelled of warm, spicy male and leather. An ache of longing rose in her chest then.

Did he feel as she did—or had her secrets ruined everything?

27

ALL IN THE PAST

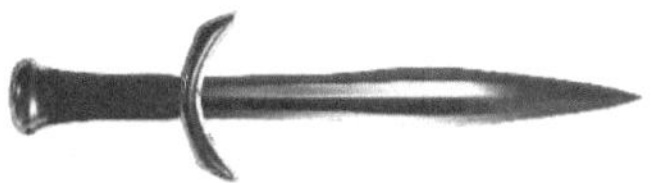

HUME CROSSED TO the washbowl, and was just stripping off his lèine, when there came another knock at the door.

"Supper," the tavern owner's daughter called out.

Fyfa climbed off the bed and went to the door. Taking the tray laden with food and a jug of ale, she thanked the lass with a smile. She then shut the door and carried the tray over to a second table that had two stools on either side of it. Her belly growled once more as she took in the huge bowls of stew and the large round of bannock.

"They've given us butter," she noted, her voice rising in excitement. The Three bless the cooks, it had been months since either of them had tasted butter. "And cheese."

Hume turned from the washbowl, his mouth curving.

Fyfa's breathing caught at the sight. Her husband had a smile that made her go weak at the knees—and he hadn't smiled enough over the years.

The ache in Fyfa's chest returned. How she wanted to change that—how she wanted to see joy in Hume's eyes and know that she was the cause. She wanted to bring this man happiness, not hurt. She wanted him to trust her with his heart.

But could he ever forgive her?

Hume turned back to his ablutions then, and Fyfa was grateful. Heart pounding, she lowered herself to one of the stools and deliberately turned so that she couldn't see him bathing. In a moment, he'd push down his braies, and she wasn't sure she could bear the sight of his muscular back, tight buttocks, and long legs—not if she wasn't allowed to touch him again.

She had to keep her wits about her—for at some point, once they'd filled their bellies and rested a little—they would need to speak about what the future held for them both.

Trying not to think about Hume's nakedness or imagine the water trickling down his chest and belly to his groin, she focused on pouring them both a cup of ale.

The delicious-looking supper tempted her—but she wouldn't dive into it, not until her husband joined her.

A short while later, Hume padded barefoot across the floor to her and took a seat on the low stool opposite. He was naked to the waist still, his dark-auburn hair damp from bathing. The scent of lye, lavender, and clean male wafted across the table, and the clench in Fyfa's stomach this time had nothing to do with hunger, but desire.

How was she going to bear being in the same room as this man, if he rejected her tonight?

The memory of their last heated coupling in Stirling Castle was still fresh in her mind. He'd looked so horrified, so deeply sad and wounded, afterward. She didn't want to see such an expression on his face ever again.

"Ye didn't have to wait for me," he admonished her.

"I know." Fyfa's gaze met his. "But I wanted to."

Their stare drew out for a few moments, awareness prickling through Fyfa. She noted the way her husband's eyes darkened and wondered if their proximity was having the same effect on him too.

Clearing his throat, Hume broke eye contact first and reached for a piece of bannock. "Come on … don't let it get cold."

They ate in silence, both devouring the supper with surprising swiftness. A short while later, only a few crumbs remained.

With a sigh, Hume leaned back before pouring them the last of the ale. "That was the best meal I've ever eaten."

"Aye," Fyfa agreed with a smile. "The silver penny was worth it after all."

He smiled back at her. "It was."

Picking up her cup of ale, Fyfa walked over to the bed and perched on the edge, taking sips from her drink. Now that they didn't have the meal to distract them, she suddenly felt awkward, on edge.

It was ridiculous really—for this man was her husband. Yet she'd hidden her true identity for so long that it was as if things were new between them. She suddenly felt naked before him.

Hume didn't move from the table, although she could see from the shuttered look on his face that he felt as uncomfortable as she did.

They lapsed into silence, each sipping at their ale and letting the delicious supper settle.

Eventually, Hume spoke. His expression was carefully neutral when he did, and only the tightness of his fingers around the cup betrayed his inner tension. "What ye said at the waterfall, Fyfa ... before we were attacked ... did ye mean it?"

Fyfa swallowed to ease the sudden tightness in her throat. "I did ... every word." She paused then, wishing she could be more eloquent. The Fyfa of old was supremely confident and had the right phrase for every occasion. But this Fyfa, the woman who was desperately in love with her husband and terrified of losing him, was at a loss for words. "I've made a lot of mistakes, Hume." She paused, tearing her gaze from his and looking down at the dregs of ale in her cup.

"Aye," he replied roughly. "Ye have."

Fyfa's pulse quickened, her belly twisting. He still hadn't forgiven her. She'd hurt him too deeply.

"But so have I," he continued.

Fyfa's chin kicked up. Hume was staring at her, and the tender look upon his face made her catch her breath.

"I'm far from blameless, lass." His gaze shadowed then. "And my jealousy only served to drive a wedge between us."

Fyfa swallowed. "But that's all done with now," she whispered. "I want us to start again … to put the past behind us."

A pause followed before he replied, "I want that too."

Wordlessly, Hume put his empty cup aside and rose to his feet. Approaching Fyfa, he took her cup from her and set it down on the table. And then he grasped her hands and drew her to her feet.

Angling her chin up, Fyfa held his gaze. He looked down at her, drinking her in, before raising a hand and tracing her jaw with his fingertips. Fyfa shivered under his touch, yet she didn't move, didn't reach for him.

This was a fragile moment, and she didn't wish to shatter it.

"I always wondered why ye chose me," he said huskily, "and when I found out the truth, it dredged up every pathetic, damning thought I've ever had about myself. I don't hate ye, Fyfa … I've been too busy loathing myself."

Fyfa's breathing caught. She resisted the urge to jump in, to tell him that he was the best man she'd ever known—that he had to stop being so hard on himself. Hume needed to be able to say it all, without being interrupted.

"But then when Stirling fell, something within me shifted." His fingertips continued their lazy path down her jaw-line. "I'm no longer Steward of Stirling … I can now choose who I become from this day forth." He paused then, his eyes darkening to jade. "I want to fight for Scottish freedom, Fyfa … at *yer* side."

Fyfa's pulse started to race, heat igniting in her belly. "And ye will," she whispered. She reached up, her hand splaying across the hard wall of his bare chest. She could feel his heart pounding against her palm. "Ye are the best of them, Hume," she whispered, her voice catching. "I've always known it … and I want ye to believe it too." Her husband's eyes shadowed. "Aye, ye had a difficult childhood and a wife who should have been honest with ye … but ye have the best character of anyone I've ever met. Yer word has always been yer bond, Hume … ye've always protected me, looked out for me, even when ye believed the worst of me."

"Aye, but my behavior has been poor at times over the past two years," he murmured, his voice roughening. "Can ye forgive me for that?"

"There's nothing to forgive." She meant it too. Fyfa wasn't one to nurse grievances, especially after the part she'd played in their troubles.

Their gazes fused. "Ye are so lovely ... so spirited," he said, his voice catching. "Ye are my light, my hope, Fyfa. Without ye, my world would be dark indeed."

Silence fell between them then, the moment stretching taut. Tears pricked the back of Fyfa's eyes.

He leaned down, his lips brushing across hers. The last kisses they'd shared of late had been brutal, rough—yet this one was tender. Hume reached up with both hands, cradling the back of her head as his lips parted hers.

Fyfa sighed, leaning into him, her eyelids fluttering closed as he deepened the embrace, his tongue sliding against hers. The heat of his mouth, the taste of him, made her melt against him. She wrapped her arms around his torso, pulling him flush against her. His body's warmth and strength enveloped her, making her feel shielded, loved, and wanted.

She was always her best self when she was in Hume Comyn's arms, she realized. He brought her home, grounded her.

The kiss drew out, gradually growing more passionate as their tongues danced, and they breathed each other in.

After a spell, Hume drew back, his eyes smoldering with hunger. He then reached out and began to unlace the bodice of her kirtle. Wordlessly, he undressed her, and as he did so, Fyfa noted the slight tremor in his hands—the man appeared outwardly calm and in control, yet she realized he was now holding himself on a tight leash.

For herself, Fyfa was aflame. Her legs trembled under her, and the tender flesh between her thighs ached. And when he stripped her kirtle and lèine from her, Fyfa squared her shoulders so that her breasts jutted between them, her nipples achingly hard.

Hume's breathing caught as he stared down at her breasts. His big hands then cupped them, his thumbs running over the sensitive tips. "So bonny," he whispered. "I've ached for ye, Fyfa."

"And I for ye," she replied. Her voice caught then as he lowered himself before her and drew one of her taut nipples into his mouth. He suckled her tenderly at first, and then harder, until she groaned and slid her fingers through his hair, drawing him closer still.

Hume took his time loving her breasts, drawing out her pleasure until she gasped and sighed against him. If he hadn't been holding her up, she'd have sagged to the floor.

How she'd missed this.

Finally, he released her breasts and rose to his feet once more. Looking down, Fyfa could see his arousal tenting his braies. When he unlaced them and pushed his braies down, the sight of his magnificent rod made a soft cry escape her.

Fyfa reached down and wrapped her fingers around his girth. The heat and strength of him made need pulse in her lower belly.

Her breathing caught then. This moment wasn't just physically intimate, but emotionally raw as well. Finally, there were no more walls between them. Looking up, Fyfa locked gazes with her husband. Hume was staring down at her as if she was the most precious thing he'd ever set eyes upon. The love she saw there made her vision blur with tears.

This would be more than a coupling, but a union of souls.

28

MINE

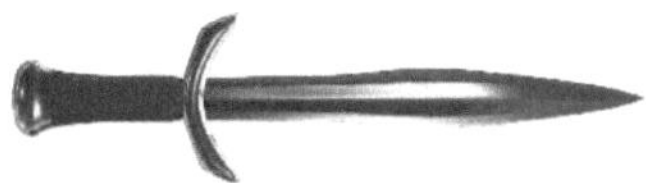

HUME DREW IN a shuddering breath and attempted to keep a leash on his hunger.

He desired nothing more than to throw his wife back on the bed, part her thighs, and plow her.

But he also wanted to draw these precious moments out.

This evening was a turning point for both of them, and he didn't want it to be over quickly. He wanted to make memories of every breath, every heartbeat.

Gathering Fyfa against him, his mouth covered hers once more, his kiss more urgent than earlier, more demanding. And all the while, his hands roamed over the smooth, firm curves of Fyfa's luscious body. In the two years while they hadn't shared a bed, he'd spent nights lying awake on the bench seat in the solar, torturing himself imagining his wife's nakedness. Clothed, Fyfa was a bonny, sensual woman who drew a man's eyes as naturally as breathing—but naked, she was a siren. She was all long limbs and creamy white skin—so lovely that his throat ached as he touched her.

Mine.

Aye, they'd been wed years now—but tonight was the first time Hume felt truly at one with his wife. For the first time, they'd both shared what lay within their hearts, their hurts and fears laid bare.

Fyfa had been living a lie, but so had he. His dour manner hid a seething mass of resentment and insecurity. How could he love his wife, if he hated himself? Strangely, the fall of Stirling had liberated him, had stripped away the identity he'd clung to—and aiding Fyfa afterward, he'd finally discovered his true purpose. Fyfa was a freedom fighter, and so was he.

Limbs tangled, mouths devouring, they tumbled onto the bed.

Hume rose up above her, his lips trailing down his wife's jaw and neck, to the rosy peaks of her breasts once more. He couldn't help it, he fell upon them, thrilling at her whispered pleas, her groans.

And when he continued his path down her body and spread her thighs wide to delve between them, her groans became cries. She arched up against Hume's mouth, and he held her tight, pleasuring her until her body trembled, until she hoarsely gasped his name.

"Please, Hume ... I want ye inside me."

She didn't need to ask again. Hume was already holding himself on a tight leash.

Spreading her wider still, he slid into Fyfa in one smooth, achingly slow stroke, burying himself to the root.

Her deep groan, when he did, caused his belly muscles to grow taut, and he nearly spilled within her there and then. Hume drew in a deep, shuddering breath. He needed to slow down, to draw this out.

Murmuring soft, sensual words, he withdrew from her, holding himself up so that he could watch where their bodies joined, could see the slide of his engorged rod into her slick heat. His body trembled from the need to let go, to plow her senseless—yet he held back, taking her in slow, deliberate thrusts.

"Hume!" Fyfa arched off the bed, her pale skin glistening with sweat, her hair a fiery halo around her head. He felt the tremors of her core, clenching hard around him, and, finally, he couldn't stand it any longer.

His wife's cries filled the bed-chamber as he thrust hard into her. Hume took her in a frenzy, each plunge deeper than the last, until his climax barreled into him with such violence that his back arched and his gaze darkened for an instant.

Gazing up into her husband's face, watching his lips part, his eyes close, and pleasure ripple over his features, Fyfa's breathing caught. She loved seeing him lose control like that. He'd never taken her with such a blend of tenderness and pure unbridled lust—her body was boneless and quivering in the aftermath.

Breathing hard, Hume lowered himself down, propping himself up on his elbows so he didn't crush her.

Then, bending his head, he kissed her.

And in that kiss, she felt every unspoken word—all the love that he'd never been able to fully articulate.

When the kiss ended, and he drew back slightly to meet her gaze, Hume's eyes were glistening. "I love ye, Fyfa," he said huskily. "So much that ye could destroy me if ye wished to."

Pain twisted in Fyfa's chest. "I will never do that," she rasped, her voice shaking from the melee of the emotions that made it hard to speak, hard to draw breath. "Our hearts are one, mo ghràdh ... and, together, we shall build a fortress around them."

They slept deeply, cradled in each other's arms. Fyfa woke first, in the early hours of dawn, savoring the feel of her husband's body entwined with hers. She felt different this morning, almost as if she were someone else.

A lightness filled her heart—a sensation she'd never experienced. For a few hours, she'd forgotten the cause, the fall of Stirling, and the English victory. All that had mattered in this room was that she and Hume were together.

No matter what happened now, they'd face it united.

Eventually, Hume stirred, stretching his long body like a cat, his auburn eyelashes flickering open. The dawn light filtered into the chamber through a gap in the shutters, illuminating his handsome features.

Fyfa smiled at him. "Good morning."

A slow smile crept across Hume's face. "And good morn to ye too, wife," he replied, his voice husky with sleep.

Propping herself up onto an elbow, Fyfa reached out with her free hand and trailed her fingertips down from the hollow of his neck to his belly. "I like seeing ye like this," she murmured, heat kindling in the cradle of her hips.

His eyes hooded, and when her gaze followed the path of her fingertips, she saw that his shaft was growing hard against his belly.

"And I never tire of seeing ye naked, mo chridhe," he replied.

My heart. The endearment made Fyfa's breathing quicken. When he looked at her like that, spoke to her like that, she forgot all else.

Hume rolled over to face her and reached out, his own hand trailing a lazy path over her shoulder and down her naked flank. His fingertips then traced the birthmark upon her left thigh. It was large and looked a little like a leaf or a splayed hand.

"Is this why yer parents abandoned ye?" His voice was soft, tender.

"Aye … Colina, the High Bandruì of my order, thought so. She found me one cold spring … there were three of us abandoned in the space of just two months that year: me, Nessa, and Breanna."

Hume's mouth quirked. "Ye will be looking forward to seeing her … and yer sisters … again."

"Aye, it's been a while."

Their gazes fused once more, and then Hume's expression grew solemn. "Will I be welcome?"

Fyfa snorted. "Of course … I'm not going anywhere without ye now, Hume. Ye will live with us."

"But ye are a coven of witches … do ye have any men among ye?"

"No, but we are about to change that."

Hume made a frustrated sound in the back of his throat. "What if they don't *want* me to reside among them?"

Fyfa leaned forward, cupping his face with her hands, her gaze locking with his. "Then, ye and I will live elsewhere." She paused there, letting her words sink in. "But one thing is for certain, Hume. Wherever I go, it will be with ye. The cause needs men like ye … together, we can do a lot of good."

His mouth lifted at the corners. "Ye are a difficult woman to argue with, Fyfa."

She grinned back at him. "Aye, that's because I'm often right." She then gave him a hard, passionate kiss.

A sunny morning greeted them when they emerged into the stable yard, a brisk south wind pushing billowing clouds across a cerulean sky. A smile stretched Fyfa's mouth as she turned her face up to the sun.

Really, she couldn't stop grinning like a fool this morning.

Hume had given her a passionate tumble before they'd risen from their bed and dressed. Standing in the yard, watching as her husband saddled their horse, it seemed as if the world around her had more color, more promise.

It was as if a missing piece in her life had just slid into place.

In her gut, she knew this was what was meant to happen.

Hume had been right to voice concerns about how the Guardians would react to her bringing him into their midst, yet whatever happened, nothing would tear them apart. Not now.

Hume finished saddling the gelding and led the horse out into the yard. He then flashed her a smile—an expression that made Fyfa's belly swoop. What she really wanted was a few days locked away with her husband so that she could get her fill of him and make up for all the lost time.

It had been an effort to drag themselves away from the privacy of their chamber. However, they still had a few days ride before them. Assynt and the Wailing Widow Falls were in the midst of the Highlands.

"Ready?" he asked.

"Aye." Fyfa stepped up to the horse's side and placed her foot in Hume's linked hands before vaulting up onto the front of the saddle. He mounted behind her, one arm looping protectively around her middle, the other taking hold of the reins.

An instant later, they rode out of the yard and into the dirt road beyond. Ben Hope rose against the horizon, every detail of its sculpted slopes brought out into sharp relief by the bright morning sun. Crianlarich was a lot busier this morning than it had been the eve before. Women were hanging out washing, and bairns played in the sun before the open doors of the white-washed cottages. It was a domestic scene, one that made something tug at Fyfa.

She wanted a home of her own with Hume— somewhere they could start afresh together and begin a family.

Hassan arrived back at Stirling as the noon sun crested the sky.

Teeth clenched against the throbbing pain in the side of his chest, the assassin rode up the causeway to the castle and through the gates into the outer bailey. He'd initially gone back to the camp but had been told the king now resided inside the castle.

The Blade swung a leg over the back of his courser and slid gingerly to the ground.

The sickly pain in his side was so great now that his knees nearly buckled.

Around him, the guards at the gate, and the men tending the horses, were favoring him with curious looks.

They all knew of the king's assassin—and they were all wary of him.

But Hassan had no need of friends. He had little time for people, except for when he was sent to kill them.

It hadn't been that way once. As a child in Acre, he'd been surrounded by a loving family. But after his parents and brothers were murdered by thieves, he'd found himself an orphan living on the streets. The Hashashin had taken him in months later, yet the loss of his family had changed him, and he'd been a lone-wolf ever since.

Throwing the reins of his horse to one of the stable hands, Hassan left the outer-bailey and limped through an archway into the inner-bailey—a wide area carpeted in fine white pebbles. Each step was an effort, and Hassan had to prevent himself from clutching at his injured ribs. Fire now burned down his side.

The stone keep, battered and blackened in places from the long siege, rose before him, its towers outlined against the sky.

A group of women emerged from the main entrance then, laughing and chattering together like a flock of exotic birds.

Hassan's step slowed further as he made his way toward the keep. The ladies' laughter died away when they noticed him, their gazes tracking his path.

"Hassan!" One of them, Lady Lamia, greeted him. She was a slender beauty with hair the color of sea foam and a pale, shrewd gaze. She stepped forward, her eyes bright, expectant. "How goes it?"

Hassan didn't answer. Instead, he kept walking.

Lamia's gaze shifted down to where blood stained his smoke-grey tunic and cloak—and the bright look in her eyes faded.

A jolt went through the assassin. Somehow, Lady Lamia knew where he'd been. And now she knew he'd failed.

Jaw clenched, *The Blade* climbed the steps, aware of the woman's gaze boring into his back.

How had the court lady come to learn about his mission? And why did she appear to care about its outcome?

Hassan entered the keep and went looking for the king. On the way, he encountered servants scurrying about, readying the castle for Edward. He found the king in what had been the governor's solar. Edward was deep in discussion with two of his knights—Aymer de Valence and Nicholas Harrington—but the moment Hassan appeared like a wraith in the doorway, the king broke off mid-sentence.

All three men's attention shifted to the door.

"We'll continue this later," Edward murmured, rising to his feet before nodding to Sir Aymer and Sir Nicholas.

Both men left the solar without another word, their spurs clinking on the stone floor. They cast Hassan pointed looks, their gazes sliding over his bloodied clothing, yet Hassan ignored them, as he had Lady Lamia. He answered to one person only.

Even so, Hassan was having trouble focusing now. The pain was making him feel queasy, and his ears were starting to ring. He really needed to see the physician, yet this meeting couldn't wait.

Entering the solar, *The Blade* shut the door behind him before he met the king's cool gaze.

"So?" Edward greeted him. "How did it go?"

"I failed," Hassan replied, drawing back his cloak to reveal the bloody gash on the side of his chest. His clothing was still damp from the river. He'd been lucky not to dash his brains out on the rocks below, and had crawled like a drowned rat to the riverbank, before gritting his teeth and yanking out the dirk blade. Then bleeding, he'd staggered back to his horse.

Glancing down at the dirk-wound, Hassan clenched his jaw. He'd avoided looking at it on the journey back to Stirling, and now he realized why. It looked grave indeed.

The sound in his ears grew louder, like someone was ringing a large bell in his skull.

Edward's bearded jaw tensed. "You did?" He rose to his feet and stepped toward Hassan. "How is that possible?"

The harsh edge to the king's voice galled. Three decades he'd served this man, and he'd never once missed a mark. Countless successes didn't matter to Edward it seemed, only this one failure. However, the weakness that now flooded through the assassin's limbs made it difficult to dredge up any outrage.

"Perhaps you should have told me you were sending me after a witch," he rasped.

An instant later, *The Blade* crumpled to the ground.

29

UNWORTHY ONLY IN YER EYES

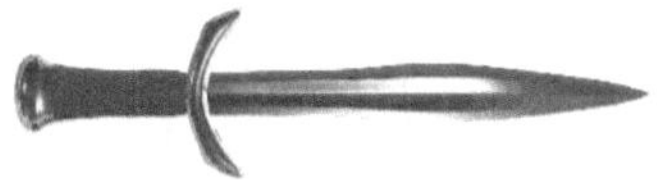

THE ROAD NORTH took them along the banks of Loch Eil and past Fort William. The village hugged the shores of the loch, huddled at the feet of emerald foothills that led up to the snow-capped bulk of Ben Nevis.

Perched before her husband, Fyfa took in the magnificent mountain to the east. Ben Nevis dominated the landscape, rising into the washed-out afternoon sky like a sleeping giant.

Clip-clopping through the cobbled main street of Fort William, Fyfa took in the ruddy faces of the women as they shopped, wicker baskets tucked under their arms, and the men shepherding a flock of black-faced sheep through the main square.

Warmth spread through her. "It's good to be back in the Highlands," she murmured, breaking the silence between her and Hume.

The farther north they'd traveled, the quieter he'd become. This afternoon, he'd barely spoken.

Fyfa knew why: their road north to Assynt took them past Fort William. And just north of Fort William was Inverlochy Castle. His birthplace.

"Aye, it's bonny country all right," Hume replied, his tone subdued. "I'd forgotten just how much so."

The fine weather had followed them, and this afternoon the sun burnished the surrounding hills and the mighty Ben Nevis.

Leaving Fort William behind, they joined the highway once more, a narrow dirt road that hugged the winding path of the River Lochy. And eventually, as Ben Nevis drew closer, looming overhead now, Fyfa saw the grey-stone towers of a fortress in the distance. Perched on the banks of the river, it was a huge castle, with an impressive curtain wall and four crenelated towers.

Hume spied it at the same time, she was sure of it, for his body tensed against hers.

They reached a fork in the road, the eastern path leading up to the castle gates, and Hume drew the gelding up.

They sat in silence for a few moments before her husband finally spoke. "It's getting late in the day … Inverlochy would be a good place to break our journey."

Fyfa heard the reluctance in his voice. She shifted in the saddle, wishing she could see her husband's face. "Ye sound as if ye're considering riding into a leper colony. I'm beginning to think yer mother is a fire-breathing banshee."

He huffed a humorless laugh. "She *is* a fire-breathing banshee," he replied, his tone rueful now.

"We don't have to stay here, if ye would prefer not to?" Fyfa didn't want to force Hume to spend the night at Inverlochy, yet she had to admit she was curious about this place and the woman who'd brought this man into the world.

Hume loosed a sigh and gathered up the reins. "Surely, just one night can't hurt?"

With that, he urged the gelding right, and up the slight incline toward the castle gates.

The moment he rode under the portcullis into the wide bailey at the heart of the castle, Hume wished he hadn't decided to stay the night at Inverlochy Castle.

Memories, few of them good, crashed over him as he swept his gaze around. He'd thought after years at Stirling Castle, Inverlochy would seem small and mean in comparison. Yet the fortress was still as grand. Four towers loomed over the bailey, the biggest of them, The Comyn Tower, casting a deep shadow over the cobbled courtyard. This tower served as the castle's keep—and it was within its thick walls that he'd grown from a bairn to a man.

Swinging down from his horse, he helped Fyfa to the ground.

And then one of the voices from his past—one he'd done his best to forget over the years, boomed across the bailey.

"Hume Comyn, I don't believe it!"

Swiveling, Hume's gaze swept over the stocky warrior striding toward him. The man stopped a few yards back, an insolent smile stretching his broad face. "And what vision of loveliness have ye brought with ye?"

Unsmiling, Hume placed a possessive hand on the small of Fyfa's back. "Fyfa, this is Garth Lindsay, Captain of the Inverlochy Guard. Garth, meet my wife."

"Good day," Fyfa greeted the captain pleasantly.

"And good day to ye," Garth drawled.

Hume swore the man was about to lick his lips. If he did, he'd shove his teeth down his throat.

However, Garth didn't. Instead, he shot Hume a veiled look. "No wonder ye've been hiding this vision away ... keeping her all to yerself, eh?"

"We've been busy at Stirling," Hume replied, his tone cool. "And in case ye are interested ... the castle has fallen to the English."

In an instant, Garth's expression changed. His heavy brow lowered, the cords of his thick neck standing out. Observing him, Hume noted that the man still looked like the bully he remembered.

Garth Lindsay hadn't been captain of the guard when Hume was a lad. Instead, he'd been one of the men-at-arms who defended the castle. And one of his favorite pastimes was to corner the shy nephew of the laird of Inverlochy. A swift punch to the guts would have Hume throwing up his morning bannocks, while Garth swaggered away with a laugh. The bullying stopped once Hume grew tall and strong enough to hit back—yet the memories lingered.

The captain muttered a curse and spat on the ground, yet Hume was already turning from him. He had no time these days for Lindsay. "Where's my mother?"

Fyfa climbed the spiral stairs inside the great tower at her husband's side. Hume's expression was inscrutable, his grip on her hand firm. Yet she could feel the tension vibrating off him.

Perhaps we shouldn't have come here.

Inverlochy was an impressive fortress indeed, yet the moment they'd ridden into the wide bailey, an oppressive cloud had settled over her.

She'd taken an instant dislike to Captain Lindsay—and when he'd greeted her husband, she understood why Hume had avoided returning here. Clearly, it wasn't just his mother that had made life difficult for him at Inverlochy.

The captain had informed them they'd likely find Hume's mother with the lady of the castle, Joan—John Comyn's wife. The two women spent most afternoons in the solar.

Reaching the top floor of the tower, Hume knocked briskly on a large oaken door. His jaw tensed then as he readied himself for the reunion. He was nervous, Fyfa could sense it—and once again, she wondered if returning to this place was a good idea.

"Come in," a woman's voice reached them.

Hume threw open the door, revealing a wide space decorated with fine mats and tapestries, with a window looking over the river. Two women sat together at a large loom by the open window.

Fyfa observed them with interest. One of the women was tall and rawboned, with a long face. A set of keys jangled at her hip as she rose to her feet. "Hume!" she greeted him, her eyes widening. "Is Red with ye?"

Fyfa supposed this was John Comyn's wife and chatelaine of Inverlochy in her husband's absence.

Hume favored his cousin's wife with a tight smile. "No, Lady Joan, we left Stirling ahead of him ... he'll be here in a day or two, I'm sure."

Joan's long face tensed. "So Stirling has fallen, I take it?"

"Aye."

The woman still seated at the loom sniffed. In her fifth decade, with greying auburn hair, Maureen Comyn was still a comely woman. Her fine green kirtle matched her moss-green eyes—the same shade as her son's

"Joan, can ye pass me the yellow wool," she murmured. "I think this needs a touch of color."

Lady Comyn's mouth thinned, yet she didn't refuse the request. Instead, she moved to a nearby table and selected a ball of wool from a basket.

"Hello, mother," Hume greeted the woman before the loom. His voice was guarded, as was his gaze. Only the tense set of his shoulders gave his discomfort away.

Maureen Comyn glanced in his direction, as if only just noticing that her son had entered the room—an impossibility, for at over six feet, the man was difficult to miss. "We're busy this afternoon," she murmured as if addressing a servant. "Joan and I want to finish this tapestry by the end of the week."

"Apologies for the interruption." Hume's voice roughened. "But Fyfa and I are traveling north, and we thought it only polite to make a stop here on our way." He paused then as if fortifying himself to continue. "After all ... ye are yet to meet my wife."

Maureen didn't even glance Fyfa's way.

Heat kindled in the pit of Fyfa's belly. Was this woman insufferably rude or goose-witted? Why was she going on about her tapestry when her son, whom she hadn't seen in years, was standing before her? She didn't even have the decency to greet his wife.

Moments passed, while Joan passed Maureen the ball of wool and shot Hume an apologetic look. "Of course, ye are welcome, Hume," she said with a brittle smile. "It's a pleasure to see ye. I shall have a chamber made up for ye and yer wife."

Hume acknowledged Joan's words with a nod, although his gaze—narrowed now—was still upon his mother.

"A little advance warning would have been appreciated," Maureen said, picking up her shuttle and weaving it through the loom.

Hume's gaze shadowed. "Such things are difficult when ye reside in a castle under siege, mother."

Maureen looked up from her weaving then, her gaze narrowing as it focused on her son. Her mouth pursed. "Lord, ye are the image of yer father these days," she said.

Fyfa's own gaze narrowed. Judging from the sharp edge to her voice, the comparison wasn't a favorable one. The heat in Fyfa's belly flickered into a flame. This woman's bitterness emanated from her like a sickly cloud.

"So what happened at Stirling, then?" Maureen asked, shifting her attention back to the loom.

"We held out for as long as we could," Hume answered. "But—"

"*We?*" A thin smile stretched Maureen's lips. "So, ye were there in the thick of things, were ye, lad?"

An awkward silence fell in the solar. Joan, who hadn't retaken her seat, tensed, her gaze flicking between Maureen and Hume.

Eventually, Fyfa cleared her throat. "Actually, Hume helped defend the walls daily."

Maureen's smile faded, yet she still didn't look Fyfa's way. The deliberate slight made Fyfa clench her jaw.

"I did my part." Hume's voice had roughened further, a nerve flickering in his cheek. "But in the end, when Edward of England unleashed his Warwolf ... a giant trebuchet ... and brought part of the curtain wall down, none of us could continue to defend the castle."

"Warwolf?" Joan shuddered. "What a terrifying name."

"Aye, it's reputed to be the biggest trebuchet ever built," Hume replied.

"And what happened after the surrender?" Maureen looked up from her weaving and reached for a beater, a wooden comb she used to push the weft down. "Does Oliphant still live?"

"Aye," Hume replied, his tone wary now. "Longshanks has taken him prisoner though … while the rest of us were given our freedom."

Maureen sniffed. "Sir William did well to hold the castle for so many months."

"He did."

"Despite the defeat, many Scots will likely hail him a hero."

"Aye, they will."

Maureen swiveled on her seat, pinning Hume with a sharp look. "They won't say the same thing about ye though, will they?" Another smile curved her lips, although this one was cutting. "Just like yer father, ye'll live and die an unworthy man."

Fyfa sucked in a sharp breath, her temper quickening. Enough. Someone had to shove this woman's forked tongue back behind her teeth. However, Hume's fingers, for he still held her hand, tightened around hers in warning.

"Unworthy only in yer eyes," he replied, his tone sharp now. His nervousness had disappeared, anger replacing it.

Maureen Comyn's smile slipped just a little.

Moments stretched out, and then Hume's mouth twisted. "I should have come home sooner, mother," he murmured. "All this time, I've imagined ye had some hold over me … but now as I stand before ye, I see ye are just a broken and bitter woman."

It was Maureen's turn to suck in a breath, high spots of color appearing upon her cheeks. When she answered, her voice was thin and high. "How dare ye?"

Hume didn't bother to answer her. Instead, he inclined his head to Joan, who was staring at him as if her husband's cousin had just torn off a mask, revealing an utterly different man beneath. "I thank ye for the invitation to reside here tonight, Lady Joan, but I must decline. Our road lies far to the north, and we must be on our way." He favored the Lady of Inverlochy with a genuine smile then. "Give my apologies to John when he arrives."

30

A NEW START

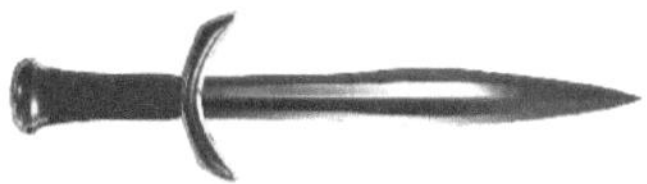

"ARE WE REALLY leaving?" Fyfa whispered as she and Hume descended the stone steps back to the ground level of the tower.

"Aye ... but first, we'll make a stop in the kitchens and get ourselves some food for supper." Hume's voice caught then, betraying him. He had shown remarkable self-control in front of his mother, but when he glanced her way, Fyfa saw that his eyes were shadowed now. "Ye don't mind sleeping rough again tonight, do ye?"

Fyfa shook her head. In truth, she'd been looking forward to a soft mattress and a hot bath, yet right now, she didn't care about any of that.

The encounter with his mother had cost him, but she was still in awe of how her husband had conducted himself before the woman.

"Ye did well in there," she murmured. "I would have lost my temper with that shrew."

"I'd not give her what she wants," he replied huskily. "Words are my mother's weapons ... no one knows how to wound like her." He took her hand then. "I'm sorry she ignored ye."

Fyfa huffed a rueful laugh. "She's never forgiven ye for wedding a scullery maid, has she?"

He barked a laugh of his own. "That's nothing, love ... she's never forgiven me for being my father's son."

Fyfa tightened her grip upon his hand. "How does someone get that bitter?"

Hume huffed a sigh. They were descending the last few steps now, and the scent of baking bread alerted them that the kitchens were nearby. "My parents' marriage was an arranged one," he replied, his voice subdued. "Even though I reputedly look like him, I don't remember my father ... for he died when I was around three in a hunting accident. But apparently, the two of them were at war from the moment they wed. John tells me that they turned Inverlochy into a battleground." Hume paused there, leading the way toward an archway into the kitchens. "Once my father died, mother took all her resentment at him out on me."

"Why did she never remarry?"

Hume cut her a rueful look. "To do so, Maureen Comyn would have to let the past go ... something she was never prepared to do. Bitterness is her bedfellow ... and so it will be for the rest of her days."

They camped for the night around fifty furlongs north of Inverlochy, in a clearing under the shadow of Ben Nevis. Despite that it was a mild eve, Hume lit a fire and fed it with branches.

The resinous scent of burning pine filled the air, and Fyfa breathed it in, a smile creasing her face. The smell of the Highlands and that of witching were one. It felt good to be back here, far from the politics and war of the south.

Her smile faded then. It was only a reprieve. Longshanks had taken 'The Brooch of Scotland', the gateway between the Lowlands and the Highlands. Where would he turn his attention next?

"Is something amiss?" Hume asked. He crouched by the fire and had just added another pine branch. Flames and sparks licked upward into the darkening sky, where moths now fluttered.

Fyfa favored him with a tired smile. "I was just wondering what Edward's next move will be … and our own."

"Well … if yer leader's prediction about Robert Bruce is true, then we should focus our attention on him. If it hadn't been for ye, he'd be dead now … but that doesn't mean others won't try."

Fyfa nodded, remembering the conversation she'd had with Robert Bruce in his tent. Aye, the man was a patriotic Scot. He'd been forced to submit to Longshanks, but it wouldn't last. Stirling had been a humiliating defeat for them all—she'd seen the simmering anger in the Bruce's eyes.

Sooner or later, he'd rise up against the oppressors. And until then, they had to make sure that no harm came to him.

"That witch in the English camp is a problem though," Hume continued, his brow furrowing. "She came close to killing both ye and Bruce."

Fyfa suppressed a shudder at the mention of Lamia Delamare. Aye, she'd seen the fury in the woman's silvery eyes as Hume had towed her away from the banquet.

They hadn't seen the last of the woman.

"I'll have to talk to Colina and the others about how to deal with her," Fyfa murmured. "She certainly poses a danger to our cause."

Hume brushed pine needles off his hands and reached into the saddlebag he'd filled with provisions from Inverlochy before their departure. "A boiled egg with yer bread and butter, my lady?" he asked, flashing her a smile.

Fyfa grinned back, Lamia and the threat she posed momentarily forgotten. She liked how easily Hume smiled these days. A weight seemed to have lifted from his broad shoulders. The meeting with his mother had been unpleasant, yet necessary. "Aye … two, if we can spare them?"

They ate their simple supper, shoulder to shoulder before the fire, while their horse rested under a nearby

tree and the sky darkened from indigo to black.
Presently, the full moon sailed high in the sky.

"I love a full moon," Fyfa said as she brushed crumbs
from her skirt. "It signifies a new start."

Hume took her hand. "Then we shall make one." He
drew her on his lap and reached up, cupping her cheek.
"I swear to ye, Fyfa Comyn, that henceforth, my life will
be dedicated to fighting for Scottish freedom at yer side."

She stared down at him, her chest aching with love.
"And I swear to ye, Hume Comyn, that I will keep
nothing from ye in future," she murmured. "Ye are my
partner in all things … and I hope to one day give ye a
bairn."

His eyes glinted at that, and his hand slid around to
the back of her neck. An instant later, he pulled her head
down for a searing kiss.

Fyfa eagerly returned his embrace, her tongue sliding
between his lips to duel with his own tongue. And then
she gently nipped at his lower lip with her teeth. The
growl that rumbled in Hume's throat in response
inflamed her, and without hesitation, she shifted astride
him, lifting her skirts so that he could slide his hands up
her thighs.

Kissing him wildly now, need wreathing up within
her, Fyfa reached down and unlaced his braies. She took
his rock-hard shaft in hand, stroking him until he
groaned, and then, raising herself up on her knees, she
positioned herself over him, teasing herself with the tip
of his rod. She was ready: wet and aching for him. She'd
wanted this ever since they'd strode out of that solar
back in Inverlochy. He'd dealt with his mother with such
strength and dignity, despite the woman's viciousness,
she'd gone weak at the knees. She'd wanted to drag
Hume into a darkened alcove off the stairwell and beg
him to take her—yet that castle wasn't the place for such
intimacy.

This quiet forest glade was though, and Fyfa was
desperate to be joined with her husband.

She impaled herself upon him, sliding down until the
entire length of his rod was buried deep inside her. This

position, the fullness of it, made her gasp, and when
Hume gripped her hips and rotated them in a sensual
roll, aching pleasure rippled through her lower belly.

Fyfa clung to Hume as he lifted her up. He let her
slide up his shaft with exquisite slowness, before he
hauled her back down, penetrating even deeper than
before.

Fyfa cried out into Hume's mouth, shuddering as he
ground his hips against hers.

They were joined, bonded—and with him buried deep
inside her, everything felt right in the world.

The Wailing Widow Falls
Assynt, Scottish Highlands

Four days later …

"Yer coven resides here?" Hume frowned as he drew up
his horse on the riverbank, glancing around. "Where
exactly?"

Fyfa smiled before digging into one of the pouches at
her waist. "Ye'll see soon enough," she murmured. "Best
keep our mount on a tight rein, lest he spooks."

"Aye?" Hume's voice held a weary edge, and it
occurred to Fyfa that their horse wasn't likely the only
one to be shocked by what would happen next.

They stood at the foot of a wooded gorge before a
towering waterfall. High above, the rocky outline of a
mountain, Glas Bheinn, reared above them, as did the
blue waters of Loch na Gainmhich. The latter spilled
over the edge of the rocks, tumbling down into the steep
ravine below.

The Wailing Widow Falls: this was the place where
Fyfa had found shelter as a bairn, where she'd grown

into a woman, a bandruì. This was the home she hadn't seen for nearly six years.

Producing a smooth river stone, she held it on her outstretched palm, so that the noon sun could warm its surface. And then she began a soft chant, an ancient sain.

The day grew quiet, the soft rumble of the falls fading to near silence—and then the wall of water before them parted.

Seated behind her, Hume uttered a curse, while the gelding snorted nervously and side-stepped.

"Aye ... it's not something folk outside our order get to see," Fyfa said softly. "Come, husband ... ride through into the cavern, and I shall introduce ye to my family."

Hume gathered the reins, hesitant, "Is it safe to pass?"

"For the moment, aye," she replied. "The charm lasts for a short while."

Muttering another oath, he urged the gelding forward. The beast snorted again yet obeyed, stepping down off the mossy river bank and onto the wet stones.

The gathered crowd of blue-robed women stared, eyes wide, at Fyfa and Hume as they slid down from their horse.

Heart hammering against his ribs, Hume swept his gaze over the cavern, hardly believing his own eyes. It seemed inconceivable that a great cave lay behind these waterfalls, and even more incredible that Fyfa had whispered a charm to part the waters allowing them to enter.

He glanced over his shoulder, watching as the veil of water drew closed once more, sealing them inside the cavern.

Not for the first time, Hume's skin prickled at his wife's abilities. Aye, she was open with him these days, yet Fyfa was still capable of surprising him. He imagined there was still much to discover about her—and the order she belonged to.

It was as lofty as a great church in here, light streaming through fissures in the high ceiling and illuminating what would have been otherwise a dark space. Sunlight pooled on the stone floor, where fowl pecked at scattered grain. Four hearths burned within the space, their heat warming the damp air. Hangings of feathers and bone crisscrossed the wide cavern, and dust motes drifted through the smoky air. Peering into dark recesses, Hume saw that alcoves, their entrances covered by curtains, lined the space.

"Christ's bones," he murmured. "This wasn't what I expected." He glanced then at Fyfa, to see she was smiling at him, a wicked glint in her eye. "Ye could have warned me."

"Aye, I could have," she replied, her tone light. "But I was looking forward to seeing the shocked look upon yer face." She shrugged then. "I didn't think ye'd believe me, anyway … this place is difficult to describe."

"That it is," he agreed, shaking his head.

"Fyfa!" A tall woman with dark hair, peat-dark eyes, and a proud bearing stepped forward from the huddle of stunned druidesses. They'd literally gathered together in a cluster at the sight of a man in their midst. The dark-haired woman wore an odd expression—a mixture of exasperation and joy. "Ye still know how to get all the attention, I see."

A wide smile spread across Fyfa's face. She left Hume's side then and closed the gap between her and the woman, flinging her arms about her. "It's good to see ye too, Bree."

Releasing the woman from her crushing embrace, Fyfa turned, her eyes gleaming with tears, and gestured to Hume. "This is my husband, Hume Comyn … Hume, meet my sister, Breanna." She then gestured to the crowd of bandruìd, young and old, who now clustered around them. "In fact, meet all my sisters."

Hume's mouth quirked. As an only child, he couldn't imagine having a family this size. "It's a pleasure," he murmured.

Breanna's dark gaze met his, her expression assessing. "How much has Fyfa told ye about us?" she asked.

"Everything," Fyfa replied, still smiling. "We've come directly from Stirling, Bree … the castle has fallen … and we have much to tell ye all." She glanced around her. "Where is Nessa … and Colina?"

Breanna's brows drew together. "Nessa isn't here," she said softly. Fyfa shot her a questioning look, but Breanna cut her off with a raised palm. "I'll tell ye about our sister later." She then gestured to where a rickety wooden ladder led up behind them. "Our mother is meditating up on her ledge … I shall fetch her."

31

THE WILL OF THE THREE

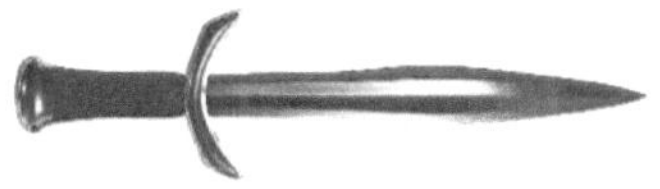

"YE SHOULDN'T HAVE brought him here, daughter … no man has ever ventured into our domain."

Fyfa tensed at the censure in the High Bandruì's voice. Colina was a gentle woman and rarely reprimanded any of her daughters. However, this afternoon, as she faced Fyfa and Hume before one of the hearths, Colina's misty blue eyes were sharp.

The High Bandruì's sight had been failing for years, something which gave her a dreamy, faraway look. Not so today. Even her familiar, Eclipse, who perched upon her shoulder, appeared to be glaring at Fyfa.

Colina stepped closer to the fire, the bone necklaces and bracelets that dangled from her small frame rattling, her mouth tightening. As always, her short brown hair was tousled and looked in need of a brush.

"I had to tell him, mother," Fyfa murmured. She was aware that all her sisters were watching her, tension rippling through the cavern. "Hume discovered the storeroom that I was using for witching." She paused then, glancing her husband's way.

Hume had said little since entering the cavern. Initially, he'd just looked about him, his eyes huge. But now that he'd adjusted to his environment, he was focused entirely on Fyfa. Their gazes locked for a moment, and his mouth lifted at the edges. He then nodded, encouraging her to continue.

"Hume is my husband … and I love him," she declared, her voice carrying across the hearth. "The secrets I once held back from him almost destroyed our marriage once. I won't keep anything back from him again." She let her attention shift around the fire.

Most of her sisters were frowning, although one or two wore deep scowls. She hadn't yet convinced any of them that this was a good idea.

Across from her, Breanna had folded her arms over her chest and pursed her mouth. Aye, her sister was gravely disappointed in her.

"I have sacrificed much for this order," Fyfa said after a spell. She chose her words carefully, even though she could feel frustration rising within her. Hume had warned her his presence might not be welcomed, yet she'd shrugged off his doubts. She now realized this would be harder than she'd anticipated. "And I've done so willingly ... but I won't give up Hume." She paused once more, tension knotting in her chest. "I'd leave the Guardians before I ever did that."

She felt her husband shift next to her. Looking to him once more, she saw his gaze was now shadowed, faint lines of tension appearing around his mouth. She took his hand, squeezing it as she turned her attention back to her mother.

"Hume knows all about us ... and he witnessed that witch in the English camp, Lamia Delamare, try to poison me and Robert Bruce."

That distracted them.

Fyfa was irritated that they'd been more interested in her bringing a man into their midst than learning what had transpired at Stirling. Their reaction frustrated her. Of course, she'd been away from this place for years now, and her absence had changed her. Life at Stirling Castle, where she'd been careful to hide her true identity, had made her more adaptable, more flexible.

These blue-robed bandruìd surrounding her were doggedly loyal to their cause, but their isolation was their weakness. Some of them were wary of the world beyond these falls—but Fyfa wasn't.

With a jolt, it occurred to her that she didn't want her old alcove back in this cavern. She still wished to protect

Scotland, but in her own way—and with the man she loved.

Breanna's eyes had narrowed as she stepped forward, her shoulders tensing. "What happened?"

Fyfa arched an eyebrow, a gesture of unspoken reproach. *Now ye ask me, sister?*

"Eclipse's message forewarned me of Lamia's presence in the camp," she replied. Her attention then shifted to Colina. "Sir William Oliphant was imprisoned after the castle fell, yet the rest of us were given our freedom." She paused then. "However, Longshanks insisted we attend a victory banquet afterward, so we were to stay on in the camp longer than I'd anticipated. It was my opportunity to learn more … to discover something that might help us, as ye had asked me … and when I took a walk, I encountered a group of Queen Margaret's ladies-in-waiting." Fyfa halted there, frowning. "One of them was Lamia."

"And she learned who ye were?" Breanna asked, her gaze still riveted upon Fyfa's face.

"I thought not … yet I was wrong," Fyfa replied. "She used a misdirection charm at the banquet so that no one saw her hand out goblets to guests. However, I spied her … and discovered that she'd poisoned the goblets she set before myself and Robert Bruce."

"We warned him," Hume spoke up then, his voice a low rumble in the cavern. "The night before, we went to his tent and advised him that Fyfa had overheard two of the king's men discussing the fact that Edward didn't trust him. As such, the Bruce believed me when I whispered to him not to touch his wine."

Fyfa nodded, grateful that Hume was helping her tell this tale. She noted the looks of interest some of her sisters were giving him. There was something about the steady, sure way her husband spoke that made one listen to him. He was also a deeply attractive man—something that wouldn't be lost upon the other women.

"Bruce wouldn't have touched the wine either," Fyfa continued, squeezing Hume's hand in thanks. "If Longshanks hadn't taken issue with the fact that he wouldn't drink a toast. He accused him of shunning his hospitality ... of insulting him ... and Robert Bruce looked as if he would indeed comply to appease him. I had to do something—so I caused a scene and knocked the wine out of Bruce's hand."

"She was a sight to behold," Hume added. "Raging at Robert Bruce for bowing to the English king, for letting him shame him. However, when Longshanks lost his temper, I had to take Fyfa from the banquet. Shortly afterward, my cousin John gave us one of his horses. We rode from the camp before Edward could have her arrested."

"But The Hammer sent a cut-throat after us, nonetheless," Fyfa concluded. Her skin prickled as she recalled the lethal grace of that grey-cloaked man. "He attacked us two days out from Stirling ... but thanks to Hume's skill with a blade and my witching, we rid ourselves of him."

Silence fell once Fyfa and Hume finished their tale. Told like that, Fyfa was surprised the pair of them had actually made it back to Assynt.

Around her, the other bandruìd stared at her. She was pleased to see that they were no longer scowling. Instead, she saw respect in many of their eyes—and awe on their faces.

Eventually, Colina shattered the silence. "Ye have indeed done well, daughter," she murmured. Fyfa was relieved to see that the High Bandruì's expression had softened. She didn't like the thought of Colina being vexed with her. "Lamia Delamare is a menace ... Nessa did well to warn us of her."

Nessa.

Fyfa's brow furrowed. "And where is our sister?" she asked. She glanced back at Breanna to see that her strong-featured face had grown taut. "Why isn't she here?"

"Nessa fell in love with the English knight she seduced," Breanna replied. "He was badly injured during the first days of the siege ... and sent home afterward."

Breanna's gaze shadowed then. "Ness returned to us, but it was clear her heart was elsewhere."

"I gave her my blessing," Colina said then, "and released Nessa from her vows. She now lives as Hugh de Burgh's wife at Grosmont Castle on the Welsh Borders."

Fyfa's lips parted, shock rippling through her. When she eventually replied, her voice came out in a rasp. "Ness left the order?"

Colina nodded, her round face softening. "Aye, lass … it was time for her to go."

Fyfa's belly cramped. She couldn't believe it. Being a Guardian of Alba wasn't something one dabbled in—it was a commitment for *life*. However, she stood on shaky ground herself right now. Hadn't she just declared that she'd leave this order if forced to choose between it and Hume? She could hardly let herself be outraged by Nessa's behavior.

But hurt dug its claws into her belly nonetheless.

"I sensed something amiss with her," Fyfa murmured finally. "When she stopped by Stirling to warn me of the English approach. She seemed … distracted."

"We should never have sent her back to the enemy." Breanna cast Colina a reproachful look—one the High Bandruì blithely ignored. "If we hadn't, Ness would still be with us."

"Hugh de Burgh was her destiny, my daughter," Colina replied with a shake of her head. Her mouth lifted into a wistful smile. "None of us can fight the will of The Three."

Silence followed the High Bandruì's words.

There was a finality to Colina's voice, a warning.

Drawing in a deep breath, Fyfa squared her shoulders. She still held her husband's hand, his presence at her side anchoring her. "Then, perhaps, it is also the Goddesses' will that my husband joins our cause." Her gaze swept over the surrounding faces. "Ye accept that Nessa has run off with an Englishman … but not that a valiant Scotsman wants to fight for Scottish freedom with us?"

Another hush settled over the cavern. Around them, the hearths crackled, and the stew for the noon meal, which hadn't yet been touched, bubbled. Nearby, one of the ponies snorted in its alcove.

Fyfa let the silence draw out, yet even as she waited, she knew she'd convinced them. Doubt and worry clouded her sisters' faces, and some of them exchanged glances, but no one challenged her.

None of them liked it, yet they would accept Hume among them.

"Fret not," she said finally, her mouth quirking. "I've lived too long in the outside world to reside happily within the confines of this cavern again. Hume and I will find somewhere to live nearby, within easy reach of the falls."

"There's an abandoned shepherd's cottage on the banks of the loch," Breanna unexpectedly spoke up. "It's in poor repair … but if ye fix it up, ye could live there."

Fyfa nodded, heat flushing through her. It meant a lot that Breanna supported her in this. Now that Nessa had left the order, the two of them had to look out for each other. Casting Breanna a grateful smile, Fyfa's attention shifted back to Colina. The High Bandruì hadn't yet given them her blessing, and Fyfa wouldn't be happy unless she did. "Mother?"

Colina's misty gaze focused upon her, and then she favored Fyfa with another, wistful, smile. "If that is what ye wish, daughter, I will not hinder it." Her familiar gave a soft caw, the crow's inky gaze piercing Fyfa. Colina's smile widened. "Eclipse agrees that Hume should stay."

Hume halted at the water's edge and let out a low whistle. "Yer sister wasn't exaggerating … it's indeed in 'poor repair'."

Fyfa halted by her husband's side, her gaze settling upon the ruined cottage before them.

Its walls were crumbling, and one end of the cottage had completely collapsed. The sod roof had long since rotted, leaving only wooden beams exposed to the air.

No one had lived here for long years.

Fyfa sighed before looking around her. Loch na Gainmhich gleamed in the late afternoon light, and the sun gilded the slopes of Glas Bheinn above them. The mountain's bulk reflected in the loch's dark, still waters.

It was a beautiful spot—and a place that Fyfa wanted to make her home.

However, Hume was right. This cottage wasn't just a hovel; it was a ruin.

Fyfa sucked in a deep breath and rolled up the sleeves of her kirtle before flashing Hume a rueful smile. "Well, then ... we'd better get to work."

"Ye won't get much done without tools." A woman's voice behind them made both Fyfa and Hume startle.

They turned to see Breanna standing behind them, a large leather satchel over one shoulder, and a wicker basket under the opposite arm. Fyfa's gaze widened; she'd thought she and Hume had climbed up here on their own, but it appeared they'd been followed.

Breanna flashed them a smile, her peat-brown eyes glinting. "And ye'll be hungry once ye've chased the rodents and spiders out this eve." Her smile widened at their surprised faces. "Ye didn't think we'd let ye deal with this on yer own did ye?"

"Aye, and ye'll need bedding too," a young bandruì with a shock of red hair approached from behind Breanna, her arms laden with blankets and furs.

Fyfa's throat constricted when she spied a line of blue-robed figures approaching down the overgrown path. Each of them carried something. One of her sisters even carried a fowl under each arm, while another led a goat behind her—Fyfa and Hume would be able to enjoy eggs and fresh milk in their new home.

Vision blurring, Fyfa smiled at them. "Yer help is very welcome," she said huskily. She stepped close to Hume then and looked up at his face.

Now that he'd gotten over his surprise, her husband wore a wide smile, his moss-green eyes warm. Fyfa leaned into him, and his arm went about her shoulders, pulling her close.

"Aye." Hume's voice was a rumble in his chest. "Very welcome indeed."

Epilogue

UNDER A WOLF MOON

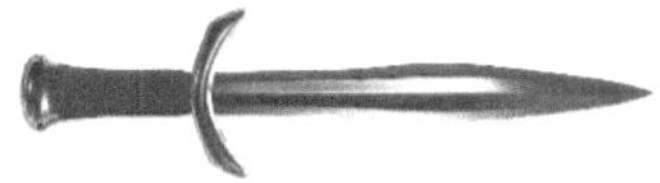

Glasgow, Scotland

Six months later ...

THE FULL MOON lit their way as the two cloaked figures crossed the stone bridge spanning the River Clyde.

Fyfa's breath steamed before her in the gelid air. The cold stung her cheeks and seared her lungs, yet she ignored it. Instead, she peered northeast, at where Glasgow's Saltmarket lay in darkness. The occasional burning pitch torch lined the cobbled way before them, yet without the moon's silvery glow, she and Hume would be traveling largely blind.

Glancing up at the bright globe above, she let its light bathe her face. An instant later, her witching stirred in response, a quickening in her veins. The Wolf Moon shone down on them this eve—a chill winter's moon—yet a full moon was a good night to take action.

"This way," Hume murmured, his boots scuffing on icy cobbles. It had snowed days earlier, melted, and refrozen. The ground was perilous, as slippery as a frozen loch, yet it also meant that few folk were out tonight. "It's almost time."

Fyfa didn't reply. She merely hurried her pace, following her husband as he entered Saltmarket. Dark houses, both in timber and stone, loomed overhead, shadowed doorways and windows peering out at them. But neither husband nor wife faltered. Hume had planned this evening meticulously. He knew exactly where they were heading, and what they'd do when they got there.

A tight smile curved Fyfa's lips. She too was well prepared.

They followed the narrow street out to a crossroad where they halted, hugging the shadows. Here, four streets converged: Saltmarket, High Street, Tronsgate, and Gallowgate.

A grand building loomed over the crossroad, its bulk casting a deep shadow: the Tolbooth. It was a huge edifice, around five stories high, with small dark windows. A large oaken door faced out onto Tronsgate—although Fyfa's attention didn't rest on the Tolbooth but upon the high tower attached to it. Capped with a turreted parapet, crown, and spire, this was known as the 'Steeple'. And despite its elegant appearance, highlighted by the hoary light of the moon, the Steeple was a prison.

Fyfa's gaze traveled to the top level—seven stories up—her pulse accelerating. Six Highlanders were imprisoned there and would be taken to the gallows the following dawn.

Her jaw tightened. *Not if we have any say in the matter.*

The English sheriff of Glasgow held the men and had condemned them with a sham trial. Their only crime was rebelling against English rule.

Reaching out, Fyfa found Hume's hand. Their fingers, chilled by the cold, locked for a moment.

"Are ye ready?" Hume whispered, his gaze glinting under the hood of his cloak.

"Aye."

"Ye know what to do?"

A smile stretched Fyfa's lips, although she knew her husband couldn't see it. "Every last detail."

"Good ... let's go."

They left the shadows and crossed the slippery square, making their way to the door of the Steeple. The light of a nearby torch bathed the building in hallowed light.

A small window faced the street. The wooden shutters were closed, although when she stepped close, Fyfa could see the chamber beyond through a crack. Indoors, she spied the four guards she'd known would be there. They sat around a table, a few feet from the narrow stairs that led up the tower, playing knucklebones. Two cressets upon the walls and a large candle at the center of the table illuminated the space and the brown-hued stone walls.

Wordlessly, Hume moved to the closed door that led into the tower and waited, while Fyfa pushed aside her cloak. Ignoring the bite of January cold, she withdrew her cairn stone from a pouch at her waist.

And then, gaze fixed upon the candle on the table, she whispered a charm, her fingers tightening around the lump of smoky quartz.

The stone flared hot against her palm, and a witch-wind rose, barreling through the previously still night.

An instant later, all the flames inside the chamber doused.

Gasps followed and then cursing.

Fyfa waited by the window, anticipating the guards' next move. More swearing followed. It was in English, a tongue that Fyfa didn't understand, yet the meaning was clear.

The men started arguing then, and Fyfa heard the heavy tread of feet approaching the iron and oaken door to the outside.

Another smile tugged at her mouth. As she'd hoped, one of them was venturing outdoors to relight his candle from the nearby torch.

She tensed then, as the scrape of the iron bar that locked the entrance to the prison echoed through the night.

An instant later, the door opened and a squinting figure emerged.

Hume stepped up sharply to his side and clubbed him across the back of the neck. The man dropped to the ground with a pained grunt.

Hume leaped over the prone figure and went inside, with Fyfa at his heels. The moment they were indoors, she thrust her cairn stone high, upon her open palm.

Light flared, blinding. She and Hume had been prepared for it—but the remaining guards weren't—and before any of them had time to reach for their weapons, her husband was on them.

He felled the guard nearest with a punch to the jaw, while Fyfa reached into another pouch upon her belt and grasped a handful of powder.

The cairn stone flared brightly once more, and another gust of wind barreled into the prison. Fyfa launched herself at one of the guards, who was in the process of drawing a knife, and she threw the dust she grasped into his face.

The guard grunted. Instead of drawing his knife, he growled out a curse and clutched at his face.

Hume's heavy punch to the belly brought the guard to his knees.

A short while later, all four men were subdued, gagged, and trussed up like geese for market. Hume had dragged the one he'd knocked senseless indoors and pulled the door shut so that anyone who happened to pass by wouldn't be suspicious.

Fyfa helped herself to the large iron key that hung upon the wall near the stairwell. Letting the cairn stone light their way, husband and wife alighted the stone steps.

Taking the steps two at a time, Fyfa followed Hume upstairs. By the time she reached the top floor landing, both of them were out of breath. Fyfa then handed Hume the key. He went to the large iron door on the opposite side of the landing and threw it open.

Moving forward in her husband's wake, Fyfa illuminated the cell beyond with the silvery glow of her cairn stone.

The men sat slumped against the walls. Dirty and unkempt, they squinted up at her, their gazes haunted, their faces resigned.

"Aye," one of them rasped. "What do ye want?"

"We're here to rescue ye," Fyfa announced. "Come on … get yerselves up before we have more company."

The Highland prisoners didn't need to be told twice. They clambered to their feet, cursing under their breaths as their cold-stiffened limbs protested, and followed Hume and Fyfa down to the bottom level of the tower. Inside the entrance hall, the bound guards still lay on the floor. All of them were awake, their gazes furious as they spied the prisoners.

One of them started making angry grunting sounds, yet the cloth Fyfa had stuffed into his mouth muffled his ranting.

Fyfa's gaze narrowed. The bastard should be grateful her husband had seen fit to save his, and his friends', lives. The following morning, these guards had planned to escort their Scot prisoners to the gallows.

Ever since Stirling, Edward Longshanks had set about putting his sheriffs in strategic spots across Scotland. Soon he'd call all the Scottish nobles who'd bent the knee to him, once more, to organize how English rule over this land would work going forward. Robert Bruce was one of the nobles, yet rumors now circulated Scotland that Bruce and a man named William Lamberton had signed a pact to resist the English, 'a friendship and alliance against all men'.

Heat flared in Fyfa's belly. Aye, the time was coming when Robert Bruce would fulfill his destiny.

She couldn't wait for that day.

They stepped outside into the freezing darkness, and Hume turned to the six men they'd just released.

"Go now," he told them, his voice low and urgent, "slip into the shadows … and continue the fight."

"I thank ye for coming to our aid," one of the men spoke up, his gaze flicking from Hume's face to Fyfa's. "But *who* are ye … and why have ye helped us?"

Hume favored the Highlander with a grim smile. "Our identity matters not," he murmured. "Just know that we are friends of Robert the Bruce … and we will not see our countrymen hanged for defending their own land. Make sure that ye tell every Scot ye meet that, one day, Robert Bruce will be king of Scotland."

The men's gazes gleamed, their bearded jaws tensing. A soft chorus of 'ayes' followed.

Taking hold of Fyfa's hand, Hume led her across the square and back into Saltmarket. Hoods pulled up, they moved swiftly along the street.

"We did it," Fyfa whispered to him. "Ye were breathtaking back there, husband."

Hume's grip on her hand tightened. "As were ye, wife."

A few yards on, Hume halted. Instead of continuing back toward the River Clyde, and their escape route, he pulled Fyfa into an alleyway and pushed her up against a wall.

He then covered her gasp of surprise with his hungry mouth. The kiss was possessive, hot—and it made Fyfa momentarily forget the danger they were still in. Leaning into the kiss, she devoured him with equal hunger. It was always like this between them—six moons had passed since their reconciliation, and if anything, Fyfa's need for her husband had grown. They'd made up for the lost time, yet the passion between them burned hotter still.

During the past months, they'd gotten to know each other all over again. With the help of her sisters, they'd repaired that cottage, and when they weren't out on a mission or task for the order, they focused on making the dwelling their home for the future. Fyfa had planted a vegetable garden, although this time of year, it didn't yield much, and Hume had built enclosures for the livestock they kept. Fyfa had also planted out a large patch of herbs, for both healing and witching. It was a simple, yet blissfully happy life—and every morning when Fyfa awoke, she thanked The Three for giving her the wits to fight for Hume Comyn.

When they drew apart, Fyfa gazed up at the shadowed planes of Hume's face. "What was that for?" she asked breathlessly.

His answering grin flashed in the darkness before he took hold of her hand and drew her out toward the street once more. "Just a promise, mo ghràdh," he murmured. "For later."

The End

FROM THE AUTHOR

FYFA'S SACRIFICE was the first 'estranged couple' story I've ever written. I was wondering how this story would turn out—as our hero and heroine have already been married for five years when the novel begins—but it was fascinating to pick apart this 'relationship gone wrong', and see if Fyfa and Hume could make things work in the end.

Of course, this is a romance, so they were always going to get their HEA … however, there were moments when I wondered if I could fix things for them. These two had plenty of obstacles to overcome.

If you've read my *Immortal Highland Centurions* series, you will have already met Fyfa in Books 2 and 3 of that series. Fyfa gives our heroine some romantic advice (an irony considering what we learn about her later on!) in CASSIAN, and then helped John Comyn organize an attack on Stirling while Edward of England is off chasing William Wallace in DRACO. She's a fun, spirited heroine—and she and Hume are perfect together!

Hume was one of my favorite types of hero—gruff, protective, and a warrior at heart. I loved giving him a chance to shine!

I hope you loved FYFA'S SACRIFICE … now get ready for a fake relationship and real rogue for a hero with Book 3 in the series, BREANNA'S SURRENDER, coming up next!

Jayne x

HISTORICAL NOTES

I did A LOT of research for this series!

Of course, this story-world blends a touch of fantasy with real historical fact (as The Immortal Highland Centurions did), however, I took care to base my witches of the Guardians of Alba order on ancient Celtic druidic and Wiccan practices, to give the order a feeling of authenticity.

My references to The Three goddesses (The Maiden, The Mother, and the Crone), come from Celtic mythology, as do my references to their power being related to the moon. Each moon of the year had a different name and significance, and each phase of the moon held a specific power. From the Wiccan religion, I brought in the use of the elements, candle magic, the use of crystals, and the use of the words 'craft', 'witching', and 'workings' to describe magic and spell casting. Both Celtic and Wiccan practices had a strong 'feminine' influence, which I really enjoyed exploring with my bandruìd. I wanted their practice to be largely positive and life-affirming.

I really enjoyed researching the historical backdrop to their novel (and indeed the whole series). If you read The Immortal Highland Centurions then you will have already met King Edward I of England (also known as 'Longshanks' or 'The Hammer of the Scots'). That series also featured William Wallace as a side character. However, this one is focused on the rise of Robert the Bruce to power (with the 'behind-the-scenes' help of our witches!).

In FYFA'S SACRIFICE, we finally meet Robert the Bruce, when he is called to Stirling, along with other Scottish nobles who had bent the knee to Edward of England, to watch the English king end the siege with the unveiling of his new weapon.

I was inspired for this incident by a scene in the movie OUTLAW KING (https://www.youtube.com/watch?v=6wx8X0yDD38), which takes place at the end of this famous siege. I altered this scene a bit to suit my story, removing Robert Bruce's father from the scene (as he'd actually died of leprosy a couple of months earlier!). Instead, one of Robert Bruce's brothers is with him at Stirling.

In 1304, Edward of England lay siege to Stirling Castle. The siege lasted from the beginning of April and ended on 24 July. Sir William Oliphant defended the castle with a garrison, while Edward attacked with a number of siege engines, including the infamous Warwolf.

Impatient with his lack of progress, Edward ordered his chief engineer, Master James of St. George, to begin work on a more massive engine, a huge trebuchet he named Warwolf. The weapon also went by the names *Ludgar* and *Loup de Guerre*.

Historians believe that this trebuchet was the biggest ever built. When disassembled, the weapon would fill 30 wagons in parts. It reportedly took five master carpenters and forty-nine other laborers at least three months to complete.

If you'd like to see a beautifully rendered reproduction of the Siege of Stirling, visit this website: https://bobmarshall.co.uk/portfolio/stirlingcastle1304/

Sir William Oliphant, the governor of Stirling, did try to surrender to Edward when he realized all hope was lost. However, Edward refused to accept his surrender until the Warwolf had been tested. Despite previous threats, Edward spared all the Scots in the garrison and took

Oliphant prisoner. William Oliphant was imprisoned in the Tower of London.

As with my previous series, I've tried to remain largely faithful to the historical representations of Edward I England. He was indeed an aging warrior king, and his son, Prince Edward, did accompany him on his campaigns to Scotland, helping him to conquer the Scots. His second wife, Margaret, also traveled with him.

Sir Aymer de Valence, Edward's military commander after the departure of Hugh de Burgh is also a real historical figure, who did serve both Edward I and II of England. You'll be meeting Sir Aymer again in Book 3!

During the story, we meet Hassan al-Aziz Muhammad, also known as 'alnasl'—*The Blade*—a Saracen assassin who had once been one of the Hashashin—a powerful order of assassins in the Holy Land. Hassan is a fictional character, although the order he belonged to is not.

The Hashashin (also known as the Nizari Ismailis), were a heretical group of Shiite Muslims who were powerful in Persia and Syria from the 11th century until their defeat at the hands of the Mongols in the mid-13th century. Secure in their fortified hilltop castles, they became infamous for their strategy of singling out opposition figures and murdering them, usually in knife-wielding teams.

The English word 'assassin' comes from 'Hashashin'. 'Assassin' is a variation of the Arabic hasisi ('hashish-eater'), in reference to these assassins' use of hashish. Apparently, the Hashashin ate powdered hemp leaves, which contain a natural psychoactive drug, before they went on an assassination mission.

In my story, Edward brings the sixteen-year-old Hassan back from the Holy Land with him. Before he was crowned, Edward did actually fight there, and one of the

Hashashin made an attempt on his life in Acre in 1272. The assassin stabbed him with a poison blade before Edward fought back and overpowered him. It was rumored that Edward's first wife, Eleanor, sucked the poison from his wound. However, historians believe this likely didn't happen. Instead, he was saved by the camp surgeon.

You can read more about this incident here: https://www.medievalists.net/2011/05/the-prince-the-assassin-and-the-mongols/

There is no evidence that Edward had a Saracen assassin in his employ, but inspired by real history, I couldn't help myself … I had to create *The Blade*!

All the settings in this novel are based on real locations:

Stirling: this fortress (which I also feature in my Immortals series) was indeed 'the brooch that holds Scotland together'. The Siege of Stirling was a landmark victory for the English during the Wars of Independence. However, it was not an easy one.

The Wailing Widow Falls: I came across a picture of these waterfalls a few years ago … and just knew that, one day, I'd write about them. Located in the northwest of the Highlands in Assynt (Caithness/Sutherland and Ross-shire), these massive falls run out of Loch na Gianmhich, crashing into a narrow gorge at the bottom. There are many tales associated with their evocative name, although the one I used is a variation of a story of a deer hunter who fell from the top while hunting in a thunderstorm. The next morning his mother, filled with grief, hurled herself to her death from the same spot. In my version, it's his wife who does so … after all, it is calling the Wailing *Widow* Falls. Of course (to my knowledge) there isn't a cavern hidden behind the waterfalls!

Inverlochy Castle: this 13th Century castle is located near Inverlochy and Fort William. This fortress was one of the seats of the Comyn clan. The castle sits on the banks of the River Lochy. These days, the castle is a ruin (as it was attacked twice over the years), but you can still see the impressive curtain wall and the ruins of four towers—the largest of which, 'The Comyn Tower', served as the castle's keep.

Crianlarich: our hero and heroine stop at this village en route north. This village was indeed known as the 'Gateway to the Highlands'.

Glasgow: the setting of the epilogue mentions the 'Tolbooth' and 'The Steeple', located on the intersection between Saltmarket, High Street, Tronsgate, and Gallowgate. Indeed, The Steeple' was used as a prison— and prisoners were housed on the seventh floor of the tower.

In the novel, I mention 'saining'—this is an ancient Scottish practice that is intended to bestow protection onto an object, a place, or a person in order to ward away evil influences or intent. A saining charm was a rhyme that often used elements such as fire or water.

I hope you enjoyed this window into the research, settings, and background to the novel. All these details help to make the story all the richer!

ABOUT THE AUTHOR

Award-winning author Jayne Castel writes epic Historical and Fantasy Romance. Her vibrant characters, richly researched historical settings and action-packed adventure romance transport readers to forgotten times and imaginary worlds.

Jayne is the author of a number of best-selling series. In love with all things Scottish, she writes romances set in both Dark Ages and Medieval Scotland.

When she's not writing, Jayne is reading (and re-reading) her favorite authors, cooking Italian feasts, and going on long walks with her husband. She lives in New Zealand's beautiful South Island.

Connect with Jayne online:
www.jaynecastel.com
www.facebook.com/JayneCastelRomance
https://www.instagram.com/jaynecastelauthor/
Email: contact@jaynecastel.com